Are You Falling for It?

An Olympus Novel

Rachel Pluck

For everyone hiding their insecurities behind a big laugh.

Playlist

"New Romantics (Taylor's Version)" by Taylor Swift
"Blame Brett" by The Beaches
"Marvelous" by Wallows
"Beach House" by Carly Rae Jepsen
"Echo" by Incubus
"Blinded (When I See You)" by Third Eye Blind
"Papercuts" by Landon Conrath
"Calling After Me" by Wallows
"Baby Blue Shades" by Bad Suns
"Gorgeous" by Taylor Swift
"Life Was Easier When I Only Cared About Me" by Bad Suns
"Brandy (You're a Fine Girl)" by Looking Glass
"Then It All Goes Away" by Dayglow
"Break My Heart" by Dua Lipa
"Dress" by Taylor Swift
"2AM" by Landon Conrath
"cardigan" by Taylor Swift
"Motorcycle Drive By" by Third Eye Blind
"day&night" by Taylor Roche
"Maybe You Saved Me" by Bad Suns
"Planet" by Aiden Bisset
"Disappear Here" by Bad Suns
"Out of My League" by Aiden Bisset
"All That I'm Craving" by Aiden Bisset

Chapter 1

If You Heard the Rumors, They're Probably True

Nobody trusts the girl who's sleeping with the boss.

The phrase blinks to life in Olivia's mind, like big, white block letters punched out of a black sheet of paper. She squeezes her eyes shut to blink it away right as her shoulder blades dig into the expansive wooden desk beneath her. As she arches her back, the sharp end of something small and thin stabs the top of her spine—a pen maybe?

She shakes her head, trying to push off yet another distraction, just as a breathless moan leaves her lips. Her toned arms are coiled tightly around Bruce Westin, pulling the full weight of his body against hers, and she tries to focus her attention there. He rocks his hips and tension builds inside her. She can feel it on her skin, like static before a lightning strike. She's close, and even though her eyes are closed, she can tell by his building speed and heavy breath hot against the shell of her ear that Bruce is too.

One more roll sends her body sliding against the desk, until her head nearly hangs off the edge of it, and she comes undone. She releases one hand's grip on Bruce's muscled shoulder and slaps it across her mouth to stifle her screams. The muffled sound of her ecstasy projected *almost* noiselessly into her palm is enough to send Bruce over the edge with her.

When they're done, there are no wistful cuddles on the plush carpeted floor. There are no sweet nothings whispered against dewy lips or sweat-kissed skin. Bruce climbs unceremoniously off her, then off the desk entirely. He runs a hand through his thick blond hair a few times until it looks intentionally mussed, like an eight-hundred-dollar blowout at the salon catering to Manhattan's elite down the block.

Olivia stands and collects her clothing from the floor. First her bra, hanging from the left arm rest of Bruce's wingback office chair, and then her sleeveless blouse, lying discarded at its base. She finds her thong across the room, a lacy little thing but nothing special. It doesn't match her bra; it doesn't need to. She doesn't dress up for Bruce.

It's crumpled on the floor in front of the window, its blinds she—*thankfully*—shut tightly the moment she stepped into the well-appointed, extremely masculine office. Her high-waisted floral skirt painted in hues of lavender, pastel blue, and baby pink lies beside it. She expertly slides each garment on her athletic figure, moving like a stage performer tearing on a new costume between acts so she doesn't miss her next cue.

When she turns back around to scour the floor for her favorite pair of nude Louboutins, she sees Bruce standing beside his oversized desk in nothing but his tailor-made trousers. Her breath nearly catches in her throat at the sight of his exposed abdomen, a single bead of sweat trickling down the center of his six pack. *Nearly* catches.

Thankfully, he doesn't notice her stare as he picks up his powder blue button-down shirt and shrugs it over his shoulders, sending his chest muscles rippling. She distantly recalls the time her best friend Hannah referred to him as a Greek god and fights to hold back her snort.

It's not that Hannah was wrong. Bruce strength trains six days each week with a *very* expensive personal trainer and rides his bike the two-and-a-half miles to work from his apartment in the Upper East Side at least four. To describe him as fit would be putting it lightly.

It's just that Olivia is reluctant to give the man a compliment, no matter what it's for. Never mind that she's been sneaking into his office every Friday afternoon for the last three months to explore exactly what that pricey personal trainer bill has done for his physique.

Bruce looks up and sees her watching him as she steps into her heels and he smirks as he fastens the buttons on his shirt from the bottom up, reminding her exactly why he's beyond her compliments. "Same time next week?" he teases, and she grinds her teeth as she smooths out her skirt.

"I meant what I said earlier. This was the last time," she replies curtly on her way to his office door.

Bruce steps in front of her and lifts a hand to her waist. He leans in close, the scent of his Tom Ford Tuscan Leather cologne filling her nostrils. She knows it's Tom Ford, not because she's a nose, but because she had to restock his toiletries, among other things, when his assistant went on vacation... three months ago.

Precisely how she ended up in this predicament to begin with.

Olivia leans her upper body away and casts her eyes over Bruce's shoulder toward the closed door, then reluctantly meets his stare. Her heart stammers in her chest at the sight of his icy blue irises so close to her. *Traitor.* She doesn't let it show as she says stonily back, "I mean it. This time was the last time."

Bruce chuckles softly, a sound that would filter through the air like music to anyone else. Except maybe the enemies he's made in his eleven-year career as a no-bullshit lawyer. Instead, it just grates on her last nerve. "Come on, Quinn. We're good together like this. It's not like there's someone else. Why end a good thing?"

For a moment, her resolve flickers.

On one hand, he's absolutely wrong. Sleeping with her boss, a partner at her law firm, is wrong. Moreover, it's completely idiotic.

On the other hand, he's partially right too. For some reason, this thing between them works. And it's a hell of a lot better than the toxic tech bros and finance frat boys she usually meets on Hinge. She inwardly cringes at the thought.

Her voice is like venom when she shoots back, "There is no *'we'* here." The way he specified "*like this*" didn't escape her notice. "And maybe there is someone else." She tries to make it sound breezy, light, lifting and dropping one exposed shoulder with ease.

She's lying, and she's ninety-nine percent sure Bruce knows it, but she stands her ground anyway, holding his calculating stare with her chin high.

Eventually, Bruce shakes his head but drops his hand from her waist to take two steps backward, out of her path. "Whatever you say, Olivia. I'll see you on Monday."

Dismissed.

Olivia beelines for the door and swings it open noiselessly, just enough for her to poke her head out first and then squeeze her lithe frame through. The law firm closes at three thirty on Fridays and it's well past six at this point, but one can never be too careful. The last things she needs are prying eyes and wagging tongues at work. Not if she wants to be considered seriously for senior paralegal anytime soon.

After all, nobody trusts the girl who's sleeping with the boss.

Chapter 2

Apologies in Advance

The elevator doors part, dumping Olivia onto The Monarch Hotel's opulent rooftop terrace. A warm breeze lifts a piece of her chestnut brown hair so it tickles her nose until she brushes it away with a hand.

The east terrace is already packed with people, some dressed in all black and sporting trays piled high with hors d'oeuvres, but most of them in cocktail attire—sequin and satin dresses stretched and glued to tanned and toned bodies for the women, well-cut dress shirts tucked into linen and cotton dress pants for the guys.

"Olivia!" a voice calls from somewhere deep in the crowd, and she slows her step to find the source. The overwhelming group of bodies parts like the Red Sea as her best friend, Hannah Maxwell, steps through, beautiful but subdued in a white silk wrap dress.

Olivia has to bite back her smile at the sight of her favorite person on earth walking toward her, thinking to herself, *At least some things haven't changed.*

Hannah hurries closer and envelops her in a crushing hug. "You made it!"

"Of course I made it," she responds through choked airways, the glossy gift bag in her hands slamming against Hannah's back as she wraps her arms around her. "Couldn't very well miss my best friend's engagement party." *Especially not when I take at least partial credit for pushing you two lovebirds together in the first place.*

Hannah laughs, and Olivia can picture her friend's ski jump nose wrinkling well before Hannah pulls back to look at her fully. She gently drags her hand around from Olivia's back to release the hug, but Hannah's fingertips snag on something on the side of her shirt. Her eyes cast down to find the source and her brows furrow deeply before she looks back up to meet Olivia's gaze. "Liv, I think your shirt might be inside out." Her voice is a whisper, as though anyone around them could even hear her over the cacophony of voices carried on the wind wafting past the crowded rooftop.

Olivia grimaces down at her shirt, which is indeed inside out, panic freezing her veins like ice. Hannah leans back and crosses her arms over her chest, cocking a hip and an eyebrow in her best friend's direction. "You didn't," she says and it isn't a question.

After a quiet groan, Olivia says, "I did. But I swear this was the last time. I made that clear." And she's pretty sure at least sixty percent of her believes it. She swivels her head left and right to see if anyone at the party is watching the two of them, then says under her breath, "Cover me."

Hannah steps closer to her best friend and forms a small blockade between her and the rest of the crowd with her body while Olivia jerks the bottom of her blouse up and out of her skirt. In less than thirty seconds, she has the blouse turned the right way and tucked back in.

"There, good as new!" she says too brightly, holding two thumbs up.

Hannah sighs and drops her arms to her sides then offers her friend a small, but warm, smile. *Oh, here we go. The comforting mother hen.*

Hannah lifts a hand to delicately stroke Olivia's arm. "Look, I'm not judging you. Not at all. I just don't want this to hold you back."

The statement is loaded with so many unspoken words. Hold you back from the promotion you've been busting your ass for this past year. Hold you back from finding someone who isn't an asshole—or also your boss.

"You're right, I should be making my rounds here. I bet Ezra's got tons of hot, rich friends just waiting to sweep a girl off her feet. Maybe we can have a double wedding." Olivia holds her breath, hoping the joke lands. Hannah's adorable little snort tells her it does, and she releases the air from her lungs and relaxes the tension in her shoulders.

Her best friend means well, of course. She's not *trying* to judge her, or her choices. But they've always existed on opposite ends of the spectrum when it came to dating. Until last summer, Hannah avoided it like the plague while Olivia has always jumped into every relationship with both feet, usually to her detriment.

"Did I hear my name?" a rumbling tenor asks from over Hannah's shoulder, and her boyfriend—no, *fiancé*—appears, hovering above her head a moment later.

Hannah's face lights up as Ezra slides his slender hands around her waist and presses a chaste kiss to her temple, and Olivia's heart nearly explodes and melts in her chest at the same time.

Given the circumstances, she's been waiting to feel something cold and dark snap inside her at the sight of Hannah and Ezra so in love while her love life is in such a shambles. She's eternally grateful it hasn't so far. All she ever feels when watching them gaze adoringly into one another's eyes or banter like an old married couple is joy. The road they took to get here hasn't been an easy or direct one... but not many average Janes can say they bagged their celebrity crush after getting a job at his record label.

"I was just telling Hannah I fully expect to be introduced to all the eligible bachelors on your guest list." She winks playfully at Ezra as he turns to face her and chuckles.

He releases his fiancée just long enough to pantomime writing something down on an imaginary piece of paper while he says, "Of course, let me just add that to the endless wedding to-do list Hannah's been making for us." He cocks an eyebrow at Olivia to add, "Although I should probably warn you, most of my friends are heathens and musicians just like me. *Definitely* not the marrying type."

At this, Hannah slaps his hands down without any real force and suppresses a giggle. Ezra catches one of her hands and smoothly slides it into his, their fingers intertwining between them as they hold one another's gaze. Olivia's heart plummets at the sight. Maybe that something cold and dark is lurking somewhere just beneath the surface after all.

"I better not hog the guests of honor before you've had the chance to make your rounds," she says, her voice sounding too loud in her ears despite the noise on the rooftop. "I need to grab a drink and drop this at the gift table." She lifts the white paper bag up in explanation and starts to back away, already searching for the nearest waiter carrying a tray of champagne flutes. She finds one mingling in a group of people she doesn't recognize to her right and sneaks one off his tray, then strides off in search of the gift table.

She takes two large gulps of the champagne, the bubbles tingling the back of her nose, and skirts the crowd until she finds a long table draped in white with boxes and bags of all shapes, colors, and sizes piled high atop it. It's against the far left side of the large terrace, against a wall made up of glass windows that peek into the rooftop's swanky main bar and lounge, dotted every few feet with expertly trimmed hedges.

On her way over to the gift table, she downs the rest of her champagne and leaves the empty glass on a bussing tray in the corner, then finds a home for her bag amongst the sea of presents, her curiosity piquing as she scans a particularly mountainous box. Her slender fingers are just reaching for the card on it when she hears a quiet tapping on the glass window to her left.

With eyebrows furrowed into a deep V in the center of her forehead, she glances up to find the source and grits her teeth when she does. Exhaling through her nose and resisting the urge to roll her eyes, she waves meekly back to Bruce Westin, who stands just on the other side of the all-glass wall. She notices he too is still wearing the same outfit from earlier, although she's sure his shirt wasn't inside out when he arrived.

Why is he *here? Am I being punk'd?*

Bruce beckons her over with his hand, his Piguet watch glinting in the low light of the sun dipping toward the horizon, but she shakes her head, gesturing with false apology on her face to the party behind her. One corner of his lips turns up, his icy blue eyes flashing. Of course he'd only be emboldened by the challenge. He drops his hand to the pocket of his trousers and slides out his phone. Seconds later, her phone is buzzing in her purse.

`Come over here.`

Olivia's jaw feathers. He's got to be kidding.

`Can't, I'm supposed to be mingling.`

`It doesn't look like you're mingling.`

`I was just about to until I was rudely interrupted.`

She knows she's skating on pretty thin ice here. For all their flawed recent history, the guy is still her boss. And as much shit as she may give him, she takes her work seriously and has high aspirations at this firm. Who knows, maybe one day she'll even take the plunge and go to law school to keep climbing the ladder.

And yet, she can't stop herself. There's a brief pause in the flit of messages back and forth and she looks up to find Bruce's gaze narrowed on her, lips curved in an arrogant grin. *Ugh, he's actually enjoying this.*

She is the first to break the stalemate.

`Why are you even here?`

`Meeting with colleagues from another firm about a case. Why are YOU here?`

`Engagement party. Invite only.`

She sees Bruce's shoulders shaking and can almost hear his laugh despite the wall separating them. She bites down on her bottom lip to hide her involuntary smile. He can't know she's amused too.

`Come over here so we can talk like adults.`
`I'm sure you can slip away for a few minutes.`

She looks up at the sky, now brilliant in slashes of tangerine and apricot and mauve cast by the setting sun. She's about to respond when she hears a deep voice behind her ask, "Work stuff?"

Jumping at least half a foot at the disembodied voice, she almost drops her phone on the gift table in front of her. Too quickly, she spins around and nearly crashes into a six foot five linebacker of a man standing directly behind her. He's dressed head-to-toe in black—an Armani suit that hugs every hard line of muscle beneath like it had been sewn onto him. When he dips his head a little closer to her eye level, a small silver nose ring catches the last rays of evening sunlight clinging to the cloudless sky overhead.

It takes the tiniest fraction of a second for her to recognize the bassist in Ezra's band before her face breaks out in a beaming grin. "Oh my gosh! Peter, didn't your mom ever teach you not to sneak up on people?" She swats playfully at his bicep with one hand, the other clutched over her pumping heart.

Peter grins sheepishly and rubs at the back of his neck with a hand the size of a grapefruit. "Sorry, I had to get away from a group of label execs or I thought I might die. Saw you over here and made a break for it."

Still grinning, she drops her hand to her side, her heart rate slowing toward normal again. "I hear you. I've been hiding on the outskirts the whole time I've been here. I'm surprised Hannah hasn't noticed yet." Although it apparently isn't a very good hiding spot after all, considering she's now been accosted twice in five minutes.

He glances meaningfully down at her other hand where she still clutches her phone in a death grip. "Working overtime again?" he rephrases his earlier question.

Her mouth pops open, but no words come out. With what she hopes is a covert glance back at the glass wall behind her, she sees Bruce still standing there, that trademark icy stare narrowed at Peter, that sharp jaw clenching and flexing. Something stretches and then recoils inside of her at the sight of it, Bruce's earlier words echoing with perfect recall in her head: *It's not like there's someone else.*

"Something like that," she says slowly, returning her attention to Peter with a sweet smile curving her lips. She reaches a hand out to squeeze his bicep in what she hopes he interprets as a friendly and perfectly normal gesture for two acquaintances through mutual friends.

He doesn't seem to question it, instead returning it with a crooked grin of his own and a pat against her hand with his fingertips. In involuntary reflex, she tightens her grip around his arm. "Don't let Hannah catch you. The explosion will level this entire block."

Olivia laughs, louder than usual, tossing her head back as though Peter has said the most brilliant quip she's ever heard in her life. She can practically feel Bruce's glare burning a hole between her shoulder blades. *Good.*

Peter shoots her a look somewhere between concern and amusement. "You okay, Liv?" *Oh no, too unnatural. Time to rein it in.*

She relaxes her neck and dims her smile to normal wattage levels. "Too much champagne on an empty stomach. Come on, let's go snag some appetizers."

"Don't need to ask me twice," he replies, wiggling his jet-black eyebrows.

As she lets Peter lead her back toward the crowd of guests, her arm still snaked possessively around his, Olivia spares one passing glance back at Bruce. Despite the distance, despite the glass and hedges running interference between them, she can see the steam coming from his ears. Biting back her smirk, she returns her attention to the man on her arm, gazing up at him in adoration.

No one else, huh?

·♥·♥·♥·♥·♥·

"Letting your hair grow out?" Olivia muses while slowly walking her fingers through the air above a table near the bar laden with small bites—baby bella mushrooms stuffed with crab, fresh shrimp cocktail, deviled eggs, antipasto skewers, the cutest little baby beef empanadas, cheesesteak eggrolls, and at least seven things she can't even identify. Her stomach growls and she eagerly grabs one of everything—plus two more deviled eggs—and piles it onto her plate.

When Peter doesn't answer, she glances up from the food to find him shoving a whole deviled egg in his mouth. She tries to hold back her cackle, but her shoulders shake with the effort.

"Huh?" he mumbles around the bite of food, and she can't stop herself from snorting.

"Slow down, cowboy. It's not going anywhere."

He swallows, the muscles in his throat working, then shoots her a narrowed stare. "Hey, I'm a big guy. Big guys gotta eat."

She bounces her eyebrows in acceptance before stepping away from the buffet table, silently beckoning Peter to follow. He does.

They find a quiet area off to one side of the terrace with a plush loveseat, two matching overstuffed armchairs, and a table, and each take a seat across from one another. She can't help but notice Peter managed to eat at least a third of his plate on the brief walk over and fights her smile.

"As I was saying before I was interrupted by your practice round for the next Nathan's Hot Dog Eating Contest, your hair's gotten longer."

He nods and swallows a bite of shrimp cocktail. A small dab of cocktail sauce stains the corner of his mouth and Olivia has the sudden urge to wipe it away with her thumb. Luckily, she doesn't need to, as Peter slides his tongue out to lick up the briny sauce. The entire movement feels like it's performed in slow motion, and she looks away to the purpling horizon, her gut clenching.

"Trying something new," he answers finally with a shrug of his broad shoulders. He hesitates, his emerald eyes going slightly wide, his hand hovering in the air on its way to bring another bite of food to his mouth. "What, don't you like it? Does it look bad or something?"

One corner of her mouth tilts up at the tightness between his brows. Peter always had big golden retriever energy. It was one of the things she enjoyed most about being around him. Back when they used to spend time together, that is. When Hannah and Ezra first started dating.

A memory of the four of them at a nightclub in Chicago last summer floods her vision. She'd left Hannah on the dancefloor with Ezra, her way of forcing them to embrace their feelings, and spent the better part of the night alone with Peter at the bar. It wasn't wholly unpleasant.

Out loud, she says, "It looks great! Just a big change, that's all. Ezra cut his shag and you started growing yours out."

Peter visibly untenses at her compliment and finishes his next bite of food before conceding, "It took some time to get it to a manageable length, but it's way better than trying to find a good place to get it cut on the road every two weeks."

Pausing, she cocks her head in thought. Has it really been that long since she's seen him? She tries to think back to their last interaction and her stomach drops when she realizes it was at the party celebrating the release of Olympus's latest studio album... four months ago.

There had been a time when the two of them texted almost daily. But that was back when they were trying to shove their best friends into a relationship they were too stubborn to start themselves. When the job was over, when she became distracted with work... well. The texts had started to trickle in less and less until they both just stopped.

"Do you think you'll be going on tour again soon, to promote the album?"

Peter chews and swallows another impossibly large mouthful. "If we do, it wouldn't be until after the wedding." He tilts his head to one side. "But I did hear rumblings the label was cooking something up for after the honeymoon. Late November."

With a gasp, she dramatically clutches a hand to her heart. "You'll miss my birthday!"

One corner of Peter's lips tugs up, as if pulled by an invisible string. The resulting lopsided grin is, she can admit to herself only, adorable. "Oh no, well we can't have that." He pauses and looks thoughtfully into the middle distance. "Actually, when is your birthday?"

She can't blame him for not knowing. It was probably her fault for being missing in action for so long, anyway. "November twenty-sixth."

He nods and taps his temple with the first two fingers of one hand, like he's committing it to memory. "I'll see what I can do, Quinn. I'll see what I can do."

She tries to hide the flush that creeps to her cheeks around a bite of a cheesesteak eggroll, and Peter takes the cue to dig into his own food. Or, what's left of it.

Not surprisingly, he finishes his plate and has to go back for a second helping before she's halfway done with her first.

When their bellies are satisfied and full, she stands from the deep blue loveseat and stretches her arms overhead to release the tightness left behind in her muscles by her 5 a.m. spin class. She also pretends to ignore the caressing feeling of Peter's eyes roving over her body before he realizes what he's doing and looks away.

"Okay, let's grab some drinks and mingle. Hannah is going to kill me if I stay hidden much longer."

Silent as a cat, Peter stands up with a grace someone as large as him shouldn't possess and offers one corded arm to her. She crooks her arm around his elbow and leads him toward the bar.

Two Aperol spritzes later and Olivia feels light on her feet, just relaxed enough to be social without completely losing her wits. At some point during their turn around the terrace, they had each managed to link up with the guests of honor, and consequently lost one another from there.

She stays with Hannah for the rest of the party, getting introduced around to some of her colleagues and Ezra's family and friends—she recognizes only two of them: Lexi, his best friend since childhood and her fiancée Camila, who both flew in from San Francisco—and dozens of other nameless faces she had forgotten almost as soon as she'd been introduced to them.

I need to work on my networking skills, she'd thought to herself more than once, the senior paralegal job hammering itself into the ridges of her brain every few minutes. Like she could forget about it even if she wanted to.

In that time, the sun has completely sunk below the horizon, bathing the rooftop in a silk wrapped night scented with hyacinths, probably wafting from the trellises tucked away in corners that crawl with the stuff. Twinkling string lights dance above their heads in the evening breeze, the candles placed on nearly every flat surface keeping the party going.

"Excuse me, I have to run to the ladies' room," Olivia leans in to whisper to Hannah and her mom, whom she'd been talking to for about the past twenty minutes.

The two of them barely break conversation, each waving a lofted hand supporting a champagne flute in her direction to acknowledge they heard her. They had been thick as thieves since the engagement, clucking like hens over linen colors, flower arrangements, and the like.

It warmed Olivia to see them so close, even while living apart. It had been a big change when Hannah moved to New York from the small town in Pennsylvania where she'd grown up. An even bigger shift when she'd been sent on tour last summer.

Now, Hannah's mom was at their apartment at least once a month. Some roommates might mind, but not Olivia. It wasn't so bad having a mom around their tiny place in Brooklyn, pitching in with the cleaning and cooking them dinner whenever she visited. It came in handy with all the late nights she'd been working lately.

The crowd of engagement party guests has thinned out quite a bit by now and, checking her watch, she realizes nearly three hours have passed. The main lounge on the other side of the glass wall is filling in with the typical weekend crowd, eager to start their night with a craft cocktail and skyline views.

Her elbows get jostled as she wades through the crowd like they're a pool of molasses, finally making it to the door on the far side that leads to the restrooms. Thankfully, there's no line yet, and she ducks in to do her business just as the roar of a speaker somewhere outside kicks to life, bleating an old Tegan and Sara song layered over a house beat.

She washes up and checks herself in the mirror, pleased to find her shirt is still right side out. Like she hadn't been running her fingers down her sides every so often, just to make sure.

After slicking on a fresh coat of glossy lip tint, she aims for the door, bursting through it with a flourish while tucking the tube of gloss back into her purse. With her eyes cast down at the contents of her bag, her body makes contact with something smooth and unyielding. A yelp of surprise escapes her lips before she stumbles back. Two strong hands reach out firmly to grip her upper arms, steadying her. She has to crane her neck to find the reason behind her collision.

"Easy there, champagne legs," a deep voice coils around her like smoke, and her gut sinks. *Am I being punished for something I did in a past life?*

Olivia rights herself, lifting her chin and, with as much gentleness as she can muster, drags her arms out of Bruce Westin's grip to smooth her hands down her shirt. "Not the champagne, I just wasn't expecting a freight train to come barreling at me right outside the bathroom."

She swears she sees Bruce flex his pectorals through his cotton dress shirt and fights the urge to call him on it. He must notice the seething glare hidden behind her gaze, because one corner of his mouth tilts up. "I thought you were going to come over, say hi."

"What gave you that idea?"

"When you ended our little text conversation."

"I ended it because I had a party to get back to."

"And a guy?" There's something low and almost lethal in the way the question slides from his lips.

A chill dances down her spine, but she can't help herself. She cocks her head, the movement purely feline. "What guy?"

Bruce squares his shoulders and feathers his jaw.

Olivia waits for a beat. Then two. Then three. "Oh! Right, *that* guy."

He tenses, waiting for her to go on. When she doesn't, instead offering him nothing more than a saccharine smile, he sighs and pinches the bridge of his nose between his thumb and forefinger. "You really should be in a courtroom."

Her smile widens and she leans into Bruce slightly, tilting her ear toward him. "I'm sorry, was that a compliment?"

"Hardly," he replies, but his lips twitch in the direction of a smile. He lifts one of his arms like he's going to touch her face, the corded muscles of his forearm dancing where he has the sleeves rolled up to his elbow.

This is how it had always been with them. The digs, the innuendo behind their eyes, all part of their little game. The game that kept her coming back all these months.

"Liv! Thank god I found you. The party's wrapping up and Hannah needs help getting the gifts loaded into her car."

She swallows hard, shoving down any lingering warmth that may have been blooming in her core, when she sees Peter's head poke around the corner. Only then does she notice the music filtering in ten times louder through the open door to the rooftop. She's unsure how long Peter stood there, how much he might have seen, and swallows at the thought.

Bruce cranes his neck around to look at the reason for their interruption, and even in the low light, she can see his jaw flex and then steel. It's clear her non-answers did nothing to quell his assumptions about who Peter is and how she knows him.

And does she really want to do that? To reassure him Peter is nothing but a friend of a friend. An acquaintance she happens to enjoy grabbing a beer with. Or used to, anyway.

No. When Bruce realizes that, she's back to square one. He thinks he owns her. Can have her whenever he wants, damn the consequences. Because there are no consequences for him, not really.

Olivia straightens and sidesteps Bruce in one smooth movement, putting on her most assuring smile as she approaches Peter in three long-legged strides. "Of course, happy to help."

She resists glancing back at the man now behind her, and judging from the wide-eyed and cocked-brow look on Peter's face directed squarely at her boss, she doesn't want to see what's waiting for her back there.

Instead, she loops one of her sunkissed arms through Peter's elbow, using her own inertia to turn him around and pull him toward the door before he can question what he did or didn't walk in on.

"Who was that guy?" Peter's voice floats down to her ears as she tugs him through the main lounge and onto the secluded rooftop terrace.

She releases a sigh through her nose and then rubs the spot between her eyebrows with the pad of her thumb. The party has almost completely emptied out now, save for Hannah, Ezra, and their parents.

"Where are Zach and Angel?" she dodges, scanning the dim rooftop in search of Ezra and Peter's other two bandmates. During the party she'd spoken to them each for only about half a second. They'd been chumming it up with two other musicians, one of them covered in tattoos, with eyelashes so thick and dark, she thought he'd been wearing eyeliner and mascara at first glance.

"They took the first load of gifts down to the garage already. Angel has to get back to his suite. I guess his girl gets really bad morning sickness around this time of day." He tilts his head and twists his mouth, then adds, "Can it really be called morning sickness if it happens late at night?"

She jerks her head toward him, her grip around his elbow tightening. "Adrianna's pregnant?"

Peter chuckles, pointedly glancing down at her arm where it's constricted around his like a blood pressure cuff. "Yeah, maybe you'd know that if you came around more often." He lightly bumps his hip against hers to take some of the sting out of it.

Wincing, she looks away as they reach the others.

Between the four band members, Hannah, and Olivia—they sent the parents home to bed, despite their fierce protests—it only took two more trips to the parking garage beneath the hotel to get all the gifts and decorations torn down and packed away for the night.

During their last scan of the rooftop to make sure nothing was left behind, Hannah had quietly told Olivia she'd be staying at the hotel with Ezra that night so they could have breakfast with their parents the next morning before they traveled home—Ezra's parents back to LA and Hannah's mom back to Pennsylvania.

At the time, Olivia had nudged her friend on, waving her toward the elevators with a broad smile that didn't quite reach her eyes. Now as she stares out at the expansive, cloudless New York City sky from the rooftop of The Monarch Hotel, she feels a chill caress her skin.

Sure, just behind her there's a crowded bar, lilting laughter, warm bodies, and warm conversation waiting in the main lounge. But as the full weight of the day sinks down upon her, she can't help but feel alone.

"You dodged my question earlier like a pro," a quiet voice whispers from over her shoulder. She doesn't need to turn around to know who it belongs to, instead keeping her sight trained on the night sky, like she'll find the answers to all of life's questions floating out there in the abyss. One of the few things she misses about living in the middle of nowhere, in her small hometown where everybody knows everybody else's business, is being able to see the stars.

"I wasn't dodging. I just had a more important question to ask," she lies smoothly, lips curving. She feels Peter step up beside her, his towering body radiating heat like her own personal campfire. Unable to resist, she steals a peek up at him and sees his full mouth has flattened to a thin line.

"What's going on, Liv?" he asks after a few beats of silence. His voice is so low it's barely audible, like he's afraid to speak the words. "You seemed... off tonight."

She sighs and folds her arms around herself, gaze training back over the skyline, the lights of cars darting in and out of traffic dancing in her eyes like fireflies. She debates shrugging him off, either dodging the question again or giving him a surface level answer: *I'm fine, everything's fine. Just tired, that's all. Just busy at work, that's all.* The kind of thing you're supposed to say when someone asks how you're doing and both of you know they don't really care for the truth.

Then that feeling of being alone creeps back over her shoulders, tickling her skin like a blanket of shadows until she's covered in goosebumps. She hears a roar of laughter bubble up from somewhere behind them at the bar in the main lounge and it further compounds the chill.

Just talk to him, she thinks to herself. *What have you got to lose?*

"I've been a little distracted the past few months," she starts, still avoiding eye contact with Peter. "There's sort of this guy I've been sort of seeing. And he's driving me sort of crazy."

"That's a lot of 'sort ofs' for one sentence," he chides, and she cracks a ghost of a smile.

"Okay. I've been seeing someone off and on for the past three months and he's absolutely driving me crazy?"

"And that was the guy I saw you talking with earlier?"

She nods.

"When you say 'driving you crazy' is that in the good, Britney Spears way, or the bad, 'Truth Hurts' by Lizzo sort of way?"

Olivia's head snaps to him like a whip.

"What? A guy can't enjoy a pop song every once in a while?"

She laughs and cocks her head to think, gaze going distant. After a brief pause, she shrugs one shoulder and decides to continue on her path of honesty. "A little bit of both, I guess?" She blows out a puff of air that lifts a stray piece of her hair. "It's complicated. I don't see anything with him long-term, but there's an... allure there." She thinks of the game, how much the two of them enjoy playing, even if it hurts.

Peter nods in her periphery, and she decides to finally face him fully just as he asks in a voice so small it's out of character for him, "Why not break it off, then?"

Stalling, she wrings her hands together. Despite the cool evening around them, her palms are slick and clammy. To answer his question honestly, she'd have to reveal things she's not ready to say aloud. "It's complicated," she repeats slowly, then clarifies, "We work together."

Her throat clogs up when his eyes go wide for a moment before he blinks them back to normal. A small smile tilts up the corner of his mouth when he responds, "This sounds like a conversation best had over greasy food. Come on, I know a place near here that's still open." Only Peter could still be hungry after the metric ton of appetizers he consumed earlier.

Her shoulders loosen and she slowly releases the lip she had pulled into her mouth. With a passing glance back at the bar behind them, she nods and lets him lead her to the elevators.

Chapter 3

Building a Wall to Crash Into

T he stretched, fire-engine-red vinyl booth squeaks beneath Olivia's partially bare legs as she shifts in her seat, pulling her arms away from the chipped laminate table so the waitress has room to deposit the heavy plates balanced in her palms.

The diner on 57th street isn't completely empty, despite it being nearly midnight—the sign on the front door says they stay open until two on weekends. There's a pair of girls, clearly college-age and clearly drunk, giggling in a booth about four down from theirs. Olivia cuts her eyes across the room and notices an older couple, possibly in their sixties, dressed in finery like they too just left a swanky event at an even swankier hotel. The man is feeding his wife—she presumes—a french fry and she's laughing around it, pretending to bat him away. It's adorable, and something about it makes her chest hurt.

When their waitress scurries off to fill another patron's coffee, Olivia and Peter waste no time digging into the warm food piled high atop their pebbled gray ceramic dishes: two half-pound burger patties topped with smoked Gouda, bacon, and caramelized onions on a brioche bun with a stack of fries that could rival the Empire State Building for Peter, and a smoked turkey club sandwich with Swiss cheese, bacon, and avocado, also with a mound of fries on the side, for Olivia. The diner's old soundsystem quietly plays Train's "Meet Virginia" and the two of them lapse into a comfortable silence.

While taking in her surroundings, Olivia notices a waitress hovering just a few feet away. It's not the same woman in her early forties, with lines at the corners of her mouth hinting at a pack-a-day smoking habit, who took their order. This one is significantly younger, maybe early twenties, with a head of raucous brown curls tied up in a bun on the top of her head. The scrunchy she's using can barely contain the mass, and tight ringlets spill out over the sides. Her dark eyes are almost cat-shaped, accented by a slick wing of black eyeliner, and the way her diner issue apron cinches around her waist hints at feminine curves.

And right now she's pretending to wipe down the same worn, brown laminate table top Olivia had watched her clean about three minutes earlier. And again five minutes before that. She narrows her eyes at the waitress for a moment, one of her dark eyebrows lifting when she realizes what has the girl so entranced. *Peter.*

Olivia purses her rosebud lips but returns her gaze to the man across from her. He's completely oblivious, entranced solely by the food in front of him. Only when Peter's scarfed down half his cheeseburger and a third of his hand cut fries does he break the silence. "So, an office romance, eh?" She steels herself for more, swallowing hard on a bite of her sandwich. "And he's in your department at the firm?"

At this, she nearly chokes, and has to suck down a large gulp of cola through her straw to stop from spewing. "Something like that."

Peter waits for her to go on, finishing his cheeseburger in the meantime.

"Like I said before, I don't see things going anywhere long-term with this guy. We've had fun here and there, but it's like we're on different paths." Olivia speaks slowly, trying to explain without oversharing. It's not often she's so unsure of herself. She decides to take a different route. "There's an opportunity for a promotion coming up that I'd like to be seriously considered for and I don't want this standing in the way of it. *But* it's awkward because we work together a lot, like on all the same cases. And it's been pretty casual up to this point, so I'm not really sure what there is to break, exactly. What I really need is something to make him back off on his own."

He swallows a bite of golden fry and cocks his head to the side, a bit like a puppy. "Like what?"

She blows out a breath that puffs out her lips and stabs one of her own fries into a dollop of ketchup. "That's the million-dollar question." She bites off a hunk of fry with more force than she intends, making her teeth *clack*. She chews and swallows, her gaze trailing thoughtfully out the plate glass window beside them to the New Yorkers bustling up and down the sidewalk outside. Without meaning to, she adds in a soft voice, "When I brought it up to him earlier—the idea of ending things, I mean—he had the audacity to ask me what the point would be, because it's not like I'm seeing someone else. Can you believe that? Like the only possible reason I could have for breaking off our little fling was if I had someone better on the hook."

"He sounds like an asshole." Peter's voice thrums through her bones, making her realize what she'd just revealed, and she winces. She hears the sound of liquid through a straw before he speaks again. "But it sounds like you have your ace in the hole. Convince him you've moved on with someone else. Case closed."

She turns back to face Peter just in time to see his mouth stretch into a grin, satisfied with his pun, she assumes. It makes her smile, too, despite the fact that he's wrong. She opens her mouth to say, *I already tried that*, when her jaw goes slack. She locks onto Peter, staring at him like she's a toddler with a sugar addiction and he's the last slice of chocolate cake at a birthday party, her lips slowly stretching into a wide grin.

Peter scoots back in his seat, the vinyl squeaking where it catches against his denim jeans. "I don't like that look. Last time you had that look, we ended up ambushing our best friends at karaoke night."

"And were we not just celebrating the recent engagement of said friends? When have I ever steered you wrong?" Her voice is pure sugar as she bats her lashes.

"No. Whatever it is, no."

"You haven't even heard my proposition."

Peter groans and throws his head back, pinching his eyes shut. "Oh great, now there's a proposition."

Olivia smiles sweetly again, the smile she's seen men crumble before dozens of times, and reaches a hand out to gently caress the backside of Peter's hand where it lies on the sticky diner table. "You said it yourself. If he thinks I'm seeing someone seriously, he'll back off. I'll tell him the fling was fun, but I'm interested in settling down. Something real. And I've found someone I think I could fall for."

He groans again, trying not to look at her face. In the short while she has known him, he's never been able to resist her harebrained schemes. And he stands little chance of starting now if she can help it.

There's resignation in his answering sigh. "What do you need me to do?"

She lets loose a high-pitched squeal of enthusiasm, practically vibrating in her seat. "I need to make Bruce believe I've really met someone. And since he already thinks that someone is you, you're the perfect boyfriend."

"Boyfriend?!"

Olivia pulls her hand away from his to wave it through the air between them, placating. "*Pretend* boyfriend."

Peter's eyes dart momentarily to his now uncovered hand and then back to her. "What does that even mean?"

She can't stop her lip from twitching in a smirk. "I thought you said you were familiar with pop culture."

He merely blinks at her in response.

She scoffs and picks up a french fry, picking at the crispy, now cold, outer crust. "On the outside, we look like we're dating. We organize a few simple dates, post selfies from them to our Instagram accounts. Maybe end up in a tabloid or two. It'll be easy."

"And that's it? That'll convince this Bruce guy to leave you alone?"

Olivia frowns. "You're right, that might not be enough. He barely goes on Instagram. It would probably take him three months just to see the photos."

Peter nearly spits out his soda. "Three months?!"

"Relax," she replies soothingly. "It's not going to take that long. It can't. They'll start interviewing for the promotion way before that." She lifts a finger to tap her chin methodically while she thinks. He watches the motion curiously, his eyes catching on her lower lip where it juts out in deep thought.

She throws her hand out, index finger shooting up toward the ceiling, and Peter nearly jumps back at the palpable excitement radiating from her every pore. "The awards banquet!"

"Ah, of course. The awards banquet. I know exactly what that means," he deadpans, and Olivia throws a french fry at him. He ducks the slightly soggy potato at the last moment.

"A few attorneys at our firm are receiving awards at a banquet in two weeks." She conveniently leaves out the fact that Bruce is one of those partners. "It's a big to-do. We bought out three tables so all the departments can attend. You come with me, he sees us together, boom."

"So that's it? We go to the banquet and then it's over?"

"No! The banquet is what piques his curiosity so he stalks my Instagram. We need to make sure we have at least a few posts together before then, and we should probably queue up a few more afterwards, just to be safe."

Peter lets out his third groan in the past five minutes, and Olivia glares at him. After a brief pause, he asks in a barely audible whisper, "If I do this, what's in it for me?"

She shrugs and looks him in the eyes. "What do you want?"

He draws back slightly like he's momentarily taken aback by her frankness. That trademark boldness she wears so well. She can see his throat bob when he swallows deeply.

He takes his time, chewing on the inside of his cheek while he considers her question. She narrows her gaze, practically able to watch the gears whirring in his head. She stares at him so intently, she can't miss the way the corners of his mouth turn down, like he's replaying something unpleasant inside that handsome head of his.

Her palms start to sweat, growing slicker with each millisecond that ticks by. When she first posed her question, she'd felt confident. *What could the guy possibly want from her?* His hesitation now makes her blood chill. *What* could *he want?*

Olivia is about to prompt him to go on when she's interrupted by a throaty giggle punctuated by a sniff coming from her left side. She clenches her jaw as the mystery waitress materializes beside their table, her dark, doe eyes locked on Peter.

"Excuse me, I'm sorry to bother you, but..." She pauses to bite her lip, the picture of innocence, and she has to stop herself from scoffing. "Are you Peter Campbell? From Olympus?"

Peter plasters on the biggest grin Olivia has ever seen as he turns to the girl. "The one and only," he replies with a wink, and the waitress teeters on her toes, her body practically floating to the ceiling.

"Could I... take a photo with you?" The waitress wrings her hands together nervously.

Peter is already standing, all six-and-a-half feet of him towering over the girl who, upon closer inspection, couldn't be more than five-foot-two. He moves surprisingly fast for such a big guy, Olivia muses to herself for the second time that day as she watches his height unfold. "Absolutely! Liv, do you mind?"

She blinks, then shoots a pointed look between him and the waitress and back, balling her fist in her lap to resist the urge to refuse. She's not sure why the simple request bothers her. The guy's a bassist in a *mildly* popular alternative band. Of course he would have some fans out there. She swallows a strange dryness in the back of her throat and plasters on a smile, though it's much dimmer than the one Peter wears, and stands to accept the waitress's phone.

A white-hot pang, like the sensation you get when one of your lungs gets stuck on a breath, stabs Olivia below her breastbone as Peter slides one of his corded arms around the girl's small waist and tugs her against his side. As she snaps a few photos of them as quickly as she can, Olivia can't help but notice the way the still-nameless girl leans in to covertly inhale the scent of Peter's cologne. It's a scent she remembers well from last summer when they first met. Earthy, like cedar and rain.

She shakes her head to clear the strange thoughts flitting through her mind and forces another wan smile as she hands the phone back to the waitress. Olivia and Peter return to their booth, the vinyl making a sound like a flock of geese flying overhead under the pressure of their bodies.

Olivia takes a deep drag of her soda then plunks it down on the table with the force of a gavel swing. "Okay, so we were talking terms."

Peter startles across the table from her, as though he thought the minor interruption would end their conversation. He should've known better. "Right... terms," he says slowly, tasting the words in his mouth. He blows out a long breath and leans forward until his elbows are resting against the sticky table, the movement closing some of the distance between them. Like what he's about to say is serious, for her ears only. Without thinking, she leans forward, assuming the same position.

"One weekend in LA with my family," he says in a hush, his eyes glancing over Olivia's right and then left shoulders before meeting her gaze again. He looks a bit like a mob boss discussing a hit.

She tilts her head. "You want to visit your family across the country?"

Peter nods.

She shifts back against the booth again, offering a loose wave with one hand before folding her arms over her chest. "Go ahead, you don't need my permission. We aren't actually dating, you know."

Peter makes a noise somewhere between a scoff and a *harrumph* and tosses his head back. "No, Liv. I want *us* to visit my family. Together." She blinks at him and he forces himself to look at her, to utter the words. "My mom, she's been badgering me lately about... settling down. Meeting, in her words, *a nice girl*. I want you to pretend to be that *nice girl* to get her off my back for a little while. Make this little arrangement work for both of us."

"You want me to lie to your mom?" Her words are slow, as though she's trying out an unfamiliar language.

"It wouldn't just be my mom. My sister and brother, too. And my dad."

"You want me to lie to your entire family?" Olivia bursts forward, her voice an octave higher than when she last spoke as she slams her palms against the table.

Peter hushes her, his gaze again darting around the restaurant. When he's assured himself none of the other patrons are looking their way, he turns to her and hisses, "So it's fine for us to lie to your coworkers and all your friends on Instagram, but you won't do me this one solid? Forget it, I'm out." He sits back in his seat, a resigned expression on his face.

Now it's Olivia's turn to groan. "Point taken. I don't know, this just feels more personal." She pauses. "Are you sure? My... coworker probably won't care by the time our fake relationship expires, but you'll have to explain to your family why we didn't work out."

"Won't your parents be just as invested?" he counters with a lifted brow.

She waves him off with a manicured hand. "My parents are a little atypical. New age-y. I don't think they'd care if I never settled down. They might be surprised to see we're dating, but I don't anticipate any questions."

His mouth twists like he's resisting the urge to say "*must be nice*," and he stares toward the kitchen of the diner, probably while he considers how his family might react.

Olivia knows they live across the country in California where he and the rest of his band, Olympus, grew up. Her knowledge about his family starts and ends there, though. She wonders if they're close, or when he'd seen them last.

Judging by the tightness in his forehead, she starts to think maybe not for quite some time. That maybe his ask in their collective bargain weighs even more heavily on him than he's willing to let on.

After a weighted pause, Peter flexes his jaw. "I can handle it."

Olivia watches him carefully, her head rolling over her neck slowly to take in his changed demeanor. A part of her wants to reach out, to ask him what it was that clouded his face, darkened his green eyes until they resembled a thick forest after dusk.

Instead, she gives in. "Fine. I think I can manage a long weekend off work later this month. But when your parents fall hopelessly in love with me and are devastated that we decided to amicably part ways over irreconcilable differences, don't say I didn't warn you."

Peter shoots her the middle finger but a small smile tugs up the corners of his lips, and she feels a golden warmth radiating from within her core at the sight of it.

Before she can stop herself, she clambers from her side of the booth and dives into his, wriggling her body against the red vinyl until it screams in protest.

"Geez, Liv, warn a guy, will you?" Peter cries in mock protest, sliding his body further to the left to make enough room for her. Well, as much room as his broad frame can allow, which is far from what the average person would consider "enough."

It doesn't matter; the close proximity is perfect. Olivia embraces it, leaning her shoulder against his muscled arm so their sides are completely flush. She whips out her phone and angles it in front of their faces, the front-facing camera already open on the screen.

"Two photos with fans in one night. This must be a new record for me," he jokes when he figures out her intentions.

She deadpans back, "Don't get used to it. Wouldn't want that giant head of yours to get any bigger," then sticks her tongue out in his direction.

Peter tries and fails to hide his smile as he gazes down at her. That's when she presses down on the side button, the tiny camera shutter closing and then opening again with a soft click.

Olivia immediately pulls the phone to her chest to check out her handiwork. In it, her tongue is still out, aimed squarely at Peter. They're sitting so close to one another in the cheap diner booth that it nearly grazes his nose ring by accident.

His eyes seem to glow under the buzzing fluorescent lights as he stares down at her, the corners of his mouth tugging upward even as he tries to open it in protest. To anyone who didn't know better, it would look like adoration shining there instead of admonishment.

She runs her teeth across her bottom lip, unable to place why she suddenly feels shy about sharing it.

"Here, let me see," he says, grabbing for the phone and breaking her reverie. He looks down at it and grins, a puff of a laugh escaping his lips. He tilts the phone back in Olivia's direction and adds, "Our first official photo together and we look like goons."

Her mouth pops open in horror, and she snatches the phone back from him in a hurry. "We do not look like goons, we look like we're having a good time. Which we are, because we're fun. The fun couple."

Peter chuckles and exposes his palms to her. "No arguments here, *girlfriend*." He cocks his head to the side to look at the screen one last time. "So, you gonna post it?"

Olivia takes a breath through her nose and looks down at the photo too. Her phone is cradled in her hands like a baby, something fragile. Her lips curve. "Soon. There's something we should do first."

Chapter 4

This is Going Nowhere

"You're doing what?" Hannah's voice is an explosion in Olivia's ears, even from clear across their cozy Brooklyn apartment. Olivia rocks her body back against the kitchen island, as though the extra inch of space will protect her from her best friend's ire.

Hazy Monday morning sunlight streams in through the sheer curtains framing their apartment's bay window, painting the hardwood floor in swirls of tarnished gold and cinnamon. She focuses on it to avoid the red in Hannah's face.

"It's just going to be for a month, two tops. And then we'll part ways amicably, deciding we're better suited for friendship," she explains after a gulp of coffee that burns going down, repurposing some of the words she'd used on Peter when they hatched their plan. Midway through another sip of the scalding, brown liquid, she realizes she's still dressed in her wide legged brown trousers, one of her favorite nude lacy bras, and not much else. The dryer pings from the hallway to alert her that her blouse is wrinkle-free from the warm up cycle, right on cue. She beelines for it.

"Olivia!" Hannah shoots up from her seat on their small suede sofa and blocks her path. "You can't just lie to everyone you know about a fake relationship."

"I'm not lying to everyone," Olivia replies carefully, pasting on a particularly saccharine smile as she pulls up short. "You know the truth. And so will Ezra." Toward the tail end of their night at the diner, she and Peter had decided they wouldn't be able to fake it with their two best friends.

More importantly, they were terrified of what Hannah and Ezra might think: would they see right through their sham? Would it freak them out, thinking the two of them were truly an item? Or worse, would they be thrilled and then devastated when the whole thing ended as planned?

It was too big a risk.

"Well gee, thanks. I'm honored," Hannah deadpans, crossing her arms over her chest. She's already fully dressed for work and, by her usual standards, late to leave for the record label. Olivia's plan to drop this on her best friend as she was heading out the door to avoid an argument clearly hadn't worked. "I'm not saying I don't get *why* you're doing it. But Peter? Really? Why not go on real dates, find a real relationship to get Bruce off your back?"

Olivia's smile melts from her face like wet sugar. "Well excuse me, Miss Engaged, but you have no idea what the dating scene is like right now. It's a train wreck out there. A war zone. I'm dodging shrapnel daily. Not all of us can stumble upon our hot, successful, celebrity Prince Charming at work. As a matter of fact, that's how I got into this mess in the first place." She lifts and lowers her eyebrows meaningfully. "If I have to force my way through one more awkward 'Get to Know You' message thread, or fill out one more 'About Me' question on a dating app, I think I might die. Right on the spot."

"I thought there was a promising guy you met online recently?"

Olivia snorts and darts around her friend, shooting down the short hallway to the stackable washer and dryer combo hidden behind a door made of white-painted wooden slats. She yanks the dryer door open—it always seems to stick shut in the summer, but June is early for it to be acting up—pulls out her shirt, and rips it over her head, effortlessly tucking it into the waistband of her trousers. She turns back to Hannah. "Han, I blew off my date with him to eat ice cream and binge watch reruns of *Grey's Anatomy* with you."

"I didn't know you had a date that night! Why didn't you say something?" Hannah's blue eyes widen like a fawn's.

"I didn't want to go anyway," Olivia says, waving off the look of surprise on her friend's face. Her shoulders slump as she breathes out a long sigh, and she can't help but imagine how differently Peter's conversation with Ezra must have gone. A vision of the two of them sitting on a couch in the latter's apartment, playing video games, flashes through her mind's eye.

"*Oh hey, Olivia and I are going to fake date for a little while,*" she imagines Peter offering casually in between a chorus of gunfire and bombs emanating from the television.

"*Oh, cool. Sounds good, man. Have fun,*" Ezra would say back as he jams his fingers down on the controller.

She bites back a smile at the mental image just in time to notice Hannah blinking expectantly, her hands braced against her hips. Olivia's cheek feathers as she grits her teeth, the vision of Peter and Ezra replaced by a memory. Her lip curls slightly when she finally says, "He didn't even make it three days of texting before he asked me to 'send him a pic.'"

Hannah recoils. "Okay, gross."

Olivia forces a cheery smile to her lips as she reaches out to gently grasp Hannah on both shoulders. "Look, I will eventually get back out there and take dating more seriously, I swear, but right now I need a break. And I believe this plan will work. Bruce will get bored and leave me alone after a few weeks, and I'll get a nice factory reset. By the time Peter and I fake break up, I'll be chomping at the bit to swipe right again."

Hannah swallows, then offers an understanding nod and allows Olivia to pull her into a tight embrace. "I guess there could be worse guys out there to fake a relationship with," she manages to choke out.

Olivia laughs and loosens her grip, if only slightly, and replies, "At least our double dates won't be awkward!"

The heel of Olivia's foot slips out and then back into her nude pumps as she races down the long, straight hallway. Four doors down from the elevator bay, left hand side. A heavy oak framed door with frosted glass in the middle emblazoned with the words "Kaplan, Kaplan, and Westin." She twists the handle and it gives with little pressure, the door swinging open noiselessly.

"He's not here yet," Madison singsongs quietly from the front desk, offering Olivia a sly smile as she moves to bustle past. Olivia lets out a puff of air, her pulse still thrumming in her ears from her sprint, and loosens her shoulders. Her mini-fight with Hannah that morning had made her nearly twenty minutes late for work. She always tries to beat Bruce to the office, and for the past one year, five months, and four days she has been successful. It seems her record will not be broken today.

She tosses a wide smile at Madison and heads to her small office behind reception and around a corner at a steady pace. Most of her colleagues are already in, she can tell by the rows of computer monitors lighting her path. The fact that each and every one of those screens is frozen on the generic factory-installed lock screen also tells her their owners are likely chit-chatting over the hiss and crackle of the Keurig in the staff lounge, waiting for their morning pick-me-up to finish brewing.

I guess none of the partners are in yet, she muses, bumping the door to her office open with a hip. The fluorescent lights overhead flame to life, triggered by her movement.

Olivia settles into her ergonomic desk chair, its chocolate-colored faux leather cracked just enough to be comfortably worn, and connects her laptop to her dock, its fan whirring to life as it boots up.

In minutes, she's lost to her emails. She archives, deletes, flags, and responds to them in a perfect rhythm, the taps of the mouse and the click-clacks of the keyboard broken only by slurps from the thermos she brought from home. This morning, it was filled to the brim with dark roast from a small-batch vendor that parks its coffee trailer in her neighborhood. Now it's nearly empty.

She's in the middle of her third read-through of an email from the opposing counsel on a particularly nasty divorce settlement—in it, they're requesting a *painstakingly* detailed list of her client's assets, a list her client is adamantly against providing, of course—when her laptop *pings*, alerting her to an incoming email.

Subject: SEE ME

There is no body. Only the auto-generated signature of **Bruce M. Westin, Esq.**

She hangs her head on the back of her neck and groans, mentally calculating how long she can pretend she didn't see the email. She's pretty sure she knows what this is about already, and she doubts it's the Kansky divorce.

She rises from the comfort of her chair with the gumption of someone being led to the guillotine, reaching for the legal pad and pen waiting dutifully at the edge of her desk, then makes her way down the hall. The door to Bruce's office is already open, quiet lo-fi beats filtering from somewhere within. His taste in music has always seemed at odds with the opulent appointment of his office, with its dark wood and deep hunter green and full-grain antique leather. It looks like something you'd find in an issue of an outdoor magazine—"Check out how this pro decorates his hunting lodge!"

His favorite playlist, at least the one he listens to when he's in a good mood, belongs in a hip coffee shop in SoHo.

At least he's playing his happy music, she thinks to herself, then lifts her hand to rap twice on his door. It opens two inches further from the knock. Unlike some of the others at the firm's office on West 25th, Bruce's does not have a frosted glass panel set in the center.

Thank god for that, Olivia can't help but think, recalling the last time she'd been here... and why.

She doesn't wait for a response to cross the threshold, the thick carpet muffling the heels of her pumps as she pads the five feet to the edge of Bruce's desk. "You needed to see me?"

Bruce's honey blond eyebrows arch as he inclines his head to peer at her over the ultra-wide monitor crowding his desk. He glances to the still-open door then back to her, the movement so quick it's almost imperceptible. *Almost.*

His jaw feathers once at the line she's drawn in the sand, his wrinkle-free face hardening. A split second later, the expression is gone. The corners of his lips tug toward his ears as he leans back in his chair and steeples his fingers in front of him, elbows relaxed on the arm rests. Challenge accepted.

Bruce wets his lips, drawing out the eerie quiet that's settled over the office despite the lo-fi playlist still whispering from the Bose speaker in the corner. "Did you prep the file for the Mooney case?"

Olivia's lips thin to hide her smirk. This is how he wants to play it. "First thing this morning."

"What about the research for next Thursday's trial?"

"Sitting in your inbox." She cocks her head.

Bruce pauses and looks at his monitor, searching for a few beats. "And the discovery request from opposing counsel on the Kansky case?" He knows that email just came in at nine. The game is coming to a head.

"I was working on it when your email came in." *When you interrupted me for no reason*, she doesn't need to say.

Bruce's smile widens and he leans forward to rest his bare forearms against his desk, the sleeves of his Armani shirt rolled to just below his elbows. She notices a small bead of sweat at his temple.

He must've biked to work today. "It was a pleasant surprise, seeing you Friday."

She pulls her gaze from his hairline to meet his gaze, her mouth twisting into a smile that doesn't reach her eyes. "Pleasant is certainly one way to describe it."

Bruce chuckles, the muscles of his chest flexing beneath the thin cotton of his shirt. He skims his teeth over his bottom lip. "Too bad we didn't get a chance to... catch up more."

Her mouth dries, and she has to swallow to get words to form again. "I was a little busy. Engagement party and all."

"And your mystery guy, of course."

Her heart stops for a brief moment, then races to make up for the lapse. She doesn't answer, instead lifting her eyebrows as though she doesn't understand.

"Big. Tall. Looks like he probably repeated a few grades."

Her nostrils flare and through gritted teeth she snaps, "Of course, you mean Peter. You know, I can't really comment on his transcript. We haven't quite made it to the diploma-comparing stage in our re-lationship just yet. But I guess none of that really mattered when he was recording his first platinum album straight out of high school. Then touring across Europe and Asia right after that."

It's Bruce's turn to lift his eyebrows in confusion.

Her smile turns sickeningly sweet. She lifts her chin, soaking in the moment, then says, "The guy I'm seeing? It's Peter Campbell. From Olympus."

She doubts Bruce is a fan—die-hards would've recognized Peter even from several yards—but even he must know some of their hits. He may be a douche, but he doesn't live under a rock.

"You're dating someone from Olympus?" Bruce sounds out the words, his voice dripping with skepticism. So he does know them.

Olivia nods, her chestnut hair bouncing around her shoulders with the movement. "The bassist."

A slow smile spreads across Bruce's lips and he sinks back in his chair again looking like the villain in a corporate drama. She resists the urge to lunge across the desk and slap it from his face. "The bassist," he repeats quietly, like it's some sort of inside joke.

She blinks.

"Well it's just... you know. No one really cares about the bassist."

"Obviously I do." She can't keep the bite from her voice.

"What, was the lead singer taken or something?" he jokes, and Olivia bristles. The fingers of her free hand curl into a fist at her side while the other clenches a death grip onto her legal pad. Bruce holds up his hands defensively, but the expression on his face looks like he might burst into laughter at any moment. "Sorry, sorry. Of course you care... for now."

"What's that supposed to mean?"

He blows out a breath and tilts his head, looking at Olivia like she's a toddler who just asked him why the sky is blue or how clouds work. Patronizing. Her blood boils in her veins and she can't believe she ever, ever slept with this guy.

"Nothing, nothing at all. I'm sure you'll make one another very happy," he condescends, then snaps his fingers in the air as though he was just struck by genius. "You should bring him as your plus one to the awards ceremony next week. I'd love to meet him."

She tenses. Yes, this is exactly what she wanted, but this wasn't how it was supposed to go. She was supposed to be in control. She was supposed to drop the bomb on Bruce's big, fat, Upper East Side head. She takes a deep breath and wills an appreciative smile to her face. "Great idea. Why don't I go email Madison now to ask for an extra ticket?"

Bruce nods, and a lock of sandy hair falls across his temple. He lifts a hand to comb his fingers through it, and for a moment he looks just like that guy who made her laugh over late-night Chinese, just the two of them at the office after dark, hustling for a major custody hearing. He drops his hand to his desk, his palm resting against the ink blotter beneath his keyboard, and the image fades.

Olivia turns on her heel and walks with poised slowness to his door. When she crosses the threshold, she practically sprints back to her office.

She taps an agitated fingertip three times against her keyboard to wake up her laptop, the screen brightening to reveal Bruce's email still marked unread in her inbox. She smashes her hand against her mouse and it whips itself into the trash bin. With another two clicks, she's composing an email to Madison in reception to request an extra ticket for the Bar Association awards banquet. The email is two sentences in length and does not reveal why she wants the ticket or who it's for. Only that she needs one and Bruce approved it.

Once she has pushed send, Olivia shifts back against her chair and folds her hands in her lap, still stewing. If someone looked at her right now, they'd probably see steam spewing from her ears. She's not sure why Bruce's comments bothered her so much. She had been expecting something of the sort—petty jabs, jealous posturing. Typical alpha male behavior.

But something in the way he insulted Peter without even knowing him, something in his joke about the lead singer and "*no one really caring about the bassist,*" has her seeing red.

"Hey! I just got your email," a bright voice chirps from the open doorway behind her, and Olivia stiffens at first, then twirls her chair around to face the source. Madison.

Olivia loosens her shoulders and forces a polite smile to her lips. She has always liked Madison. She's nice, organized, always brings the best candies for the bowl on the front desk. Olivia could tell immediately upon first meeting her that she's ambitious. She's currently going to school at night to get her paralegal certification with hopes of moving up at the firm.

"Madison, hey. Yes, sorry for being so last minute, I wasn't sure he'd be able to make it until today," she fibs, searching and failing to come up with a better excuse.

"He?" Madison fishes, taking a few steps into Olivia's office, lowering her voice when she asks, "Got a hot date or something?"

Olivia laughs softly under her breath and waves a hand through the air. "Something like that." She pauses, her vision going distant before she muses in a barely audible voice, "My boyfriend, actually."

"So you're really dating Peter Campbell?"

Her eyes snap to Madison, going as wide as saucers.

Madison winces, biting on the corner of her bottom lip as she closes the remaining distance between them to perch one thigh on the edge of Olivia's desk. "Sorry, I didn't mean to eavesdrop. I was bringing the mail around and Bruce's door was open when you two were talking."

Olivia lets out a sigh and reaches up to twist a strand of her caramel brown hair between her thumb and index finger. "It's fine. We weren't exactly being quiet. So you know Olympus?"

Madison lifts and drops one shoulder. "Sort of. I don't follow them closely or anything, but one of their songs was trending earlier this year. I may have checked them out a little."

Olivia frowns, her brows knitting together. God, had she really been that out of it this year? She had no idea their new album was doing so well.

"He's pretty hot, actually..." Madison was saying, pulling something up on her phone. She turns the screen toward Olivia. It's a video from Olympus's Instagram account, one she's pretty sure Hannah took on their tour last summer, actually. Peter flashes a wicked smile at the camera while his fingers fly across the frets of his Fender. His hair is a little shorter than it is now, but pieces of it are still stuck up in different directions, like he just ran his hands through it. His throat works as he swallows, then his eyes cast back down to the strings of his bass. Olivia's breath catches in her throat when she watches him suck his lower lip into his mouth in concentration.

Fortunately, the video ends, and Madison pulls her phone away to tuck it back into the pocket of her slacks. Olivia tries to brush it off with a playful wave of her hand. "Yeah sure, but look at me."

Madison laughs, a chorus of tinkling bells, and she hops off Olivia's desk. "Well, I got you. Ticket will be on your desk first thing tomorrow."

Olivia's heart hammers against her breastbone and her legs quake beneath her, the steady thrum of the treadmill belt echoing through the soles of her feet as she pushes herself for one more quarter mile. She hasn't glanced down at the screen on the state-of-the-art Life Fitness machine once, shooting daggers at the lime green wall on the opposite end of the gym. The woman over there doing medicine ball squats probably thinks Olivia wants her dead with the severity of her gaze, but she doesn't care.

For the life of her, she still can't figure out why she's so upset, which only makes her push harder, stretch her legs further. Why does she care what Bruce thinks about Peter or their fake relationship? It's just that—fake! He's not wrong. This *is* only temporary.

And yet something about the smug look on Bruce's face, the upward tilt of his full lips, makes her want to marry Peter out of spite.

The thought shakes her and her toe catches against the treadmill belt, causing her to stumble and tilt forward. At the last moment, she slams her palms against the handrails so hard it sends a shock all the way up her arms to her shoulders, but it's enough to brace herself until her feet can find the safety of the deck on either side. Panting, she hangs her head, partially in relief and partially in frustration, all the while struggling to slow her beating heart.

She pushes a button without looking, and the belt slowly comes to a stop. It's only then that she lifts her head to look at the screen. Five miles in just under forty-five minutes; it's a new record. She hadn't even realized she'd been running that long.

Olivia steps onto the now-still belt and grabs her phone from where it's nestled in the treadmill's cup holder to pause her running playlist, cutting off a Tiesto remix mid-lyric. Then she taps over to the settings menu to turn "Do Not Disturb" mode off. She always uses the focus setting when she's working out. Otherwise she'd be instantly distracted by the first incoming notification.

Unlike every other time, the moment she turns notifications back on, her phone starts vibrating incessantly. Text after text after text rolls in, popping up so quickly on the screen she can barely make out who they're from, let alone what they say. She sees three missed calls from Hannah and a series of Instagram direct messages from old acquaintances not close enough to her inner circle to have her number. Her brows knit together.

Texts first, she decides, navigating to them. Most are from Hannah, but there are also a few from college friends she hasn't seen in a while.

What the hell is going on? she thinks to herself, then opens up her thread with Hannah.

Have you seen this?!

Did you tell someone?

Helllllloooooooooo?

Olivia wrinkles her forehead even further, slowly shaking her head back and forth. There's a link below Hannah's first text. She sucks in a deep breath and holds it in her lungs as she clicks it.

It opens a page on abouttown.com, a popular gossip and local news site focused on Manhattan's elite and celebrities who call the city home, which only makes her more confused. Her throat dries as she scrolls down in search of meaning. An explanation. Anything that will make the billions of notifications make sense.

Finally, she sees it toward the bottom, sandwiched between a story about a woman accusing her billionaire ex-husband of defrauding his hedge fund investors and another boasting some socialite's top tips for entertaining. The headline asks her, "Does Peter Campbell, the Sexy Bassist from Olympus, Have a New Girlfriend?"

The blood drains from her face as she clicks the article. It's extremely brief, no more than five sentences. Those five sentences, and the stupid headline, mock her just the same.

How did this happen? she asks herself as she reads the article over and over and over until she has every stinking word memorized.

Sorry ladies! Peter Campbell, fresh off a sell-out U.S. tour and a new platinum album, may be off the market. A source close to the lucky lady tells AboutTown that the sexy bassist of alternative rock band Olympus is spending his nights with a Plain Jane who goes by the name Olivia. She's a paralegal (!!) at a law firm here in the city, of all things! The pair haven't been spotted together yet, but this columnist is keeping an eye out for evidence.

She feels her fingers clenching a death grip around her phone and tries to force them to relax before she breaks the expensive piece of metal in half. Deep breath. Loose fingers. Good. But she still can't stop herself from reading the article again.

Some publicity had always been part of the plan, sure, but she'd wanted it on *her* terms. They would soft-launch themselves on Instagram first with a photo of her choosing, *then* get picked up by the gossip rags.

This was hardly the plan.

At least the article didn't mention her last name. Or the law firm! She winces at the thought of Bruce calling her into his office a second time about this. They aren't anti-publicity per se, but the partners prefer media hits on their own terms. Articles about their accolades and courtroom victories. Not who one of their staffers is sleeping with.

And I'm not even sleeping with him! she wants to shout.

Her phone starts to vibrate in her palm and the webpage is obscured by a new incoming call. It's Peter.

Shit, Olivia thinks, then presses the green button and puts the phone to her ear.

"I assume you've seen it by now," he says by way of greeting, then clears his throat. She expected his tone to be tight, terse, annoyed. Even angry. She's surprised to find a slight bounce in his vowels, the sound of his breath coming in heavy even through the phone. Almost like he's nervous.

Her eyebrows furrow. "Yeeeees," she enunciates slowly. "I was at the gym when my phone started blowing up. Hannah sent it to me."

"I'm so sorry, I have no idea how this got leaked. I swear I haven't told anyone but Ezra yet, not even my mom. It's just AboutTown. No one takes that crap seriously anyway, I'm sure. Don't take what they said to heart." Peter's words come out rapidly, like word vomit, and she blinks.

Oh my god, he is *nervous.*

"Peter, Peter, stop," Olivia cuts him off. "It's fine, really." Just saying the words out loud calms her nerves. The powerlessness she felt moments ago fades, replaced by an intense desire to comfort her friend. "I mean, I'm a little insulted. Plain Jane does not do me justice. In fact, I feel like the article should've said it was a miracle an incredibly smart and talented paralegal such as myself would even *consider* dating a musician, but at least they didn't give out my last name or where I work." She forces a laugh and finds that it comes more easily than it should have, given the circumstances.

He chuckles, and the sound eases the last remaining tightness in her chest, replacing it with something warm and gooey, like a chocolate chip cookie fresh out of the oven from her favorite bakery down the street from the law firm. She bites back her slowly spreading smile.

Then it hits her—the law firm. *Madison*.

"Oh no, I think this might be my fault," she says with a groan, letting her head roll back on her neck. "I had to ask a girl at work for your ticket to the banquet next Thursday. She said she was loosely familiar with your band, but I never thought she'd rat us out to the press." She pauses, another faraway revelation slowly climbing its way out of the caverns of her mind. "I completely forgot her sister writes for AboutTown. God, I'm such an idiot!"

"Hey, hey, hey. You're not an idiot, okay?" Peter's voice is low, soothing, and even though he could be a hundred miles away right now, she can almost feel the rumble of his chest against her ear. Against her will, her toes curl in her favorite pair of purple running shoes. "It was bound to happen sooner or later. This is probably a good thing. All part of the plan, right?"

Olivia nods, then realizes he's not actually with her and can't see it, despite the weird tension coiling through her body. "Right, of course. The plan."

"I'm sure once they see us out together the tune will change. They'll be asking why you settled for an ogre like me," he teases, their roles suddenly reversed, and she makes a sound somewhere between a chortle and a scoff.

"Listen, I should probably give my mom a call before she sees this. I'll never hear the end of it if she finds out I'm seeing someone over the Internet instead of directly from me. Are you gonna be okay?"

Olivia's smile widens. "I don't know, I may need to find a bunker to hide in to escape the incessant DMs and texts from old acquaintances wondering if I'm Peter Campbell's mystery girl—" he cuts her off briefly with a *pfft* sound but doesn't say anything. "But I think I'll be just fine."

The two of them say their goodbyes, Olivia wishing Peter luck with his parents and Peter wishing her luck with Hannah, and they hang up. As she packs up her gym bag in the women's locker room at an unhurried pace, she breathes out a satisfied sigh, feeling calm for the first time in hours.

She may be hovering at the edge of a precipice now—toeing the line between her current life of anonymity and a new one, albeit a fake one, in the spotlight—but for some reason she's ready to leap.

Before she stows her phone away to exit the locker room, she pulls up Instagram. Ignoring the queue of messages blinking at her from the top right of the screen, she presses the button to start a new post.

One action to answer all the people in her inbox, en masse.

She pulls up her most recent photo. No caption. No hashtags. Just two people in a diner after midnight.

Chapter 5

When the Light Hits Just Right

The staccato *tap-tap-tap* of Olivia's heels driving against the concrete pad outside The Pier echoes off the gently rolling waters of the Hudson River before her. She's been pacing nearly the entire time she's been here, hardly pausing to admire the magnificent view of the sun lowering itself into the water's chilly depths.

She points her feet toward the river and takes five steps until she's standing just before the railing, its sole purpose to prevent drunk Manhattanites from falling into the chilly water below. She smooths her hands over the designer dress she bought off-*off* the rack for nearly sixty-percent less than the retail price because it went out of style two seasons ago. Olivia didn't care when she bought it; she thought it was gorgeous, with its form-fitting nude bodice extending just below her knees, the deep gold and black lace overlay, the open back that dips down to just above her behind, and the demure slit up her left thigh that makes her legs look even longer than they are.

It had taken her three outfit changes to decide on the dress. Normally she wouldn't wear something this bold to a work event, but she couldn't shake the feeling that a lot was riding on this evening. The awards banquet. Her and Peter's big reveal.

Well, the big reveal on her terms, at least.

With the cat already out of the proverbial bag, she and Peter had decided their fake relationship wouldn't need much more of an online paper trail. Bruce already knew. Peter's parents already knew.

Hell, Olivia's tragically offline parents down in Pennsylvania even knew and had sent their blessing over FaceTime from a tandem kayak in the middle of a pristine lake, not a ripple in sight save for the ones they etched with their oars.

She had been surprised to find them there when she'd called.

"Is that Marsh Creek?" she'd asked with a furrowed brow, disbelief plain in her voice. She knew the Pennsylvania state park well from her time growing up twenty minutes from it, and she was pretty sure it didn't butt up against white-capped mountains.

In fact, she was one hundred percent sure.

Her mother had laughed, the trill of a flute. It sounded like a noise Moira Rose might make in an episode of *Schitt's Creek*. "Oh no, sweetie. We're in Colorado!"

Olivia had paled, unable to stop the corners of her mouth from turning down. "You went to Colorado and didn't say anything?" She shouldn't have been surprised. Not only were her parents chronically offline, they'd always been avid travelers. Her parents had practically celebrated when she had finally turned sixteen and been deemed old enough to stay at home on her own for some of their adventures.

She had always tried not to let it bother her. It wasn't that they didn't want her there. It was that she had school, and a part-time job, and friends, and a life at home. She couldn't take off to Maine for a long weekend or backpack through Acadia National Park on a whim.

Her parents loved her. But she'd always suspected they loved one another just a little bit more. They had the type of soul-bond most people can only dream of. Two halves of one heart.

"We didn't think you'd mind from all the way up in New York City!" her father had sung from behind Olivia's mother on the tandem kayak.

Her mom had wiggled her fingers at the phone then, a beaming smile on her lips. "Our big city girl."

It was supposed to be a term of endearment. And they did have a point. What's a few thousand more miles between folks who only see each other four or so times a year?

Even so, it stung a bit. A dry sensation at the back of Olivia's throat, like when the pollen surges in springtime.

As quickly as it had gotten off-track, the conversation returned to her fake relationship. "We just want you to be happy," they'd told her. "Boyfriend, no boyfriend, whatever floats your boat!" Her dad had been especially proud of that pun, hoisting his paddle high up in the air, sending a spray of off-color water down on his wife, who had merely laughed.

They could be sickening at times, but adorable, too.

Still, she couldn't shake the feeling of being an outsider, even amongst her own parents. Always observing their love from afar. In this case, literally.

Now, Olivia taps her manicured nails against the steel rail as she waits for Peter to arrive. It's still early. The cocktail hour had just begun when she had arrived. But her nerves are wearing thinner by the second.

"Waiting for your date?" a cool voice asks over her shoulder.

She clenches her fingers once around the railing, then releases it to spin around. She can't help but feel a little smug when she notices Bruce's eyes widen at her figure before he can catch himself and steel his features into a neutral expression. Which, for Bruce, is somewhere between self-righteous and pompous. "He had an interview that ran late, but he should be here soon."

In truth, Olivia has no idea what is delaying her fake boyfriend, but she'll be damned if she lets it show.

Bruce nods, then takes one more step toward her until he's fully inside her personal bubble. He leans down to place his lips inches from her ear to whisper, "I'd never keep you waiting. Not in that dress."

She swallows and runs her tongue over her teeth, searching for a way to snap back but unable to muster the words. Luckily, she's rescued when a towering man with dark hair curling around his ears, emerald eyes so bright they shine like a beacon in the darkness, and a tailored black tuxedo cut so well to his frame she'd have thought he was born in it, steps into her view.

Her jaw goes slack as she watches him scan the nearly empty pier, most of the other guests having already stepped inside for drinks and hors d'oeuvres, then land on her. His handsome face splits into a double platinum grin that shows off his straight, white teeth. It's like the setting sun shifts in the sky to cast its rays down upon him when he crosses the few yards between them. His approach feels like it's in slow motion.

Bruce turns around and stiffens in front of her, but Olivia doesn't focus on him. She can't.

"Hey babe, sorry I'm late!" Peter's voice carries through the air so she can hear him perfectly. "We were working on something new in the studio and Ezra decided that was the moment he needed to learn bongos. The new single must have bongos, and he must be the one to play them." He rolls his eyes playfully as he reaches Olivia, then adds, "Two hours of my life I'll never get back."

Peter must notice the odd expression on her face and assume it has something to do with the blond man he has pointedly ignored thus far.

He makes a show of snaking his arm around her back, his fingertips finding the flushed skin revealed by the deep V cut of her dress. His hand flexes against her bare skin, as though he's surprised to find it there instead of fabric, then settles to press flat against her spine. Goosebumps instantly erupt in their wake.

"You look absolutely stunning, by the way," he tells her in a thick voice, leaning down to press a kiss to her cheek. She can't help but notice just how much further he has to bend at the waist to reach her compared to Bruce. The thought warms something deep in her core. Or maybe that was the caress of his pillow-soft lips against her hot skin.

He always seemed so large. Broad and burly, like a frat boy or a football player. She never imagined his lips would feel so delicate.

You shouldn't be imagining what his lips would feel like at all! Get it together, she thinks to herself and snaps her gaping mouth shut.

Peter lets his face linger next to hers for one more tense moment, then he straightens and pretends to see Bruce for the first time. To anyone else, the look of surprise would appear genuine, but Olivia can see the tiniest hint of amusement dancing in his eyes. He's acting the part for her. It brings a smile to her lips for the first time all evening.

Bruce, on the other hand, is tightlipped by the time Peter introduces himself on Olivia's behalf. He immediately makes an excuse to go inside ahead of the pair of them.

"Thank god he's at the other table," she says quietly, her eyes locked on Bruce's receding form until he's through the doors and swallowed up by the sea of networking professionals.

"That's the guy, right? I figured by the weird look on your face," Peter says, stepping back into her line of sight. He's still grinning, but something about it seems boyish again, like a little kid who just hit his first tee ball in front of his parents. It's clear he doesn't recognize Bruce from the engagement party, a small miracle. "He looked so pissed when he saw me! We've got this fake dating thing down. Hashtag teamwork!" He holds up a hand like he wants a high five.

Olivia looks pointedly at his raised palm, then back to his face. *Right*, she thinks, *it's all pretend. Head in the game, Quinn.*

"Okay, lesson one in the *How to Fake Date Olivia Quinn Handbook*: no one says 'hashtag' anymore. And high fives are reserved for sporting events only."

"People definitely say hashtag still."

"No, they do not."

"Do too."

"Do not."

Peter opens his mouth to keep the debate going, but she cuts him off with a wave of her hand. "I need a drink. Time to really put this fake dating thing to the test."

Olivia loops her arm through Peter's elbow, her palm fitting perfectly around the bulging curve of his bicep, and tows him toward the entrance. Dozens of people are still milling about the beautifully appointed ballroom, while the rest have already found their seats at the large round tables organized in neat rows throughout the space.

She admires the muted gold linens that hug the tables tightly and the large glass bowls set in their centers, each filled with smooth stones the color of sand, succulents of varying heights, and a short, fat candle flickering in the very middle. The late evening sun still streams in the wall of windows lining one side of the ballroom, bathing the room in a dusky glow that makes everything look just a little bit better. Magical, even.

Then she notices the small stage at the front of the rectangular room and the light within them dims. The stage where they'll have to watch stupid Bruce accept his stupid award with his stupid pompous smile.

She's going to need every last drop of that magic.

She shakes the thought away and turns her attention to the bar on the far-left side of the ballroom. Despite her heels, her feet pad silently across the plush red carpet adorned with gold accents, beelining for it.

After waiting two turns from the back of a short line, they order drinks at the bar—a glass of Riesling for Olivia and a bottle of some hoppy IPA she's never heard of for Peter—and make their way to their table just before a tall, slim man in a navy blue suit announces from the stage that dinner is about to be served.

"What did you order for me?" Peter asks in a hush from his seat beside Olivia when their tablemates begin to sit down around them.

"Steak, duh," she whispers, flicking her cream linen napkin and layering it onto her lap. She sees Bruce taking his seat at the table next to them out of her periphery and purposely avoids eye contact with him.

Their group inadvertently divided itself by hierarchy. At least, she thinks it was inadvertent. Bruce is seated with nine other lawyers—some are partners, like him, and others are senior counselors or associates. Olivia and Peter sit with three other paralegals and their significant others and two legal assistants who came solo.

Despite ordering tickets for everyone, Madison is thankfully not in attendance. She'd apologized profusely to Olivia for spilling the beans about her new relationship. And, in truth, she wasn't even angry anymore. She hadn't been since she'd talked to Peter on the phone that night. But it felt right to let Madison squirm a little bit longer. Maybe owe her a favor or two.

Without turning her head, Olivia shifts to look at the table of attorneys beside her. She knows she should have fought her way to the big kids' table and spent the evening buttering up the people with the power to promote her, but the thought of holding her charade for the entire evening at a table filled with some of the best bullshitters in the state had nearly made her pass out earlier in the week.

Not to mention having to stare down Bruce Westin all evening.

Dinner is carried out to each table on gigantic round trays impossibly balanced by expert servers dressed in all black who move in a silent, practiced dance. While they eat, Olivia and Peter are asked the usual questions by their tablemates—questions they should have seen coming and better prepared for, but didn't.

How they met is an easy one: they tell the truth. An abbreviated version of it anyway. Their best friends started working together, then dating. Olivia and Peter met through them, grew closer, and the rest was history.

Both of them stumble over the question of how long they've been together. Olivia immediately opens her mouth to say three months, but Peter says six months at the same time. When met with the furrowed eyebrows and downturned mouths of their companions, they're forced to backpedal.

"Oh well, what Peter means is that we've been casually dating for about six months, but we didn't make things official until just three months ago. Isn't that right sweetie?" She throws a tight smile in Peter's direction that screams, *Just go with it.*

He nods back enthusiastically. "Yes, of course, that's what I meant."

It's a lie in every sense of the word, but no one at their table seems to question it.

With a skill Olivia did not expect from him, Peter turns the conversation around and takes the two of them out of the hot seat by peppering the others in their group with a never-ending list of icebreakers. He sets everyone at ease, lending a genuine ear to their answers and laughing at all the right moments, until the discussion eventually takes on a life of its own without his help.

Olivia can't stop beaming, most of the tension she'd been carrying at the beginning of the night evaporating from her body as they talk. She wants to blame it on the two glasses of white wine she downed during dinner, but she knows deep down it has more to do with the tall drink of water seated beside her.

While one of the other paralegal's husbands tells a funny story about the time he tried to dig a hole to China in his childhood backyard because he was convinced he was a wilderness explorer like the one he'd seen on television, she glances over at Peter to find his attention is already on her. Her cheeks flush at the unexpected attention and she offers him a tentative, close-mouthed smile, almost imperceptibly nodding her thanks to him for salvaging the evening.

During the next lull in conversation, Peter pushes his chair back from the table and stands, taking Olivia's empty wine glass with him. He excuses himself from the group to get them both a refill at the bar.

"He seems like a keeper," one of the legal assistants says with a wink in Olivia's direction. She thinks the girl's name is Marcy.

"Nice guy. Definitely not what I would have expected from a rockstar," agrees one of the paralegal's husbands. Olivia doesn't even try to remember his name.

"Don't let him hear you call him that. His head will get even bigger than it already is," Olivia jokes half-heartedly, unable to stop her gaze from following Peter's receding form as he weaves through the chatter-filled ballroom. The black-clad waiters are back to clear the dinner dishes, and from her peripheral vision she notices two people standing on the corner of the stage, whispering to one another.

She breathes out a sigh that lifts a piece of hair from her face, the loose curl bouncing against her cheek when it lands. The awards are about to begin.

Stealthy as a cat, Peter returns to their table and smoothly slides a full wine glass toward Olivia before taking his seat. Feedback echoes from the sound system when someone, an older woman, adjusts the microphone on the podium at the center of the stage, and the room immediately goes quiet from the sudden screech.

Olivia takes a sip from her glass and smiles to herself—Riesling. He remembered.

"Hello! My name is Miriam Whitmore, and on behalf of the New York State Bar Association, I want to thank you all for joining us on this momentous occasion, honoring some of the most distinguished professionals in our industry for their contributions to the legal profession in New York," the woman on stage says eloquently into the microphone, her voice strong and clear through the now-silent ballroom. She pauses for a moment to flip over a piece of paper on the podium. "We are so pleased to recognize 115 winners tonight, including the illustrious Attorney of the Year, who will be announced officially for the first time tonight."

At this last sentence, an eruption of applause breaks out from one group of tables near the windows then migrates across the room like a cascading wave as hundreds of hands pick it up. Olivia's hands meet unenthusiastically for a few weak claps until the woman on stage, Miriam, picks up where she left off with renewed gusto. She all but tunes her out as she blabbers on about the wealth of talent in the room, the history of the awards, and the qualifications of this year's judges.

She already knows the recipient of this year's Attorney of the Year award. It's why her firm shelled out a pretty penny for two tables here tonight.

Olivia tries her best to listen as the awards are rattled off by different presenters. She waits carefully for at least five minutes in between each sip of her wine, counting the seconds in her head. She dutifully claps when she's supposed to and laughs on cue during the few awards worthy of speeches. She even applauds extra hard when one of the partners at her firm, Alexander Kaplan, is honored for his Lifetime Achievement Award, and when one of the associates is named a Rising Star recipient.

Peter looks sidelong at her after one particularly large gulp from her glass and lifts one of his brows. She shrugs, pushing her bottom lip out as if to say, *Why not?*

His mouth curls up in a sly smile and he takes a long swig from his own beer, holding the bottle to his lips for just one second longer than Olivia had. She resists the urge to swat at his arm and call him a one-upper in front of their table. She also ignores the way her eyes catch on his throat as it works to swallow the cold, foamy liquid.

Fortunately, or unfortunately, her attention is drawn back to the stage when the presenter declares to the captivated—albeit buzzed—audience that it's time to name this year's Attorney of the Year. It's Olivia's turn to swallow.

Her pulse thrums so loudly in her ears she can barely hear the presenter's words. He's saying something about this year's nominees, how they all had such a significant impact on the legal community over the past year, but only one could be named this year's MVP. She fights the urge to roll her eyes at the theater of it, choosing to blink them rapidly instead.

"This year's recipient needs little introduction. He is well known to everyone in this room for his contributions on the Executive Committee of this very association, as well as the work he does as an adjunct professor in Hofstra's Criminal Justice program and as a volunteer for Columbia's pro bono program. He has been praised as an incredibly astute litigator, a strategic trial lawyer, and a devoted advocate for his clients..." It feels like the presenter is going on and on and on, drawing out the moment she's been dreading all night, until finally— "Please give a round of well-deserved applause for this year's Attorney of the Year, partner at Kaplan, Kaplan, and Westin, and pillar of our community, Bruce Westin."

A symphony of applause thunders in her ears, and she remembers only at the last second to lift her own hands. To bring them together in a near silent clap. She stays trained on the stage as she feels Bruce stand from his seat at the table beside hers. Keeps them focused forward even as she feels Peter's jaw drop open, and when his head turns to her mere moments later. She forces a polite smile to her lips when Bruce takes the stage, knowing in her heart he'll find her in the crowd.

A shark zeroing in on its prey.

Olivia only moves when she feels Peter begin to pull away from the table, ready to push his chair back and step away. She strikes out like a tiger, her hand gripping his forearm tightly, but not enough to hurt.

Like she could do damage to a guy like Peter even if she tried.

She turns her head toward him for the first time in minutes, her eyes pleading. Sure, she fibbed a bit. But he can't walk away, not now. Bruce will see, he'll know something's wrong. It will ruin everything.

Without her uttering a word, Peter seems to understand. His muscles relax only a fraction, enough for him to be fully seated in his chair once more just as Bruce begins his speech. With the blood still rushing in her ears, Olivia can't make out a word he says, but she can feel Bruce watching her even as she keeps her attention trained on Peter. Like she's afraid he may still bolt at any second.

When she's finally sure he won't, she turns her attention back to the stage and finds a pair of icy blue eyes waiting for her. They slither down to where her hand still rests on Peter's forearm.

For the two of them, it's a restraint. A plea not to walk away from this fool's bargain they've made. But to Bruce, she quickly realizes, it's a touch of affection. A lover's caress. A vein bulges in his forehead so hard that Olivia can see it from clear across the ballroom.

She smiles and strokes a finger over the top of Peter's tuxedo jacket. She can feel the corded muscles jump in his forearm at her gentle graze.

The two of them sit like that until Bruce ends his speech and exits the stage. Before he can take his seat, though, Peter is gone.

"Excuse me," Peter mumbles to the table, not that they could've heard him even if they had been paying attention. They're still watching Bruce make his way down the four small steps to the ballroom floor, where he is met with handshakes and congratulations from everyone down in front.

While their attention is still focused elsewhere, Olivia pushes her seat back with a force that nearly sends it careening to the carpeted floor and dashes after him. She could be considered pretty tall at just under five-foot-ten-inches. And though she's graced with long legs honed from years of distance running, she still struggles to catch up to Peter as he slices a path through the crowded ballroom, heading for the doors that lead to the pier. He's through them in the blink of an eye, and Olivia quickens her pace.

In moments that drag on like hours, she finds him leaning against the same painted steel banister she had paced in front of just a few hours earlier. Olivia slows her pace until the tap of her heels against the concrete is almost entirely muffled by the sound of waves beating against the dock below their feet. She stops two feet from Peter.

Sensing her presence, Peter turns his head slowly to her. The area is dimly lit by a mix of off-white, purple, and blue incandescent bulbs, the muted colors making the sharp lines of his jaw and high cheekbones look like they're chiseled from marble. She sucks in a sharp breath, all thoughts of what she might say to him vanishing.

"The guy we're trying to make jealous is a partner at your firm?" He says the words slowly, his volume so low she almost can't make them out over the rushing water. "I thought he was just some paralegal."

Olivia tenses, her hands balling into fists at her side. "*Just* some paralegal?" She knows this isn't her fight, but she can't help it.

Peter sighs and drags the fingers of one hand through his dark hair. It bounces back into place as soon as he lets go. "You know what I mean. Just that I thought he was a colleague, someone on your team, on your level. Or maybe even someone beneath you. Not the freaking head of the firm."

"He's not the head of the firm," Olivia interjects haughtily, then pauses. Again, not the point, and she knows it. She takes a cautious step forward until less than a foot of space remains between them. Peter removes his forearms from the banister and turns to face her fully. Even in near darkness, she can feel his presence, the space he takes up in the world, more than just see it.

She goes on, "If we're getting everything out on the table now, there's something else you should know. I didn't lie to you when I said he was on my team. He is. He's also a partner at the firm. Bruce is... my boss."

Peter's emerald eyes look almost inky in the darkness but she can see the whites of them as they widen. "Your... boss?"

Olivia winces but nods.

"Geez Liv, why didn't you tell me?" Likely without even realizing it, he inches closer to her.

Throwing her hands out to her sides, she turns her body toward the river. "I don't know! Would it have made a difference? Does it make one now? He's still some guy I'm trying to get off my back so I can earn a promotion, fair and square. Not to make him jealous, might I add for the hundredth time. It doesn't change anything about the plan." She steps up to the banister and drapes her forearms over it, allowing the cool, late June breeze to lift the curls framing her face.

There's a part of her, deep down, screaming the real reason she hid the truth from Peter. She tries to muffle it, throw a bucket of water on the embers, but still it burns just beneath the surface.

Because she's embarrassed. Because she was afraid of this very reaction.

And now her secret may blow the entire plan up before it really even begins.

While she stares off into the dark waters of the Hudson, a silent war raging in her mind, Peter breathes. Considers.

After a pause that feels like an eternity passes, he says quietly, "No, I guess you're right. It doesn't change anything. I just..." Peter pauses to scratch at the back of his neck. "Wish you'd been honest with me, I guess."

Olivia blows out her own breath. She's surprised he caved so quickly. A more companionable silence passes between them then, her heart still thrumming a mile a minute in her chest, the only sound she can hear.

Eventually, Peter breaks in to say, "As if I didn't already want to break the guy's nose enough."

She gasps and rolls her head around on her neck to look at him in her periphery. "You've known the guy for like five seconds, how could you possibly want to disfigure him already?"

He arches an brow in her direction. "What, like you don't?"

"Okay, fine, but I work with the guy. Every day. I've earned that right."

One corner of Peter's mouth tilts up. "I'm actually a little surprised you gave him the time of day."

In spite of herself, her mouth twitches. A small stroke to her ego. She asks casually, "What do you mean?"

Peter moves to join her back at the banister, standing so close his tricep brushes her shoulder. "Well, for starters, the guy's a total douchebag. I mean, that speech? Come on."

Olivia snorts involuntarily, eyes still trained over the river despite his closeness. She can smell his cologne, something fresh and woodsy, like cedar and bergamot.

"Not to mention his smarmy little smile, his too-white teeth. Oh! And the way he was eyeing you up and down like a prize Gibson Thunderbird in the showroom window he just couldn't wait to take home." He shakes his head and rolls his shoulders like a chill just raked up his spine.

She pauses for a moment with her mouth hanging open, then she throws her head back and cackles. The force of it rattles her chest and shakes her shoulders.

Peter narrows his eyes at her for a second, then a slow smile breaks across his face. And then he's laughing too, a rumble of thunder in the distance slowly crescendoing to a heavy boom that wraps them both up like a blanket.

Through his laughter, he adds a bit breathlessly, "He reminds me of my brother in like, the worst possible way."

Olivia lifts a brow at him. It's the first time he's brought up his family since their talk at the diner. She wants to prod further, but she only just got back onto his good side after lying. Probably best not to poke the bear.

There would be plenty of time for that in the days to come.

Instead she reaches out to bump his arm with her elbow. "You know, you do this eyebrow thing when you get all uppity." It's not really a question.

"Uppity?" he cries, throwing his hands out toward the rushing water of the Hudson.

"You know, all wild and flustered about something. Like the Bruce thing. It doesn't happen often, but when it does, your eyebrow sort of wiggles and gets really high on your forehead. It's tough to describe."

She pauses and shoots him a glance, then smirks. "Yes! There, you're doing it now!"

Peter forces his eyebrow down with his fingertips and then glares at her. He blows out a breath that sounds like a can of soda opening. "You are the worst fake girlfriend ever."

This only encourages her. "I didn't say it was bad! It's cute, your little errant eyebrow. I like it." She reaches out like she's going to poke it, but Peter swats her hand away without force.

"Well if we're calling each other out, I will say: your taste in men is terrible. I always thought you had a thing for dark-haired beauties, like me," he chides.

Olivia rolls her eyes so hard at him she thinks they may actually get stuck, but she can't help but bark a laugh. The man has a point. Her horrible taste in men is how she ended up here in the first place.

She tries to playfully bump her shoulder against his but is only able to reach his upper tricep.

After a weighted silence, Peter's expression turns thoughtful. She can see him chewing on the inside of his cheek before he says, "So if it doesn't matter like you said it doesn't, why didn't you tell me he was your boss in the first place?"

Her spine stiffens. *Did he somehow read my thoughts a few moments ago, see them pass over my face like words on a page?*

She opens her mouth, unsure if any words will even come out. She surprises herself when she admits the truth, of all things. "I think I was a little embarrassed? We're friends, but we don't know each other all that well. I guess I... I didn't want you to think less of me, if you knew I was sleeping with my boss."

Peter's mouth twists in what Olivia assumes is the same surprise she feels. "Liv," he breathes, reaching out to tuck a stray curl behind her ear. Her skin heats faster than an electric stove top where his fingertips brush against it. "I would never think less of you, no matter what. And I'm looking forward to getting to know you better."

She smiles down at the river and runs her teeth along her bottom lip.

His eyes quickly catch on the motion and his nostrils flare. He shakes his head, like he's trying to clear an oncoming thought. "After all, you are supposed to be the love of my life," he tries to joke, but it comes out a little flat.

Olivia wrinkles her nose, not quite willing to let herself wonder what it was that distracted him. "Come on, open bar only lasts about another half hour. Let's go get Kaplan, Kaplan, and Westin's money's worth."

Chapter 6

Staring at the Sun

"So the cat is officially out of the bag then, huh?" Hannah's voice has a tinny echo to it as it floats over the crisp white dressing room door and reaches Olivia's ears. Everything about this place is shades of white. The eggshell walls, the powder doors, the pale smoke carpet, the bridal white dresses.

She has been inside this oversized dressing room once already, when they first arrived to She Said Yes! Boutique. Its four towering white walls are home to a small, cushioned loveseat the color of a freshwater pearl and a seemingly endless row of hooks for dress hangers. It has no mirrors on purpose. Brides aren't supposed to peer behind the curtain, lest they see the stretched or loose fabric hogtied behind their backs with clips and ribbons so a dress five sizes too small or big looks perfectly fitted from the front.

Brides need the big reveal outside the dressing room. The one where everyone gasps, someone inevitably tears up, and well... she says yes.

"Which cat? Which bag? There have been so many strays cutting loose lately," Olivia says lightly, her smile actually reaching her eyes when she hears her best friend snort with laughter. She's pretty sure she hears the saleswoman helping Hannah into her dress cough to hide a laugh of her own.

She had begged Hannah to let her hole up inside the fitting room and help her try each gown on. "I'll have to learn the ins and outs of getting you into these things anyway for the big day," she'd whined. Despite her jaded personal opinions on the wedding industry—Olivia is convinced the business side of marriage has gotten out of hand, forcing poor brides into an overspending frenzy to try and outdo everyone else with a party that, at the end of the day, fades from memory with the passage of time just like everything else—she couldn't be more thrilled to be here for her best friend. If there's one thing she can do, it's admire a great dress, and there's something about a wedding gown that makes anyone look like a supermodel.

But Hannah was determined to get honest opinions out of her trusty bridal boutique brigade, which is actually just Olivia and Hannah's mom, Elizabeth. Hannah wanted to see the looks on their faces the moment they first glimpse her in each gown. The big bridal reveal.

Ever the control freak, it's all very on brand.

"True, we have lots to unpack with the whole 'Bruce meets Peter' thing, but this time I was referring to your first *official* tabloid photo together."

Olivia sighs. Right, that cat.

Someone at the awards banquet must have recognized Peter. Whoever it was, they never came up to him, never said anything to Olivia either. She had no idea who it was. What they did do was snap a few photos of the two of them talking closely with one another out on the pier after the ceremony, including one slightly grainy picture of them heading back inside with secret smiles lighting up their faces, and send them into AboutTown.

The ifs and maybes were gone, just like that. Olivia and Peter became an item in the court of public opinion. The only one that truly matters.

"It had to happen at some point," she offers now with a shrug. "That was sort of the point, right? And honestly, I'm relieved it was a good photo of me. It could've been a lot worse." Thinking back on that night, after the awards had been given out and she and Peter were left to their own devices at an open bar, Olivia realized there were more than a few opportunities to snap an unflattering picture of her. Like that time Peter made her laugh so hard she nearly spewed wine out of her nose.

Hannah snorts loudly again, making her best friend smile. "It *was* a really good photo. Of both of you. If I didn't know any better, I'd have been just as fooled as the tabloids."

Olivia wrinkles her nose, trying to bite back a smile. She isn't sure how they caught the moment; it had seemed so fleeting at the time. So inconsequential. A blip.

It was right after their little heart-to-heart at the riverside. She had casually looped her left arm through the crook of his elbow, her other hand meeting it halfway to squeeze his bicep. They were looking into each other's eyes, Olivia's neck long as she craned it up to meet Peter's gaze, even in her heels. They were both smiling. Not over-the-top, voracious grins, but the sort of private smiles passed between two people who know each other extraordinarily well. A shared look over an inside joke.

She couldn't even remember what she'd said, or maybe it had been Peter making another ridiculous joke, to bring that look to the surface.

"You know, it's not too late to find that for real. With a real guy," Hannah says, reading Olivia's thoughts. Her voice sounds strained, like she's wrestling a bear. A bright white bear made of lace and tulle and exposed boning.

"How dare you? Peter *is* a real guy," Olivia scoffs. "He'd be devastated to hear such an insult from you."

Hannah scoffs under her breath, and her voice sounds much clearer when she retorts, "You know what I mean. A real boyfriend, then."

Olivia barks a laugh, like she's just discovered exactly how a magician performed his latest trick. "I'll have you know, Peter has been by and large the best boyfriend I've ever had. He gives me plenty of space. He looks great in a suit. He's best friends with my best friend. He's not asking me to send nudes or expecting me to put out because he bought me a cheap dinner at The Foundry," she says, referencing a casual brewery near their shared apartment. She hears Elizabeth clear her throat from a few feet behind her and hides her grimace. "It's the perfect arrangement."

The muffled sound of Hannah stepping into a pair of high heels off the rack has Olivia stepping back from the door to join Elizabeth in the padded Chiavari chairs that line the edge of the small, elevated dais just outside the fitting room. An audience of two, visible in the dozen mirrors surrounding the space.

She is sure Elizabeth overheard the entirety of their conversation, but because it's Olivia, she's too sweet to offer judgment or advice without an invitation. Now if it had been Hannah up there talking about tabloid photos and fake boyfriends, that would be a different story.

Together, they eagerly watch the dressing room door when it opens at Hannah's tentative hand. Her heels echo as they clap against the hardwood flooring of the small stage while she slowly makes her way out. Her mouth is twisted like she's ready to continue arguing, but the pout drops the moment she sees Olivia and her mom's expressions.

Olivia sucks in a sharp breath, steepling her fingertips and raising them to her open mouth. Tears are already pricking at the back of her eyes.

Beside her, Elizabeth stands slowly, a hand pressed to her heart. "Oh, honey."

This is probably the tenth dress Hannah's tried on today, and yet it's the first to evoke such a reaction. Hannah lifts her brows high on her forehead, her eyes darting back and forth between her best friend and her mother.

"You are going to be the most beautiful bride ever," Olivia whispers as Hannah takes a few more tentative steps toward them. The boutique's saleswoman slowly closes the dressing room door and invites Hannah to look at herself in the series of mirrors lining the front of the stage. When she does, Olivia can see her own mouth hanging open in the reflection.

From far away, the dress looks elegant, yet simple. But upon closer inspection, it's truly a work of art. Thin, beaded straps and a modern square neckline top a bodice of exposed boning that meets folds of lightweight tulle at the high waist, the fabric floating down to the floor to create a dreamy, voluminous skirt. The entire thing is topped in a barely-there floral pattern sewn into the lace.

Despite the clips in the back holding it together, it looks like the dress was made for Hannah, clinging to her every line and curve. The skirt gently swishes around her feet as she twirls slowly in front of the mirror, her eyes beginning to line with silver.

Sensing this might be her moment, the saleswoman steps up behind Hannah and gently slides a veil into her hair, adjusting it around the waves that hang down around her face. And then the tears truly start to fall. First Hannah's, then Olivia's and Elizabeth's not far behind.

"This is the one. I can feel it," Hannah breathes as she strokes her fingers over the floral lace on the bodice.

Olivia gives Hannah's shoulder a squeeze as she joins her at the mirror to get a closer look at the dress. "I'm so glad I got to be here for this," she whispers. And despite her cool views of the dating scene and the wedding industry, she truly is happier for her best friend than she's ever been.

"I can't imagine doing any of this without you," Hannah breathes through her own happy tears, looping an arm around Olivia's waist to pull her in for a side hug while the two of them find each other in the mirror. "One day it will be the other way around," she adds with a wink.

Olivia blows out a loud puff of air, grimacing in mock horror, and bumps her hip against Hannah's. "Not for a very, very long time."

Hannah laughs, her nose wrinkling. "Just try not to upstage me with your maid of honor dress."

Olivia guffaws and reaches a hand out to adjust Hannah's veil. "Couldn't even if I tried."

Chapter 7

Just Loosen up a Little

"You ready for this?" Olivia's voice is muffled by the chaos erupting around her as she rolls her slightly battered carry-on through the final barrier of the TSA PreCheck line at JFK, Peter in tow.

"Of course, I'm not a nervous flier," Peter retorts breezily, wheeling his own blacked out Samsonite. Despite the amount of use it must have seen, it looks practically brand new. "Would be a serious problem for my career if I was."

She twists her mouth and turns to face her travel companion for the next four days. "I meant seeing your parents. You know, introducing your new, *fake* girlfriend to your family?"

"Oh, right," he says slowly as though he hadn't even considered it, though Olivia can see one corner of his mouth twitch upward. Like he seriously enjoys messing with her.

Peter had picked her up from her apartment in a town car, two first class boarding passes for a 2 p.m. flight tucked into his bag. She was pretty sure all of it had been arranged by Olympus's management team, but he didn't explain and she didn't ask.

Never look a gift horse in the mouth, that's what her father always said. And a first class trip to LA was a gift horse if Olivia had ever seen one.

As soon as they reach their gate, Olivia startles when Peter asks for her Starbucks order then promptly heads off in the direction of the coffee stand, his hood pulled low over his brow to hide his identity.

Sheesh, maybe I should date this guy for real, she thinks to herself as she watches his receding back, then quickly smacks the heel of her hand against her forehead. *Shut up, brain.*

The six-hour flight passes faster than she would've thought possible, thanks in no small part to the previously forbidden comforts of first class. She's pretty sure the reclining leather seats are more comfortable than her bed at home, saying as much to Peter no less than four times while they're in the air. He manages to smile and even laugh politely at the joke each time, like it's the most amusing thing he's heard all day.

Neither of them checked a bag, so the deboarding process is painless, and there's another town car waiting for them at the arrivals queue, identical to the one that picked them up that morning.

I could get used to traveling with famous people, Olivia muses to herself as she tucks her legs into the backseat while the driver stows her bag in the trunk. It's at this moment she realizes she's not sure what to expect at Peter's childhood home. Or of his parents, for that matter.

He told her his parents live in Pueblito del Sol, a tiny suburban neighborhood outside the hustle and bustle of central LA and just a short drive from the Santa Monica beaches, but she neglected to do any research (read: stalking) like she normally would have.

She should have asked more questions during the flight, but she'd accidentally dozed off in the middle of the movie she'd downloaded to her phone to pass the time and completely forgot.

Do you think he'd notice if I Googled him now? she wonders and shoots Peter a covert glance from her seat beside him. Even in the spacious SUV, his six-foot-five frame takes up his entire seat and then some, his left knee almost touching hers as it bounces quickly up and down. He's scrolling though something on his phone, but she can't fully make out what's on the screen. It sort of resembles a social media feed, but for a platform she's never seen before.

Olivia shrugs and pulls her own phone out to check her text messages, deciding against digitally stalking her companion for the next four days. If she's close enough to see some of his phone, then at his significantly higher vantage point, he'd have no problem seeing what she's up to, too.

The drive to Pueblito del Sol is shorter than she would have expected at just under thirty minutes. If television and movies have taught her anything, it's that LA is notorious for its traffic, so she expected the worst.

The blacked-out town car slows to a stop at the entrance to a gated community, and Olivia perks up in her seat while the driver punches a code into a keypad outside his window. She glances over at Peter as the gates roll open, but all he offers in explanation is a shy smile and a subtle lift of one of his massive shoulders.

When the car slowly pulls through the gate, she can just barely make out the whirring sound as it shuts behind them. They travel up a small incline, the paved road lined with nothing but brilliant grassy expanses, lush sycamore trees, and palms. Palm trees of all shapes and sizes, everywhere.

They make a right turn onto an adjoining street and Olivia's eyes bulge out of her head as she takes in the sight of sprawling spring green lawns and wide driveways leading up to beautiful multi-story family homes. Some of them have gardens out front overflowing with palm trees and exotic-looking flowers of the brightest pinks, reds, yellows, and purples, as if they were brought to life with the flick of an artist's paintbrush.

There's a trio of small children running in circles through another, their high-pitched squeals loud enough to penetrate the closed car windows. Olivia smiles to herself as they take turns jumping through a sprinkler, the laughter bubbling higher each time the cool water from the hose hits their slightly sunburnt skin.

It seems like the perfect place to grow up, not so different from her parents' neighborhood back in West Chester.

Eventually, the car turns right again, this time into one of those expansive driveways, coming to a stop in front of a charming stone house with an attached three-car garage. A towering willow tree stands sentinel in the front yard, obscuring some of the house and property from view, though Olivia can tell that it must have at least five bedrooms judging by its size. Her breath hitches in her throat.

Peter unlatches his seatbelt and climbs out of the SUV to circle around to the trunk and help the driver with their luggage. Olivia is much slower moving as she follows suit.

The moment she steps outside the SUV, the smell of a charcoal grill wafts toward her, the smoky scent filling her nostrils. She inhales the familiar scent deeply and her stomach growls, the last remnants of the iced lemon loaf Peter grabbed her at Starbucks that morning completely gone.

When she closes the door to the car, she's drawn back to the house when the large, solid-wood front door bursts open to reveal a woman who could be Peter's twin—minus a foot in height and the linebacker build. Olivia watches as the woman takes off at a horse's gallop, her petite frame slamming into Peter with such force it all but knocks him backward, a feat she would've thought impossible if someone had asked her just five minutes ago.

"Mom, you're crushing me," Peter gasps, straining to suck fresh air into his lungs. His mom lets go with a tinkling laugh. Now that she's closer, Olivia can see some subtle differences between them. They have the same jet-black hair and brilliant emerald eyes, but his mother's nose is narrower with a pronounced uptilt to the tip where his has a sturdier bridge that makes it more masculine. Her face is lined subtly with age, but still achingly beautiful, lit up by the ten-thousand-watt smile she now turns on Olivia.

"You must be Peter's special someone," his mother sings and Olivia can't stop herself from flushing.

Her words stick in her throat, and she has to swallow the dryness before she can respond, "I'm Olivia Quinn. It's so great to meet you."

Olivia holds out her hand but the older woman bats it away playfully and envelops her in a full body hug instead. "Sorry, but we're touchy-feely in this family! You'll get used to it."

Olivia laughs breathlessly and loosely returns the hug until Peter's mother pulls back just enough to add, "I'm Rebecca, but everyone calls me Becca. I am just so thrilled that Peter's finally brought a girl home!"

Peter's mother—Becca—takes a small step back from Olivia but keeps her hands rested on her shoulders. "I can't wait to learn more about you! Peter hasn't told us much." She pauses to lean in conspiratorially. "In fact, I think if it were up to him, he wouldn't have told us at all." Becca laughs, the sound light and airy, like sleigh bells chiming far off in the distance.

"Come on, Becca, let the kids get settled in a bit before you grill them," a deep voice jokes from the front door. Becca releases Olivia, and she looks up to find a man who must be Peter's father standing on their front porch with a coffee mug in one hand.

She can immediately tell where Peter gets his height from as the man on the porch must be at least as tall as he is, possibly even taller. His father's hair is brown, a much lighter shade than his wife's and son's though, and peppered through with flecks of silver that hint at his age. As he slowly descends the two steps down to the concrete path leading to the driveway, Olivia notices he is at least two shades tanner than the rest of his family, too. His skin more of an olive shade where Peter and Becca are pale.

She also immediately notices he's handsome—all sharp lines and broad shoulders, just like his son. Warmth creeps up the back of her neck when she realizes she's been staring too long and a conversation has taken place around her without her realizing. Even their bags are gone, already wheeled through the front door by the driver.

Olivia must have a bewildered look on her face, because Peter steps up to her side and rests one of his large palms gently against the small of her back. "You okay? I know they can be a lot," he leans down to whisper in her ear, his warm breath tickling the sensitive skin below her ear.

The heat in her neck rises to her cheeks as she nods. She twists her head to meet his gaze and offers him a small, encouraging smile. She's here to do a job, to be the best pretend girlfriend she can be. Now is not the time to chicken out.

"Come in, come in!" Becca interrupts their quiet moment, clapping her hands together. "I've got dinner ready for us on the terrace. Tex-Mex, your favorite," she adds with a pointed look at her son.

This makes her spine straighten, her muscles tensing. His favorite food. That's something a good girlfriend should know, and yet it's the first time she's even thought about it. About what Peter likes.

Am I going to be able to pull this off? she thinks to herself.

Peter again registers her distress and strokes the tops of his knuckles against her spine reassuringly. He rolls his head to the side to look down at her, his eyes nearly glowing in the late day sun, as if to say, *Come on, Liv. We got this!*

Olivia visibly loosens and leans a fraction into his touch. She tells herself it's because that's what a good girlfriend would do.

The dinner Mrs. Campbell—Becca, she keeps reminding her to call her—prepared was one of the most delicious homemade meals Olivia had ever had. The spread had taken up the entirety of an eight-person glass-topped table out on the Campbells' spacious terrace.

Terrace is putting it lightly, Olivia had thought to herself when she first stepped onto the veranda overlooking the valley their neighborhood is nestled in. The concrete deck juts out at least fifteen feet from the back of the house, well-appointed in green and bronze outdoor rugs and sturdy wicker-style chaises, couches, and chairs.

Becca had lifted the lids off her lavish set of matching patterned dishes to reveal steaming plates of steak, chicken, shrimp, and peppers and onions. The scent alone had practically knocked Olivia over. The family-style fajitas were served with all the fixings—three different types of cheese, sour cream, freshly made pico de gallo and guacamole with chips, red rice and beans, lettuce, limes, and warmed flour tortillas.

The Campbells had uncorked a bottle of Pinot Noir, an expensive one judging by the label, and the tightness in Olivia's shoulders fully melted away as her belly filled with more food than she had room for and three full glasses of wine.

It had taken them all over two hours to finish dinner, the sun slowly descending toward the horizon and casting the terrace in a golden glow. Despite her initial misgivings, it had been some of the most fun Olivia had had in a while. The Campbells had peppered her with questions about her job, her family, her life back in New York. It wasn't anything she hadn't expected, and she felt more prepared this time having had a little practice with her coworkers at the awards banquet.

Becca had eagerly indulged her questions about Peter's childhood, especially the ones offering the best opportunities to embarrass him.

During that meal, she'd realized she liked Peter's parents. Being around them made her miss her own hippie-dippie mom and dad back in Pennsylvania.

And his parents seem to like her, too.

Peter, on the other hand, had remained quiet during dinner. Reserved. It seemed odd, given his usual boisterous personality. He'd still managed to find excuses to touch her throughout the meal—first draping an arm loosely around the back of her chair so his fingertips grazed her shoulder every so often, then reaching out to swipe his thumb at a little bit of salsa that had caught on the corner of her lip. Enough to sell the ruse of who they are and why they're here (and make her knees quake a little under the table, but that's neither here nor there).

She couldn't shake the feeling that something was off, though. But now, as her second yawn in five minutes breaks through her lips, she doesn't have time to contemplate it.

"Come on, you must have room for a small bite of dessert," Becca presses gently, waving a plate with what looks like tres leches cake in the shape of a bundt atop it. She really had pulled out all the stops to welcome her son home.

Olivia rubs her stomach and wrinkles her brows, though a sated smile still curves her lips. "I couldn't eat another bite if I tried. Those fajitas were life-changing."

Becca laughs and shoves the plate in the direction of her husband—who had introduced himself as Andrew partway through the meal. He too waves it off with a tender smile of his own. "If I have that much sugar now, I'll never get to sleep tonight," he jokes.

A quick look at her watch tells her it's already after nine, and Olivia's lips part in mild surprise. The jet lag seems to hit her all at once and she has to lift a hand to her mouth to hide another yawn.

Right on cue, Peter reaches out to squeeze her free hand, their fingers lacing together as though they'd done it a hundred times before. He's still looking at her when he says to his parents, "Speaking of, we should probably get some sleep. I think the time change is starting to catch up to us."

"Can I help you clear the plates or wash up?" Olivia asks, already sliding her chair back to stand. Peter's hand snakes to the small of her back as they both rise.

Becca sets the plate of cake on the table and waves her off. "No, no, you're a guest in this house. That's what husbands and dishwashers are for."

Olivia sniffs a laugh as Peter's father pats his stomach and widens his eyes. There's a sparkle in them when he returns his wife's gaze though, and a dull ache gnaws at Olivia's chest as she watches them.

Peter pushes his chair in then turns to head inside the house with Olivia in tow. He pauses at the edge of the threshold suddenly, and she nearly runs into the back of him. "Uh, Mom... where do you have us staying while we're here?"

"Oh! I've got you all set up with fresh sheets and towels in your old room. We converted it to a guest room a little over a year ago, but it's got one of the most comfortable beds in the house."

The color drains from Peter and Olivia's faces at the same time, though neither of them dares to look at the other. Andrew coughs quietly into his hand at the mention of the bed. Singular. As in one. Not two.

Because of course, why would there be two? Why would Olivia and Peter need separate beds, separate rooms, if they are, in fact, a couple?

Although The Campbells don't seem to be quite as progressive as her parents, they clearly aren't the old-fashioned type, either. *Shit*.

Swallowing deeply, Olivia notices Peter is still frozen in shock and the moment is starting to draw on far too long, loops an arm under his, tugging him a few inches closer to her. "It's fine, we'll be fine," she whispers so only he can hear with a confidence she doesn't quite feel. "Good night, Mr. and Mrs. Campbell," she adds louder over her shoulder, hoping they can't detect the false cheer in her voice.

He nods curtly and pats her hand robotically with his own. "Right. Good night, guys."

The two of them ascend the steps at a snail's pace, Peter carrying all of their bags like he doesn't feel their weight at all. Olivia reaches the room at the end of the hall first but stops and waits for him to open the door. She knows it's been converted into a guest bedroom, but it still feels wrong to turn the handle herself. Like it still belongs to him, even if he hasn't lived here in a decade.

Peter swings open the door slowly and flicks on a light switch, revealing a modestly furnished room decorated in shades of blue and white and gray.

Mr. and Mrs. Campbell keep a tidy home, and they've got great taste; that much was evident by the first floor and the sweeping terrace. The guest bedroom is no exception. There's a king-size bed centered against one wall, situated under a large clerestory window that overlooks the backyard. On the opposite wall is a large dresser in the same light wood finish as the bed frame, a narrow writing desk beside it.

It's nice, but it feels empty. *Peter's entire childhood was erased from this room*, she can't help but think to herself as she takes in the space. Like he'd never laid on his back beneath that window, staring up at the ceiling. Like he'd never squeezed his broad shoulders through it to sneak out and meet up with his friends, shimmying down the trellis to avoid waking up his parents.

Like he'd never filled these walls with posters of his favorite bands, or his favorite actresses, or blurry Kodaks developed at the CVS by his patient mom.

Like he never crowded in here with his band long before they were Olympus, the four of them shouting over one another or listening to Zach rattle off an impossibly long and complex riff, Angel keeping time for him by slapping his hands against his thighs because there wasn't enough room for a drum set.

Something sharp stabs at the left side of Olivia's chest, and she presses a palm to the spot as if she can knead it away with the heel of her hand.

There's no trace of the boy who once laid on this floor listening to pop punk CDs and shook these walls with a bass guitar.

"You can have first dibs on the bathroom," Peter says, breaking her train of thought, and she's grateful for it. He points to a half-open door at the far end of the room that must lead to it.

At some point while Olivia dresses in her pajamas—a thin, gray cotton tank top with matching tartan shorts—brushes her teeth, and removes her makeup for bed, Peter sneaks out to the hall closet and pulls out every spare blanket the family has to make himself a nest on the floor.

She frowns at it when she emerges from the bathroom. "Are you sure you're going to be alright down there?"

Peter quirks an eyebrow in her direction, a mischievous look lighting up his face. Finally, some normalcy returns. "Who said this was for me?"

She makes a *humph* sound with her mouth and shakes her head, then crosses the room to carefully place her folded dirty clothes into a clear drawstring bag tucked inside her suitcase. "I take back any sign of concern I just showed you."

His back shakes with a chuckle and Olivia smiles to herself as he shuts the bathroom door behind him. By the time he emerges wearing nothing but a pair of basketball shorts, she's already crawled into the king-size bed in the center of the room and made herself comfortable beneath the sheets and down comforter.

She tries not to notice the dips and planes of his muscled back as he bunches his clothes from the day into a pile and throws them haphazardly into his suitcase. She absolutely doesn't take note of the way his abdominal muscles contract with the motion, because she's too busy looking at the ceiling. Its crisp white paint fades to black when Peter switches off the light.

The room falls into darkness, the only speck of light coming from a dull night light plugged into the bathroom outlet. It takes a moment for her to adjust to the pitch-black, for her ears to adjust to the silence.

A few quiet minutes pass with nothing but the sound of their breathing to fill the space. She isn't sure if she's emboldened by the darkness or by the wine at dinner when she opens her mouth to ask, "You okay?" Even at a whisper, her voice feels too loud.

Peter doesn't respond right away and Olivia wonders if he's already fallen asleep. Finally, with a note of false cheer in his voice, he says, "Of course. Why do you ask?"

She shrugs, then realizes he can't see her. "I don't know. You seemed quiet at dinner. Introspective. It was weird."

He scoffs loudly, the sound echoing in the darkness. "Me being introspective is weird?"

Scoffing right back, she fists the sheets tightly at her sides. "Don't get smart. You know what I mean."

"Hmm," Peter murmurs, and the sound feels like a concession. "I guess it's just strange being back. Seeing how excited they were to meet you, to get to know you. It was amazing, but something about it also felt wrong."

"Because we're lying to them?"

"It's not just that," he says quickly, like he can sense the guilt starting to twist in her gut. "Things have been different for me with my parents for a long time. A little strained, I guess." He pauses again, like he's not sure of himself. But maybe he's emboldened by the darkness too, because he continues. "When I was a kid, we were crazy close. Especially me and my dad. But when things started getting serious with Olympus junior year, everything changed. I almost feel like…"

After she can't take it anymore, Olivia prods, "Like what?"

Peter sighs. "Like they saw me leaving with the band as a mistake. Like I was turning my back on the life they'd built for me, what they wanted for me. To be fair, at the time none of us knew if we'd make it. No one ever does. It could've blown up in our faces just like that—" He snaps his fingers to emphasize his point and it rings out like a gunshot, jolting Olivia beneath the sheets. "When it didn't though, when things were good, I thought we would go back to the way we were."

"It's normal to drift away from our parents when we step out into the world. Start to grow up. It doesn't mean they love us any less," she offers quietly.

"No, I know. We're in different places now, literally. Sometimes I just wonder if they still feel that way."

Olivia bites her lip. She so badly wants to ask, *What way*? But she's pretty sure she knows what he'd say and it just may break her heart to hear it out loud. Instead she says, "This weekend will be perfect then, trust me. You guys will catch up and they'll see how amazing you are. I'll make them see. I'll be like your hype man."

Peter laughs and it's barely audible, but it's real, and it brings a smile to her lips. "I can't wait to see this."

Chuckling quietly, Olivia closes her eyes and rolls over onto her side. "Good night, Campbell."

"Good night, Quinn."

Chapter 8

Are You Ready, Darling?

A jagged sliver of light falls across Olivia's closed eyelids and she stirs, slapping a hand lightly to her face in search of her eye mask, only to realize it's not there. Slowly, she blinks awake and a blurry sea of gray and blue transforms into a mostly unfamiliar bedroom. Her ears prick at the sound of someone else's soft, heavy breaths rising and falling in a constant rhythm. Their pace is slow, even. Sleepy.

Then she remembers: she's in Peter's old bedroom-turned-guestroom, sleeping on a bed he swore up and down had not been his as a teenager, and he's the source of the breathing coming from... ah, right. The floor.

She bites her bottom lip and glances to the still ajar bathroom door then back to Peter's prone form, which she can just barely make out over the foot of the bed. She isn't sure why, but suddenly she feels self-conscious about her mussed hair, her makeup-less face, her thin, barely-there pajamas. An anxiety she didn't have last night in the dark.

Careful to be as quiet as she can, she leans toward the edge of the bed to peer down at her roommate for the weekend. He's lying on his side, facing away from her so she can only see his back and side profile. He's cradling his pillow against his face with one muscled arm tucked underneath it, his other arm draped across his broad chest. His broad, *bare* chest.

Olivia tenses looking first at his rounded right shoulder, then down the lines of his defined tricep. Her gaze jumps down to his side, where she can make out the edges of his obliques, sharp against his skin even in slumber. She forces herself to stop where his blanket meets the waistband of his basketball shorts, her breath already coming in short, successive bursts.

She'd be lying to herself if she said she'd never thought about him like that before. Not romantically, of course. But about the way he looked, and the ways it made her feel.

The first day she'd met him, almost a year ago in a Chicago amphitheater where his band was running through sound checks, her jaw had just about unhinged on sight. And his torso hadn't even been bare that day.

She chews the inside of her cheek and shakes her head to banish the memory.

Without making a sound, she peels back the sheets on the bed and climbs out, silently thanking the universe the like-new mattress springs don't squeak beneath her. She tiptoes to her suitcase and pulls together an outfit for the day followed by her makeup bag and beelines for the bathroom.

After a too-brief shower—for being a former teen boy's bathroom and now a guest bath, the shower has surprisingly incredible pressure—she dresses in what she hopes is cute but casual: a scoop neck blush bodysuit from Amazon that went viral last summer and her favorite pair of high waisted white jean shorts that she'll pair with pristine white sneakers. Perfect for a day of sightseeing... a day Peter has no idea he's about to take her on.

She uses the small, lit mirror on the bathroom's large countertop to do her makeup, opting for a more natural look than she typically wears back home. Olivia has never been to LA before, but everything she's seen on TV and movies screams airy. Beachy. Light on the concealer and the foundation. A dash heavier on the bronzer. She uses her favorite nude palette for the eyeshadow, topping it off with a slash of brown pencil liner and two coats of dark brown mascara.

Her hair is naturally wavy as it air dries and she decides to wear it that way, scrunching in a little coconut curling mousse to prevent frizzing. She slicks on a coat of pale pink lip oil and smacks her lips together for one final look in the mirror.

Good enough.

A puff of steam releases into the bedroom when Olivia pushes open the bathroom door. She isn't sure if it's the heat from the bathroom, the scent of her self-care products, or the sound of her bare feet padding across the cool hardwood floor that makes Peter stir in his sleep until he's lying flat on his back. Either way, before he wakes, she grabs a stack of papers she had neatly tucked into the interior pocket of her carry-on bag and crosses the bedroom to hover over his still half-asleep form.

The paper makes a snappy *thwack* sound when she rolls it into a tube and bats Peter on the chest with it. He instantly shakes awake, his eyelids flying open to reveal murky forest pools fogged with sleep. "What the hell," he grumbles, his voice like gravel. He lifts a hand to rub his chest in the spot she'd smacked.

"Wakey wakey! We've got a busy itinerary today."

Peter rubs the heel of his hand against his eyes and rises slowly onto one elbow. The movement unintentionally brings him so close to Olivia their noses nearly brush. "Itinerary? What itinerary?"

"Come on, you didn't think I'd come all the way to LA, for the first time I might add, without planning a full day of sightseeing, did you?" she asks sweetly, but backs out of the man's personal space.

He groans and hangs his head. "You've got to be kidding me."

She whacks the tube of paper against his temple, gentler this time. "Get up. Get dressed. We're going."

Reluctantly, Peter does as he's told, carrying his own toiletry bag to the bathroom for a shower Olivia swears is longer than the one she took. When he finally opens the bathroom door, releasing a cloud of steam and the mild scent of cedar and rain with it, she can't help but notice the way his bottles of products look next to hers on the edge of the sink.

She looks away.

He's wearing a pair of carbon gray chino shorts that hug his muscular thighs and a black V-neck, a look Olivia has come to recognize as his signature. "Alright, before we go anywhere or do anything, I need coffee. Like, the biggest mug of the strongest coffee we can find," Peter says, his voice still a little thick.

It's kind of cute. She can't help but smile. *Shut up*, she tells herself.

Peter rubs a plush navy bath towel against his damp hair with one large hand, squeezing some of the moisture out of the ends as he crosses the room to deposit his basketball shorts into his suitcase. "And breakfast. Like, the biggest plate of breakfast we can find," he adds, oblivious to her mental jumping jacks. He stops dead in his tracks in the middle of the room, suddenly looking the most awake he has all morning. "Do I smell bacon?"

"And pancakes," Olivia answers, rubbing her empty stomach. "I think your mom made breakfast. Let's go, I'm starving."

She lets Peter lead the way to the kitchen downstairs. She still hasn't fully adjusted to her new surroundings and would've definitely turned left at the bottom of the stairs when she was supposed to go right.

"Oh good, you're just in time! I made the works," Peter's mom says brightly, like she's been awake and refreshed for hours... or finished a pot of coffee by herself while the rest of the house slumbered.

Olivia can't help but close her eyes and take a deep inhale, letting the scent of buttery flapjacks, maple syrup, bacon, eggs, and sausage wash over her. Her mom had never been much of a cook—in fact, her dad usually did most of the cooking. But neither of her parents were big breakfast eaters. Without work to wake them, they would sometimes sleep until almost noon on the weekends.

Olivia, on the other hand, has always loved breakfast. And right now, she feels like she's died and gone to heaven.

"Wow Mom, expecting an army?" Peter asks lightly as he takes in the feast his mom has prepared, sprawled before them on their massive marble kitchen island like something straight out of a historical drama. He's not exaggerating.

Becca tosses her head back in a laugh and goes back to loading the dishwasher instead of answering.

Peter and Olivia pile heaps of food onto their plates, taking a little bit of everything on display, then fill oversized coffee mugs with freshly brewed dark roast from the family pot—Peter takes his black while Olivia stirs in one sugar and a splash of creamer. They sit side-by-side at the six-person breakfast table nestled in the corner of the kitchen.

The two of them eat in a comfortable silence for the first five minutes, the sound of Becca washing dishes and humming a few feet away serving as their soundtrack. Finally, Peter comes up for air to ask around a bite of pancake, "Tell me more about this itinerary of yours." His eyes have more of their usual sparkle back, thanks to the coffee and his mom's cooking.

Olivia grins, takes a long sip of her coffee, and pulls out the bundle of paper she had tucked into the back of her jean shorts upstairs. "So glad you asked." She spreads the paper out on the table between them, careful to avoid the small dab of maple syrup Peter had slopped over the edge of his plate while stuffing his face. "While doing my research in preparation for this trip—"

"You did research before this trip?" Peter interrupts with an arched black eyebrow. *His little errant eyebrow.*

Olivia tucks her chin and shoots him a smug look from beneath lowered lashes. "Have you met me before? Obviously. I wasn't going to come to Los Angeles for the first time and not do all the things."

She may have neglected to look more into her housemates, but she isn't completely unprepared.

Peter raises his fork, a sausage link still speared to it, in surrender.

"As I was saying," she begins again, scanning a pale pink mani-cured fingertip down the piece of paper as she reads out the list of tourist-y activities, like *visit the Hollywood sign* and *have lunch at*

Santa Monica pier and *pretend to shop on Rodeo Drive even though I couldn't afford a scrap of cloth, let alone an entire garment, in any of those stores.*

Peter's eyes have steadily grown wider with each item she has ticked off on her list until they look like they might burst right out of his skull.

Olivia rolls her lips together and looks away from him, deciding to ignore it. *He'll come around*, she thinks to herself. Out loud, she says, "I couldn't find a ton of things to do here in Pueblito del Sol, so feel free to add things you know to this list."

"You kids planning an outing? You should check out the Tischler. It's only a few minutes away," Peter's dad says from where he's materialized over their shoulders. He must've joined his wife in the kitchen at some point during Olivia's spiel. She hadn't even heard him come in.

She turns around to look at him curiously. "What's the Tischler?"

Peter groans beside her.

"Hey now, you used to love going there," his dad says, shooting his son a stern look. There's a slight uptilt to one corner of his mouth though, softening it. Andrew turns to face Olivia. "It's a classic car museum right here in the neighborhood. Home to some of the most beautiful works of machinery in the world." His expression turn wistful as he speaks.

"Sorry Dad, I don't think looking at cars from the early 1900s is on Liv's bucket list," Peter says with a snort under his breath, nodding with his chin toward the piece of paper on the table.

Olivia cocks her head, considering. On one hand, he's completely right. It's not on her list. And even if she had a whole week to spend here instead of the few days they'd planned, it likely still wouldn't make the cut. But the opportunity to prove Peter wrong *and* get a small glimpse into his childhood is too tempting to resist.

She shrugs and holds Peter's gaze as she says, "I'm in. We can go there first." Then she looks back to the eldest Campbell with a smile so sweet it's won over every parent she's ever met. "Would you like to join us?"

Peter tenses at her side. Again, she ignores him.

Andrew lifts a hand to his face, scratching his chin thoughtfully. Olivia's never seen a real-life human do the thinking face before, but somehow it works on him. "Well, I am off today. And it's been a little over two weeks since my last visit. Why not?" His face splits into a wide grin that could rival even his son's.

"Check this one out, Olivia. She's a true beauty," Andrew says brightly after letting out a low wolf whistle. He's standing in front of the shiniest cherry-red car she has ever seen. As she walks over to him, she notices a Chevrolet emblem on the back and the words "Bel Air" embossed on the fin. It looks like it's from the 1950s, but truthfully she has no idea.

To say she's a little out of her element would be putting it mildly.

Sure, she can appreciate a nice car. She's familiar with the luxury brands and some of the zippy sports cars, too. But antiques? There's a learning curve, to say the least.

"Still staring at Sally every time you come here, I see," Peter muses, his feet silent as a cat as he sidles up to them. Just before they left, Peter slid on an all-black Yankees hat and the way the wavy ends of his hair are pooling out the bottom of it, curling over the shells of his ears, does something to Olivia's insides that she'll take to her grave.

Sally. The name bounces around her mind, vaguely familiar, but she can't quite place it.

Andrew laughs boisterously, his mustache wagging, interrupting her race down memory lane. "She'll always be my favorite."

Peter smiles, small but affectionate. Olivia's chest warms at the sight of it and she starts to back up slowly until Peter and his father are standing side-by-side in front of the car. She steps up on Peter's other side but gives them room. It's not like she can follow their conversation anyway, completely lost somewhere between the words "chassis" and "knee-action suspension."

Peter slides a hand out of his pocket to brush a piece of black hair out of his eyes as he leans in to look at the interior of the red Chevy. "Is that '61 Thunderbird still here?"

"Oh yeah, Rick would never let her go," Andrew responds, referencing the owner he befriended over the years during his many, many visits to the museum. "She's in her usual spot. Come on."

Olivia lags behind Peter and his dad, watching them gradually grow more and more comfortable around each other with each car they admire. Though she'd never admit it to Peter—because he'd probably throw her over his shoulder and then straight into the Pacific Ocean—this had been one of the reasons she'd agreed to come here. Trying to force them together. Force them to talk.

Right behind proving a point, of course.

The museum itself seems to weave on endlessly, the building looking more like the interior of a small airplane hangar stuffed to the brim with cars dating back to the 1920s, possibly even earlier. Some of them are organized in neat rows, roped off to avoid fingerprints from overeager visitors. Others are on center display, smack dab in the middle of the room with their doors flung open, allowing a sneak peek at the interiors.

Those are usually Olivia's favorites. The showiest ones they have.

If they had followed the typical self-guided tour route, the three of them would have wound through time, starting with the earliest Model Ts on one side of the museum all the way through some of the most modern cars the Tischler has, which still date back to at least the late '70s.

Instead, Peter and Andrew seem to have made up their own route through the place, moved not by the date or the model or the color of the car but by some moment in their collective memory. The time they spent here together.

Peter's shoulders seem to loosen with each stop. His smile grows a little brighter with each shared inside joke.

Through it all, she finds herself paying more attention to Peter and his father than the cars.

Eventually, they circle back around to the front of the museum and Andrew steps away to talk to the owner about an event the museum is hosting in August. Peter angles his body toward Olivia and takes a few steps forward to close the distance between them until he has her pinned between himself and an old Dodge. "I know what you've been up to," he whispers, his eyes sparking.

Her belly dips, but outwardly she cocks her head to the side innocently. "I'm not sure what you mean."

The corner of Peter's lips turns up in a crooked smile. "Don't play dumb with me. I know you. You're too smart for your own good."

She tries to bite back her smile unsuccessfully. "I assure you, I am one hundred percent innocent. I just really like looking at... old cars." She shrugs, waving a loose hand toward the one behind her.

Peter laughs, the sound low and husky, like it's meant only for her. "Oh, so it had nothing to do with proving me wrong earlier when I said you're not into this kind of thing?"

Olivia's smile turns saccharine and she folds her hands together in front of her thighs. "I am honestly offended you'd even think such a thing."

"So it wasn't your master plan all along to get me and my dad talking again?"

She lifts and drops a shoulder. "You give me too much credit. I just really love museums."

Peter nods slowly, but the slick smile playing on his lips shows his skepticism. He reaches out and rests a gentle hand on her hip. His palm is so large, he can practically grip her entire hipbone. He gives her a small squeeze and leans in until his lips hover beside her ear. "Well, thank you anyway. I had a great time."

Her breath catches in her throat at his sudden closeness, the scent of his cologne melded with his shampoo filling her senses and making her dizzy. She's thankful Peter can't see her face, sure she's lost control over it. She can't even form words.

Almost as quickly as he moved in, he steps back to put a few feet between them again when he hears his father's deep voice from somewhere over his shoulder. "Peter, can I talk to you for a moment?"

He stiffens for a moment, but then nods his head and joins Andrew in the reception area of the museum. Olivia tries not to watch him walk away. She tries not to watch the two of them talking less than ten yards from her. She pretends to be extremely interested in the plaque on display next to this... *Ah, yes, Challenger. I knew that.*

When she hears a peal of deep laughter, she looks up just in time to see Peter's father patting his son's back with one hand while sliding something into his palm with the other. Her mouth twists in interest as Peter waves to his father once over his shoulder and begins the slow trek back to her across the showroom. He's still grinning ear to ear when he reaches Olivia.

"What was that about?"

"Super-secret father-son business. You wouldn't understand."

She cocks an eyebrow and folds her arms over her chest.

Peter sighs in mock frustration, but his lips are still stretched wide. "Okay, fine. He may or may not have been singing your praises."

Olivia smiles triumphantly, pumping a fist in front of her chest.

"Clearly he doesn't know you like I do."

Her grin turns into a very pointed scowl, earning a soft snort from Peter.

"More importantly, he called my mom for a ride home. He's letting us take the Mustang for the day. So, I guess your sucking up really was good for something."

She bites back a laugh and shakes her head, looking up at Peter from lowered lashes. "I told you your parents would love me by the end of this."

His smile thins slightly, a muscle feathering almost imperceptibly in his jaw. "Yeah, too bad for them this whole thing has an expiration date."

Olivia's heart stutters, her mouth running dry, but she tries not to let it show. She forces her smile to widen as she loops her arm around Peter's elbow and tugs him toward the door that leads to the parking lot. "Come on, car nerd. We've got a full itinerary and a convertible waiting for us."

Chapter 9

Baby Blue Shades

"I'm pretty sure we have these back in New York," Peter says, his footsteps slowing when he realizes where Olivia is dragging him. She refused to "spoil the surprise" on their thirty-minute ride. He looks over the sparkling gold cursive letters adorning the store's front door for the second time, like the words might change the longer he stares at them.

"Hey, I just spent two hours looking at moldy old cars so you and your dad could create a core memory. Spare me." A silver bell chimes when she tugs open the glass-paned door, the sound ringing around them like Christmas. Or a cash register drawer opening.

His feet still don't move. "So you admit it was all a setup."

She drops her head back on her neck to look quickly at the sky and gestures to the empty doorway with her free hand, using the other to prop it open. "If I say yes will you get your ass inside?"

Peter grimaces and wrinkles his nose, but it isn't enough to hide the real smile peeking through. Victory in battle.

He takes a step forward and stretches one of his large hands out to press it to the door, just above Olivia's head, his sinewy arm pushing back against its weight with ease. "After you, Quinn."

She swallows, thrown off by his sudden closeness, then quickly turns and stomps inside Luxe LA Bridal. At least he ditched the baseball hat after the museum. It did unspeakable things to her insides and she's not sure how much more of it she could take.

She's immediately greeted by an older woman dressed all in black with gold accent jewelry. In a few words, she explains why she's there and what she's looking for, and the attendant immediately races off to the far side of the store.

When she disappears, Olivia swivels back to where Peter stands behind her. Her eyes linger on a few of the racks closest to them, each one filled with white garments.

"I think you might have forgotten who I am. My name's Peter. Not Hannah," he taunts, his eyes bouncing around the store but unable to rest on anything for longer than a second.

Olivia steps up to him and rests a placating hand on his bicep, feeling the muscle flex beneath her touch. "This shouldn't take long. I need to order my maid of honor dress for the wedding, and this place has the exact one I want."

"Aren't you and Hannah supposed to like... I don't know, do this together?"

She sighs and drops her hand. "That's when the bride picks out her gown. Despite being the most type-A person I know, Hannah's actually letting us choose our own dresses. It just needs to fit the theme."

"Which is?"

At this, Olivia smiles softly, her gaze going distant. "Colors of the night sky. Han will be our stars and moon, obviously. The rest of us fall somewhere in the midnight black to dusky magenta range. I'm going with a deep navy."

"Isn't it bad luck for the best man to see the maid of honor's dress before the wedding?" Peter asks, one corner of his lips tugging up as if pulled by a string.

"You're thinking of the bride and groom," she corrects him right as the attendant wanders back.

"I pulled the dress you asked for, plus a few in the same color in case it's not a winner," the older woman says, her mauve-painted lips stretching around two rows of perfectly white teeth. "I'll show you and your boyfriend to a fitting room. We have chairs just outside the door so he can relax while you try these on."

Olivia and Peter both open their mouths at the same time to protest the word *boyfriend*, then each pause to let the other speak, which results in neither of them saying anything before the attendant walks away, expecting them to follow. They stare at each other, caught off guard, then quickly look down at their feet and trail after her before she's sucked into the maze of mannequins and metal racking.

"I'll be just over in the next aisle restocking some dresses if you need help with anything, dear," the saleswoman says after she unlocks a fitting room and swings the door wide to allow Olivia through. It looks just like the one she visited with Hannah, only about half the size. Not intended for brides. The attendant follows her inside to hang up the dresses she pulled—three from the looks of it—then steps out and closes the door to give her privacy.

Taking herself in in the the floor-to-ceiling mirror at the back of the fitting room, she takes a deep breath. This had seemed like such a good idea when she first came up with it. A quick pit stop on their trek through LA to try on one dress, find that it fits perfectly, order it, and be on her way. But now with Peter sitting just outside the fitting room, she's unsure.

What if he doesn't like it?

She shakes her head. It doesn't matter if he likes it or not. He's not really her boyfriend. And even if he was... well, Shania Twain said it best. He better damn well say it looks great anyway.

She takes another deep breath then disrobes, folding each item of her clothing up carefully to place it in a neat pile on the little settee in the corner. *You're stalling...*

Olivia digs for the dress she selected at the back of the pack. She knows how this is supposed to go—try on a few others first in some other styles just to see. More expensive ones, no doubt. But she isn't the bride and she's confident she knows exactly what she wants.

She carefully steps into the open center of the chiffon pool at her feet, sliding the cool fabric up her body until she can zip up the back. She checks her reflection only long enough to ensure nothing is out of place, then reaches for the handle of the dressing room door with a shaking hand. She pushes it open with the force of a truck barreling unchecked down a hill, stepping out of the changing room before she can lose her nerve.

Olivia takes a few tentative steps, glancing between Peter's six-foot-five frame sprawled across a plush armchair and the wall of mirrors behind him. When he doesn't immediately speak, she asks in a small voice, "Well, what do you think?"

Peter's emerald eyes are wider than she's ever seen them and, from only about three feet away, she can just make out a rim of gold blossoming around his pupils. As she fully steps into his focus, he sits up straighter and presses his palms against the tops of his thighs. His mouth flounders open, but no words come.

She takes the odd look on his face for disapproval and begins smoothing out the soft folds of chiffon clinging to her legs, her fingers brushing against the slit that goes up to her thigh to help with mobility. She takes a few steps closer.

The dress itself is crafted from a fabric so deeply navy it nearly looks black, the airy woven chiffon billowing around her feet every time she takes a step, like a midnight breeze whispering through summer willows. Staring at her reflection, Olivia runs her fingers over the plunging V-neck and adjusts the ruffled empire waist.

In the mirror, she can see Peter stand and take two steps toward her, a strange look on his face. It's almost... glazed over. She turns to face him, biting her bottom lip. "Well, what is it? Is the dress overdoing it? I don't want to draw attention away from Hannah."

His eyes meet hers in the mirror then move lower, trailing slowly down her body. They catch for a long, weighted moment on the sliver of her tanned thigh where it peeks out from the side slit, then return even more slowly to her face. A silent pause passes between them.

"It's... underdoing it?" Olivia asks slowly, her forehead creasing.

"No, it's—the dress is fine. It's good, but you..." he trails off again, his line of sight hovering somewhere just past her left ear, like he can't quite meet her gaze full on. "You look..." Peter's throat works as he swallows, his words lost to the movement.

He never gets the chance to try again, interrupted when the sales-woman rushes over with a beaming smile on her lips. "I guess I shouldn't have bothered pulling those other dresses after all."

Olivia's lips curve, and she forces herself to abandon Peter's gaze and look at the older woman instead. "I think this might be the one."

The older woman laughs and steps up behind Olivia, turning her back around to face her reflection with two sure hands on her shoulders. The saleswoman immediately begins pinching and plucking and smoothing at the fabric in a practiced rhythm. "It could maybe do with a little hemming, but I'm honestly not sure I would alter it much. It fits you like a glove."

Olivia's smile grows, her confidence growing with it. She tucks a loose piece of hair behind her ear, trying to imagine the whole look with her hair and makeup. Her eyes catch on Peter's in the mirror, just in time to see him slowly wet his lips. It sends a shiver up her spine.

"Oh, sorry dear, my hands are always like ice," the attendant says good-naturedly, mistaking the shiver for a sudden chill. "Do you have shoes in mind for this already? If not, I think we have the perfect pair."

Something about the prospect of shoe shopping breaks whatever trance has fallen over Peter, and he snaps his attention to the attendant with a horrified expression sharpening his face into a series of harsh lines and angles.

Half-tempted to let him hang, Olivia relents after a moment. "I think I've got that covered already, but thank you so much for your help."

Peter sighs loudly with relief, his shoulders drooping, and resists the temptation to playfully swat him. He finds her once again in the mirror, that glazed look replaced by something that feels even more intimate. It takes everything she has in her to look away.

·♥·♥·♥·♥·♥·

"That wasn't so bad now, was it?" her voice is carried up and away on a swift wind, wisps of her hair billowing wildly around her tanned face as Olivia and Peter cruise at seventy miles per hour on the 405. She had insisted on putting the top down before she'd allow Peter to leave the Luxe LA Bridal parking lot, already braiding her brown hair in a side plait as he tried halfheartedly to argue.

"What's that? I can't hear you over the wind," Peter booms jokingly from the driver's seat. He pulls his eyes from the road to look at his companion and immediately catches on the beaming smile lighting up her face, the way loose pieces of her hair whip back and forth around her.

Olivia shakes her head playfully at him and throws her hand out the open window, wriggling her fingers in the airstream flowing past. Her other hand thrusts down to crank the volume up on the car radio, the sound of Taylor Swift's "Gorgeous" blasting out of the sound system at her command, thanks to a little Bluetooth magic and the carefully crafted playlist she prepped before leaving New York. She relaxes her head against the seat, content.

He doesn't even complain about the choice of music.

Less than fifteen minutes later, Peter has steered the car into a parking spot near the Santa Monica Pier: the second stop on the Olivia Quinn tour. The car museum doesn't count. He leads the way out of his super-secret parking location—though Olivia teased him that it's not such a secret anymore if he shared it with her—and toward the bustling seaside.

"Oh my god!" she yells, thrusting a hand out to stop Peter in his tracks. Her palm accidentally slaps against his washboard stomach, the muscles firm enough to be felt in great detail through his black T-shirt. She jerks her hand back as soon as she's sure he's stopped walking.

Peter looks at her, eyebrows arched in unspoken question. She can practically hear his stomach rumbling—after all, she'd promised him lunch at their next stop.

In answer, Olivia points her manicured finger straight ahead to a woman about five yards away, who looks to be only a few years older than them, and her...

"Wait, is she walking a—"

She nods her head enthusiastically. "Mhmm! A tabby from the looks of it."

"I take it you're a cat person?"

Olivia grins up at him then takes off at a speed walker's pace toward the duo. Before Peter can catch up to her, even though his legs are each half a foot longer than hers, she has already learned the cat's name (Cheddar), gender (male), and if he's safe to pet (of course).

When she squats down to scratch Cheddar under his chin, the orange tabby leans into her touch like he's been deprived of it his entire life. "Aren't you just the cutest?" she coos in a baby voice that makes Peter snort.

The noise draws Cheddar's attention and, before Peter knows what's happening, the orange fur ball is winding his way between Peter's legs, brushing up against his calves like they're scratching posts. In spite of himself, he smiles down at the little guy, bending at the waist to offer him a few soft pets on the top of his head.

Reluctantly, after more than five minutes have passed, Olivia bids goodbye to Cheddar and his mom at Peter's not so subtle hints about their lunch reservation.

"I would have like, a whole brood of Cheddars at my apartment if my landlord allowed pets," Olivia says with a deep sigh as she and Peter weave through throngs of people toward a burger joint called The Sand Dune with a 4.5 star rating on Google.

It's known best for its breathtaking, panoramic views of the Pacific Ocean, thanks to its open-air dining room that makes it feel like you're practically sitting on the beach while you dine. And for having the best burgers one can find in all of Santa Monica.

That definitely wasn't why she'd picked it, though.

Peter chuckles under his breath and shoves his hands into his pockets, keeping his eyes trained on the cerulean ocean sprawled before them as they walk.

"Not a cat person?" She looks up at him, her elbow lightly colliding with his forearm as she dodges a guy on rollerblades.

"Oh, uh. No, it's not that. I guess I don't have strong opinions about them. My dad's allergic to all furry friends so we never had pets growing up, unless you count a beta fish my little brother tried and failed to raise in middle school." He laughs, the sound more of an exhale than anything.

Olivia nods, her arms still swinging at her sides as they walk. "Ah, understood. But *you're* not allergic?"

Peter smiles over at her and shakes his head. "Nah, and thank god for it. Angel's got a whole farm back home. Everything he wears is covered in pet hair at all times, even after it's been washed on the road."

She snorts and her hip bumps against his unintentionally as they reach the restaurant. "Good, because otherwise this relationship definitely wouldn't work out."

Peter's mouth lifts at one end, but he looks down at his feet as though he's learning to walk for the first time while they climb the rickety wooden steps to the propped-open door of The Sand Dune. Olivia can just make out the slightest pinch to his brow as he pushes it open for her.

One shared appetizer, two craft beers apiece, and two of the biggest burgers Olivia has ever seen later, and Peter's mood has improved drastically, much to her delight. Gone is the twinge in his forehead and the downcast eyes, replaced instead by the voracious grin she's used to seeing tug up his lips.

They're very kissable lips, she had thought to herself when she watched him purse them together while calculating the appropriate tip to leave. She nearly slapped herself to shake the thought.

Must be the beer talking.

When the bill is paid, Peter points his chin in her direction, a small smirk playing on those *"very kissable lips."* "So what's next, captain?"

Olivia's answering look has his eyes widening.

She tugs him not-so-gently down the front steps of the restaurant by his forearm to a still-bustling Santa Monica pier. Nearly two hours had passed while they dined, and the pre-dinner crowd is already filling in around them.

"You can't be serious?" he asks when they reach their next destination: a chintzy little tourist shop a few doors up from The Sand Dune, heading back toward where they parked the car. "Haven't you done enough shopping for one day?"

"Come on! Lighten up. I realized on our drive here that I forgot my sunglasses at home and need to get a cheap replacement pair. Help me pick some out."

With a note of false reluctance that doesn't dim the spark in his eyes, Peter starts slowly rotating a rack of cheap, plastic sunglasses set out in front of the little shop with his two forefingers. After less than ten seconds scanning the frames on display, he bites back a smile. "Call off the search, I think I found the perfect pair."

Olivia puts back the black oversized frames she had been eyeing and peers around his shoulder, then immediately lets out a groan. "Absolutely not." Apparently his version of trendy and cute are mini, round, metallic frames with solid black lenses. They look like something a mad scientist in the 1920s would've worn.

Peter's full-on grinning now, pinching the thin, silver temple tip of the glasses in question between one thumb and index finger. "Come on, you'd look great in these."

"I'd look like a bad John Lennon knock-off." She wrinkles her nose and goes back to scanning another rack while Peter tries, and fails, to hand the glasses to her. "I may be gifted with good looks, but even I couldn't make those work."

Peter's laugh booms around them, drawing the attention of a few other patrons, before he slides the pair back into their holder. Olivia picks up another oversized pair, this one with hazy brown lenses and tortoiseshell frames. She slides them easily over the bridge of her nose and inspects her reflection in the funhouse mirror stuck to the side of the display. She twists her head this way and that, but ultimately decides to put them back.

"Ooh, here!" Peter shouts from her right, reaching for another pair. The worn plank boards beneath his feet groan in protest when he shifts his weight to bring them closer to her.

This time, she doesn't even look up. "Let me guess, snowboarding goggles?"

"I'm serious this time, just try them on."

Reluctantly, she turns and finds his face glowing with sincerity. His eyes look a little like a grassy knoll in the center of a secret garden, gentle but untamed. She rolls her lips into her mouth, skepticism plain on her face.

The glasses he holds aloft are baby blue, almost the exact color of the cloudless California sky overhead, and have a waxy sheen to them like rock candy. Not her typical color. But the glasses are surprisingly trendy, with wide temples and rectangular frames holding light blue lenses. They look like something Malibu Barbie might wear.

When she reaches to take them from Peter's hands, their fingertips brush and a chill rakes up her spine. She snatches the sunglasses back a little more forcefully than she intends, but Peter doesn't seem to notice. She slides them smoothly onto her face and dips her head until it's eye level with the mirror.

They look good. Surprisingly good. Like they were made for her slightly angular cheekbones and ski jump nose.

Her mouth twists to the right in a reluctant smile, and she can practically feel Peter vibrating from beside her with self-satisfaction.

Slowly, she rolls her head on her neck toward him. "I guess it's true what they say."

Peter's brows furrow together.

Olivia smirks. "Even a blind squirrel finds a nut once in a while."

His mouth pops open in mock outrage, one of his broad palms soaring up to flatten against the hard planes of his chest.

Olivia lets loose a burst of laughter that draws the attention of a family of four passing by on the boardwalk. She turns her body so her back is to Peter and slides her phone out of her back pocket in one smooth motion. "Come on, we're commemorating this moment for you. The first time you picked out something mildly fashionable."

"Hey! I am always fashionable," he argues, but presses his chest to her back anyway as she angles the phone up and away so it's pointed down at their faces. He bends down until his face is just a few inches higher than hers, his chin pressing against her right ear, and slides his arms around her from behind until they're wrapped around her sternum in a loose hug.

Her lips twist in a teasing smile. "I would hardly call wearing a black T-shirt and jeans every single day fashionable. Your closet probably looks like it belongs in a cartoon."

Peter fights his growing grin and gives her a little squeeze that sends a jolt of electricity straight to her core. "Just shut up and take the picture."

Against everything in her nature, she obeys instead of arguing.

She slides the sunglasses up on her forehead to more closely inspect the photo once she's taken it. In it, their grins are sloppy. Goofy. Hinting just a little at the beers they had with lunch.

Their faces seem to fit together, like two pieces from the same puzzle finally finding home after being buried in the back of a closet for a decade.

"Damn, now *that* is a good-looking couple," Peter jokes from over her shoulder, earning him a dirty look from a passing woman who has to be at least seventy wearing a vibrant, rainbow-colored tracksuit. She hustles her stride, the tiny weights in her hands pumping faster.

Olivia's about to quip back when she's interrupted by the sudden succession of beeps on her phone that signal an incoming email alert. She visibly tenses at the sound.

When she left for vacation, she set up several auto-forward commands to divert her incoming work emails into folders by sender, so she can easily sort through them when she returns. With the exception of one person: Madison from the front desk. Despite the girl's blabbing about Olivia and Peter's relationship to the press, she had trusted Madison with a job while she was away—to email her if interviews for the senior job start. After all, she owed Olivia a favor.

That pinging alert could only mean one thing.

Olivia swallows hard and slides open the message to confirm what she already fears. "Brady? They're considering Brady for the promotion?"

Peter looks her over like she's suddenly sprouted a second head, gaze darting between her face, the baby blue shades he picked out still balanced atop her head, and the phone in her hand. "What's going on?"

She sighs heavily, the whoosh of breath blowing a loose piece of hair out of her face, and drops the hand holding the phone to her side. "They've started interviewing for the job I want. Some guy in my department was going around bragging about it after his meeting with the partners." She's not worried about Brady. He's hardly the toughest competition she's up against. In fact, he's probably the least qualified candidate in the running.

But the fact that they started interviewing the day after she leaves doesn't sit right in her stomach. It's probably her competitive nature eating her up, but the feeling gnaws at her nonetheless. Now, she tips the baby blue shades back down over her eyes, like they're a wall she can hide behind, but their light-colored lenses aren't enough to hide her rapid blinking or the crease in between her brows.

Peter takes a step closer to her and rests a reassuring hand on her shoulder. "Hey, it's okay. You said it yourself, they're just getting started, and this guy doesn't hold a candle to you. You'll be back in a few days for your shot." He gives the spot where her neck and shoulder meet a soft squeeze. "They're probably saving the best for last, that's all." He sounds so confident, like he believes with his entire being she's earned this job, despite the fact that he barely knows what she does at work, let alone if she's good at it. To him, it doesn't even matter. His blind faith in her is unshakable.

Olivia wants to smile at that thought, but the pit yawning open in her stomach makes her feel like she might spew up her lunch if she does. She picks at the frayed hem of her jean shorts, gazing unseeingly at the interior of the boardwalk shop. Without realizing it, she leans into Peter's touch, enjoying the way it almost helps her relax. *Almost.*

He worries at his lower lip with his teeth in the silence that hangs heavy over them. Eventually, he slides the hand gripping her shoulder down her arm until his fingers twine with hers. "Come on," he says, lightly tugging on the hand in his grasp.

"Where are we going?" she asks distantly, her mind still three thousand miles away.

"First, we need to pay for those. I'm up for an adventure, but preferably one that doesn't include shoplifting," Peter answers as he forces her to move along with him toward the store's checkout counter.

Olivia snorts. Now she only sounds fifteen hundred miles away. Progress.

"Second, I know a spot. The Olivia Quinn Tour has been a blast, but it's time for the Peter Campbell Detour."

Chapter 10

That Pull Feels a Little Too Strong

The engine hums as the red Mustang decelerates beneath them at a racehorse's pace. Olivia's body slings toward Peter in the driver's seat when they round a particularly sharp curve onto another boulevard.

When the steering wheel slides slowly through Peter's calloused palms to right itself again, she perks up in the passenger seat to take in her surroundings. He refused to tell her where they were going. Or that it would take over an hour and a half to get there in that infamous traffic she'd been waiting for.

"All you need to know is it'll be worth it," he'd said with a crooked smile.

Something about the upward tilt to the corner of his mouth had set butterflies loose in Olivia's stomach, their flapping threatening the dense lunch she had earlier. She'd decided to stay quiet for the rest of the ride, save for a few verses hummed along to her trip playlist.

They hook a left into a neighborhood that looks oddly similar to Peter's parents', though by the time it took to reach, she knows that's not where they are. The car shifts gears as they start to climb a hill and seconds later, their destination comes into view.

"You're not serious?"

He smirks but keeps his eyes on the road.

"Peter Campbell, I am not dressed for hiking."

This earns her a rough laugh, the sound like fine-grain sandpaper scraping against the shell of her ear. "You think I would subject you to a six-mile hike in your white sneakers? I know you a little better than that, Quinn. I'm honestly insulted."

She blinks up at the sky and chews on the right side of her cheek to keep from smiling while Peter smoothly navigates the car into an asphalt parking lot at the top of the hill. The ground surrounding the lot and its driveway is littered with beige dirt. Or maybe it's sand. She can't really tell what the rolling hills and valleys of California are made of. She had never been great at geology.

It's nearing dinnertime now, and many of the spaces are empty or home to groups of people packing up their cars for the day. Peter easily slides the Mustang into a spot. It's only after he activates the car's emergency brake that Olivia tilts her head up far enough to see their true destination. Not the Hollywood Sign, like she'd first assumed when they passed a directional sign for it, but something far less familiar to her.

From the parking lot, she can just barely make out what appears to be two gigantic, black domes on the top of a large, pristine white building. Something prickles at the back of her skull, a tiny hint of recognition—the kind you get when you've seen something before in an old movie or television show, but can't quite place it.

The sound of a car door slamming jolts her back to the present, and she realizes Peter is already beside the driver's side door, stretching his legs. The fabric of his shorts stretches and strains around the thick muscles in his thighs as he presses his left foot back into a small lunge. She forces herself to look away when he switches feet, climbing out of the car herself.

He comes around to her side of the car and follows her line of sight to the right, up the small incline leading to the massive bone-white and black structure. Then he turns to her with a wide grin. "I know I said no hiking, but I'm hoping you can manage a few yards on pavement."

She scowls at him and holds out an upward-facing palm. "Lead the way, tour guide."

Peter lets out a breathy laugh and starts up the asphalt path just wide enough to allow one vehicle through.

Olivia's thighs ache the slightest bit by the time the path finally cuts a semi-circle to the left. She follows Peter onto the adjoining sidewalk, which juts out in varying directions to form several aisles around a center courtyard that is marked by a towering, column-like monument.

With nothing but the sounds of other passersby and the rush of their breath keeping them company, she trails him by a half-step up one of the paths that rounds the small monument and skirts around the right edge of the huge domed structure behind it. It's even bigger than she'd thought when viewed from up close. "What is this place?" she finally asks when she can't resist any longer.

Peter rolls his head in her direction, that same grin still tugging at his full lips. "You'll see."

She purses her lips but doesn't argue, and eventually their path leads them around to the back of the building. A second later, she realizes it isn't just any building, but an observatory. And then she's met with one of the most impressive views she's ever seen. Her jaw falls open on sight.

"And that is just the look I was hoping for," Peter murmurs from her side, his long strides slowing so he can watch her, that grin going crooked.

"You must be able to see the entire city from up here," Olivia whispers, her strides lengthening to carry her faster to the thick stone wall lining the far edge of the property, blocking hikers from the hilly drop-off beyond it.

The observatory is set high on the hills of Los Angeles, offering a sweeping view of the valley below. It feels like they're on top of the world. Endless miles of sandy steppes and shrubs butt up to quiet residential access roads and bustling highways littered with cars in a slow dance toward anywhere.

Peter leans up against that wall at the edge of the world, resting his thick forearms on the cool white stone. "It's pretty amazing, isn't it." It isn't a question.

Olivia says nothing but nods, still taking in the vast and full landscape before her, eating it up like she'd been starved for the scene her entire life. The sun is just beginning its slow descent toward the horizon, golden rays slicing up the hills in swirls of harvest gold and amber.

They stay like that for what could be moments or hours, time marked only by the sun's shifting slants of light. Like a sea of fireflies, the lights of the city all seem to come alive at once. Only then does she speak. "When you said you knew a place..."

He lets out a breath, tearing his gaze from the dipping sun to look at her. She feels his eyes on her like a warm caress against her cheek. "Don't sound so surprised."

Her mouth twitches and she tilts her head a fraction to look at him out of her periphery. "Not surprised, just curious."

When Peter doesn't say anything, she turns to look at him fully. "The way you said it, it sounded like there was some hidden meaning. Obviously you're familiar with this place, but you sounded so sure of yourself that we had to come here when..."

Peter nods his head slowly and sends his gaze back out over the darkening valley. "When you were freaking out." The words are barely audible, like he's afraid to say them. Not for himself or what she's prying at, but like he doesn't want to upset her again. Make her relive what had caused it.

Another quiet moment passes between them. Finally, Olivia asks, "Do you want to talk about it?"

Peter hums, like he doesn't understand her meaning.

"What used to draw you out here?" she presses in that way that is so absolutely Olivia.

His lips tilt up in spite of himself. "You know. Teen angst. Rebellion. Anarchy. All the usual things."

She snorts and rocks her body sideways to nudge his arm with her shoulder. A silent request.

Peter lets out an almost inaudible sigh and peers down at her from the corner of one eye. "You're very persistent, has anyone ever told you that?"

Her face warms, bathed in gold in the growing dusk, when she replies with a mischievous grin, "Only anyone who's ever known me."

He sniffs a laugh and peeks back at the yawning valley. He weighs his words carefully before saying, "I told you before that things got strained between me and my parents around the time I turned sixteen."

"When you joined Olympus," she finishes for him and Peter nods. The glow of the streetlights, even from so far away, flash like diamonds in his eyes.

"My dad was really pushing the whole engineering thing. He wanted me to follow in his footsteps. Firstborn son and all that. He refused to see that my grades were nowhere near good enough to get into UC Berkeley, his alma mater. Refused to accept that I was way better at music than I was at math. Or science." Peter shrugs his shoulders like he's brushing off a memory he'd rather keep far back in the depths of his head.

"That was around the same time my younger brother became a self-proclaimed genius. And he never missed an opportunity to point out my less than stellar grades. Looking back on it, it's probably par for the course. Typical sibling rivalry bullshit. But it drove me crazy at the time." One corner of Peter's mouth tilts up, and her gaze snags on it as he adds, "I was always way better than that little shit at sports, though. Way bigger, too. I knocked him down a few pegs more than once."

It's so easy to picture him in shoulder pads and a football helmet, or wearing shin guards and bouncing a soccer ball between his feet. Finding every excuse to launch it square at his brother's head. She shakes her head and says, "Boys."

Peter barks a laugh, the sound sweeping around Olivia like a brisk winter wind. "I can't wait for you to meet Eric, actually. I think you'll give him a run for his money. It'll be the showdown to end all showdowns. World War III-scale."

"Hey! Don't try to change the subject, we're talking about your formative childhood memories." She remembers her desire to stalk him online yesterday and remembers too late to hide the eagerness behind her nudge.

"I think I came up here on a field trip once in elementary school or something," Peter picks up the story again at her prodding, not seeming to notice her sudden interest. "One night when I needed to get out of the house, I just started driving. Before I knew what I was doing, I was driving up that hill." He jerks his head back in the direction the two of them had just come. "After that, this became my spot when I needed space. To think."

"To freak out," Olivia muses quietly.

He smiles and meets her eyes again. "To freak out."

"You talked a lot about your dad and his plans, but what about your mom?"

Peter rolls his bottom lip into his mouth, then lets it go. "I think she worried for me. Music obviously isn't a very secure career path. But ultimately, I think she just wanted me to be happy. To be passionate about something and go for it." He pauses, his smile growing. "Plus, she absolutely loves Ezra. He's like her third son."

She finds herself smiling with him. "And your sister?"

"Jennifer got all the best genes from the Campbell pool," he answers without hesitation. "If my brother thinks he's a genius, then Jennifer really is. She's a lawyer, actually."

Olivia blinks, surprised it hadn't come up before. A strange feeling akin to guilt pangs in her gut when she realizes it's the first time she's asked.

"She works for a pretty big firm based here in LA. I don't know much about that world, but I know they represent a lot of celebrities in just about any area they could possibly need legal help. Which is a lot, apparently. Even though she lives no more than an hour from my parents, she probably only sees them about as much as I do."

Attorneys. She nods her understanding and makes a mental note to find out more about her practice when she meets Jennifer.

"I think you'll like her. And I'm pretty sure she'll love you," Peter says, his voice trailing off at the end like he began to regret the statement the moment it started to form.

Olivia picks up on the hesitation, though she won't let herself think about what it means, and leans over to bump her elbow against his arm. "I thought we already established this. Everybody loves me."

He drops his head back on his shoulders and shakes it up at the sky. She tips her own neck back to follow his gaze, catching one lone, bright star just winking into existence over their heads.

Twilight has completely fallen at this hour, their faces lit only by moonlight. It feels closer up here on the mountaintop, the moon. Like Olivia could reach out and touch it just as surely as she could caress Peter's cheek.

"Thank you," she whispers, almost certain the breathless words are lost to the night sky until she feels the warmth of his side press a little bit closer to her.

"For what?"

"For distracting me. For bringing me here. For agreeing to this whole crazy scheme in the first place."

Olivia can't hear Peter's answering chuckle, but instead feels it in the ripple of his muscle where it meets her arm. After another weighted pause, he finally says, "I've got to ask. Why do this?"

Jerking her head around, she searches his face for a hint of judgment. "I told you. I needed a legitimate excuse to get Bruce off my back if I wanted to be seriously considered for this promotion."

He tosses his head from side to side. "No, I get that part. What I meant was, why a fake relationship? Why not find someone to date for real?"

"You sound like Hannah," she says, wrinkling her nose.

He sniffs and lifts an eyebrow in her direction.

What is it about him that makes him so damn good at drilling down to the center of her heart? Like he has a giant truth ray pointed straight at her set to full-blast. "Well, Peter, if I could just wave a magic wand and manifest the perfect boyfriend, I would've done it by now. Have you tried dating recently? It's a freaking war zone out there. I'm dodging bad dates like it's ninth grade gym class."

Peter's answering laugh is so husky and genuine that it envelops her like a cocoon. He keeps one hand braced against the stone wall in front of them but tilts the rest of his body toward her. "You mean to tell me the great Olivia Quinn is having dating problems?"

"I gave up serious dating months ago," she says honestly, jutting her chin out, but there's a small waver to her voice. "I think maybe love and I weren't meant to mix."

"Woah, now. This does not sound like the same girl who helped me 'parent trap' our best friends into a relationship last summer when they were too dense to do it themselves," Peter comments, narrowing his gaze at her.

Olivia sniffs a laugh and rolls her shoulders. *Point taken.* "Sure, I love love. Big romantic gestures are my weakness, so if the chance to orchestrate one pops up, I'm going to go out of my way to jump on it. But if I've discovered anything over the past few years, it's that it just wasn't meant for me."

It's not from lack of trying, either. God, has she tried. Unfortunately, everyone she tried with was inclined to take her love for granted. Chew her up and spit her back out. A small speed bump on their way to find the one.

When her thought trails off there, it's Peter's turn to nudge her arm with his elbow.

"I'm not going to be the girl who has a guy standing outside her window at dawn with a boombox and an epic speech declaring her his one true love." She's not even sure if she said the words out loud or only in her head until Peter pulls a face and coughs into his hand.

"I'm even more confused than I was before."

She narrows her gaze at him. "You seriously have no culture. It's from a classic romcom."

Peter nods slowly, but his brow never unfurrows.

"Instead, I'm meeting finance bros still stuck in their fraternity days who can barely string a sentence together on a date."

"It can't all be that bad." There's a goading challenge in his voice.

"Oh sure, it's not all bad," she tosses back, her voice dripping with sarcasm. "The last guy I dated for more than a few weeks seemed perfect... until his secret fiancée messaged me on Instagram." She pauses to blink at the Los Angeles skyline. "Actually, I guess I was the secret in that love triangle."

Peter's mouth drops open when she finishes, his brows shooting up so far on his forehead they nearly collide with his hairline.

"She had some very choice words for me. Despite the fact that I never would have dated the guy if I knew he was engaged."

Peter lets out a low whistle. "So you've met a few bad apples."

"I haven't just met them. I attract them in droves. I'm a magnet for bad apples." She lets loose a deep sigh and shrugs. "I know I won't be the one getting proposed to on an airplane or sung to on the steps of the school bleachers."

Olivia can see Peter's frown deepen and she rushes to add, "And that's okay! Because I get something better. I get to see my best friend marry the love of her life in a few short months and know that I helped make it happen."

One corner of her mouth tugs up, as if drawn by a string. "And hey, look at us. I get to pretend-date the bassist from a mega rock band, how cool is that?"

Peter tosses his head back in a roaring laugh, the movement drawing his body even closer to Olivia's. The earthy scent of his cologne floods her nostrils, and she can't stop herself from sinking forward a fraction of an inch, drawn to it like a moth to one of those outdoor zapping lamps. The kind that burn.

He swallows, and she can't help but watch his throat work. Her breath seems to stall in her lungs.

His voice is so quiet it's almost inaudible when he says after a moment, "You say that like it means something."

Olivia slowly lifts her gaze again, that string still tugging at the corner of her mouth. Her eyes shine when she answers, "Because it does."

In the heavy silence thickening between them, Peter lifts one of his massive hands to brush a fingertip against the highest point of her cheekbone, the touch tender despite the thick calluses etched into his skin from years of pressing down guitar strings.

And maybe it's the quiet seclusion afforded to them in the settling darkness. Or maybe it's the blinking lights of the city far below that make it feel like the two of them are alone on top of the world, separate from time and space, hidden in the safe and cozy cocoon woven by Peter's brusque laugh. Whatever it is, it pushes Olivia to lean into his touch.

Peter trails his fingertips up to gently tuck a piece of hair behind her ear, his jagged calluses tickling the sensitive skin on its shell and making her shiver.

He leans forward a millimeter at a time, his tongue sliding across his lower lip. The hand now caressing the nape of Olivia's neck tremors faintly. She lifts her chin, as if to meet him halfway on his descent, like the gentle waves of the Pacific Ocean rising to meet the sun on its journey below the horizon.

When Peter's lips hover no more than an inch from hers, an aggressive and insistent vibrating sound cuts through the perfect silence that had fallen over the two of them. Like two hypnosis patients woken from a trance, they each rush a step backward and return their attention to the expansive valley at the bottom of the hill.

Peter reaches into his pocket to produce his cell phone, the source of the interruption. "It's my mom," he rasps by way of explanation. Even in the dim evening light, Olivia swears she sees a flush running up the side of his thick neck as he lifts the phone to his ear to accept the call.

She wrings her fingers together in front of her, the blood rushing in her ears so loudly she can't even hear Peter's side of the conversation.

What were you thinking? she asks herself, that hissing voice inside her skull pitched with both warning and reprimand. She can't even enjoy the company of the view anymore, her brain ringing like a fire alarm. They'd come so close to crossing an uncrossable line. If she'd leaned in just a hair more—

"We are being summoned for dinner," Peter whispers from beside her when he hangs up the call. The words come out slowly, like he's approaching a volatile toddler with a spoon full of mushy green beans.

Or his fake girlfriend who just tried to really kiss him.

He tried to kiss me!

Olivia shakes her head to stop the internal warring and forces a smile, her head nodding robotically. "Of course, better get going."

Her stomach roils the entire hour and a half drive back to Pueblito del Sol, and it's not from hunger.

Chapter 11

What a Reason to Breathe

A fter trying to stretch out dinner—Peter's mom had made the most incredible from-scratch spaghetti and meatballs Olivia had ever had—for as long as possible, Peter and Olivia are finally forced to retire to their shared bedroom upstairs when his parents drop their eighth hint of the night that they want to get to bed.

Calling the meal awkward would be an understatement. They had taken tiny, frequent sips from their glasses of Malbec and earned more than a few confused glances from Andrew and very pointed stares from Becca each time they covertly looked at, then promptly away from, one another during the meal.

The only thing that hadn't felt strained was the conversation between Peter and his dad, a far cry from the heavy silence and stretched pauses from the night before. They seemed to go on for what felt like hours about engines and pistons and tires and who knew what else. Olivia hadn't minded. It drew the heat away from her. From where she and Peter had just been. From *what* they had just been doing.

Unfortunately, as she couldn't participate in the conversation without sounding like a complete idiot, it left her thoughts with plenty of room to wander.

They wandered to the way Peter's breath felt somehow hot and cold at the same time when it brushed against her flushed cheek.

They wandered to the way the muscles in his bicep flexed and strained against the sleeve of his black T-shirt when he lifted his hand to cup her jawline.

They kept on wandering, past the pair's near-kiss and straight into *Whatcouldabeensville*. A place those thoughts had absolutely no place being.

Now, a damning silence stretches to the vaulted ceilings of Peter's old bedroom, expanding into every nook and cranny and crevice it can find until it becomes a presence in its own right. A third person. An elephant in the room.

Olivia rushes through her nighttime skincare routine in the adjoining bathroom, keenly aware of how loud the recessed lights are, shining down from the ceiling of the remodeled space with their deceptive cheer.

She is *not* the self-conscious type. Never had been. She had never shrunk away from letting a casual boyfriend or a random hookup see her without a full face of makeup on.

But something about it being Peter on the other side of that door and not just some random guy, about him seeing her with nothing to hide behind aside from her unbearably thin cotton pajamas, makes her feel stripped bare. Too exposed.

She swishes her mouthwash for longer than she needs to, relishing in the simmering burn of the alcohol in the formula as it works its magic.

Eventually, when she can draw it out no longer, she rushes from the bathroom and leaves the door gaping wide behind her to beeline for the bed in the center of the bedroom.

Peter seems just as intent to avoid her, his heavy-lidded eyes stay trained on the ground when he rushes into the bathroom. The sound of the sink turning on full blast drowns out any sound from beyond the closed door. Olivia throws the warm covers over herself and plugs the end of the charger into her iPhone.

When the door to the bathroom opens again ten minutes later, she is already twisted beneath the sheets, trying desperately—unsuccessfully—to fall asleep. Her back is to Peter, but she hears him pad quietly to his suitcase and deposit his clothing inside. The sudden blackness that descends over the room when he switches off the lights has her nearly jumping out of her skin.

She stifles a yelp, unsure why she's still so wired after such a long day, while the rustling sounds of blankets moving and a heavy form settling onto the floor echo through the cavernous space.

Olivia chews on the inside of her cheek, wishing her bottle of melatonin wasn't halfway across the room. She rolls onto her back, tucking the blankets underneath her arms and folding her fingers together over her chest while her eyes trace invisible patterns on the ceiling. She's about to force her them closed again when the sound of more rustling from the floor, followed by a loud *thud*, reaches her ears.

Peter swears softly under his breath, the sound hard to make out despite him being just six feet away, like he doesn't want her to hear it.

"You okay?" Olivia whispers into the darkness.

The sound of him sighing softly followed by even more rustling answers. Then he says a bit reluctantly, "Yeah, just banged my shin on the bedpost. I'll be fine."

She sucks her bottom lip into her mouth and inhales a deep breath. Making him sleep on the floor seems cruel, even with all the blankets he scrounged up. The man's so tall, they probably don't even fully cover him.

It's inhumane, a caressing voice whispers in her head.

He's a big boy, he'll be fine, another shoots back.

You're sleeping in his bed. In his family's home. It hardly seems fair, the first voice taunts.

"Why don't we share the bed?" that first voice asks out loud, using her mouth like a megaphone before she can stop it.

She can feel that sliver of subconscious smiling smugly.

"Uh... what?" Peter sounds out, like she just spoke in a different language.

Olivia balls the top of the sheets into her fists and winces. *No going back now*. "I said we should share. We're both adults and this bed is pretty big. I think we can make it work."

A beat of silence followed by the creak of floorboards as Peter sits up. "Are you sure?"

"Just get up here before I change my mind," she sasses and scoots all the way to the far left side of the bed. She rolls over onto her side facing the wall of the bedroom again, angled completely away from the space she just freed for him.

Her heart skips a beat when she feels the mattress behind her sink under a heavy weight, the silky sheets sliding a few inches across her bare legs to accept Peter's broad frame beneath them.

The room is still and silent for what feels like an eternity but in reality is only seconds. Olivia has to remind herself to breathe, her lungs raging and straining inside her from a lack of oxygen. At the same time, she hears a deep breath release from between Peter's lips, like he's doing the exact same thing.

This is ridiculous, she thinks to herself. *Like I said, we're adults.*

Taking her time, careful not to disturb the sheets too much, she turns over onto her back and rolls her head along her neck until she's looking over at Peter. Despite knowing full well how large he is, she hadn't been expecting just how much room he'd take up in the bed. With both of them lying flat, there are only a few inches of space separating their shoulders.

She swallows hard, the sound loud in the empty quiet surrounding them. Desperate to find some sort of normalcy, she says, "You and your dad seemed to be getting along at dinner."

He clears his throat. "We're really going to talk about my dad right now?"

"What are you implying? That now is an inappropriate time to talk about your father? I can't imagine why," she answers haughtily.

Peter blusters, "No, no, you're right. Not implying anything. It's a great time to talk about my dad."

She smiles, though she knows he can't see it. "You guys wouldn't shut up about cars."

Peter laughs, though it's less of a sound Olivia hears than a rumble she feels through the mattress. His shoulder involuntarily slides a fraction of an inch closer to hers. "It's our thing. I think the museum got him amped up."

"I like that you two have a thing."

"It was you that brought us back together," he chokes out, like he's reluctant to say the words.

"Tell me about Sally. What's the story there?" she deflects, recalling the name that had been thrown around a few times, once at the museum and then once again at dinner. She knows it has to do with one of the cars they saw that day, but something about it keeps niggling at the back of her head, like there's a hidden meaning there she should remember but can't quite pick out.

There's a warmth in Peter's voice when he answers, "It's dad's favorite car at the Tischler. The fire-engine-red '67 Camaro we stopped to look at today. He swears he had one just like it when he was in his twenties." He pauses. His voice takes on a hint of admiration when he adds, "When he first met my mom."

She rolls over to face him. "Go on, I'm sensing a story here." In the darkness, she can just make out the outline of Peter's face as he mirrors her movement to look at her. A second later and she can see the peaks and valleys of his mouth as it spreads into a grin.

"My dad, in addition to being a classic car buff, is also a major classic rock fan," he begins, tucking an arm underneath his head to prop himself up a little. The motion shifts his chest until no more than four inches separate them. Not that she notices, or anything. "So he's in his early-twenties or something like that, cruising around the Sunset Strip in this bright red Camaro he and his buddies fixed up. It's like, 1989 or somewhere in that range. And they're going to the House of Blues to see Eric Clapton.

"Long story short, my mom ends up being there, too. They bump into each other at the bar, or maybe it was the line for the bathroom—the story sounds a little different each time they tell it. One thing leads to another and they end up spending the rest of the show together, completely inseparable. Attached at the hip."

Olivia's cheeks strain under the pressure of the grin she's wearing, butterflies fluttering in her belly. Though she may have given up on love for herself, she's still a hopeless romantic at heart. Susceptible to cute romcoms, adorable *how we met* stories, and big romantic gestures.

"Clapton closes the show with 'Lay Down Sally,' and my mom and dad declare it their song that very night. They listen to the entire setlist, or at least what they can remember from it, every anniversary," Peter finishes, his voice taking on a wistful tone. "Dad always wanted to name his favorite car after Mom, but she was absolutely against it. Said being compared to a car is disgusting and cheap." This elicits a huff of agreement from Olivia. "So he named her Sally instead."

"Well, that is the most adorable thing I've ever heard."

He laughs, his minty breath tickling her nose as it whooshes out of his mouth. It makes Olivia shiver, despite the warm down comforter covering her.

In a rush, it hits her. The prickle at the back of her brain. "Sally! I knew that name was familiar. Last year when we first met in Chicago, you told me that's what you called your bass guitar."

Peter beams back at her, his white teeth glowing in the dark. "You remembered."

Before she can stop herself, she swats at him, her fingertips colliding with the hard muscle of his bare chest. It lands between them on the bed and she absently leaves it there. "Of course I remembered. I have an excellent memory. It's all part of my charm."

He scoffs playfully and runs his tongue over his bottom lip. "She's fire-engine-red, just like the car, so I had to. She's my lucky bass."

"Is your dad part of the reason you started playing, then?"

There's a long pause during which she convinces herself Peter has fallen asleep, but his breathing is still a little uneven, and she's pretty sure she can see the glisten of his eyes looking off into the middle distance.

Finally, he says, "I never really thought about it before." Olivia gets the weirdest feeling that he's not being completely truthful. "But I guess so, yeah. Sort of. Every time he drove me somewhere as a kid, he'd blast the same classic rock station on the radio. Those oldies became my first favorite songs. And probably one of the reasons I got interested in music."

"So then what happened?"

Despite the lack of light in the room, she can see the upward curve of Peter's lips. Feel it in her bones. "Like any teenager worth his salt, I rebelled against the machine. And by machine, I mean the old ass radio in my dad's car." He chuckles, and the sudden vibration she feels from it has Olivia drawing her legs a little more tightly together, until one calf overlaps the other under the sheets.

"By then, I'd already been friends with Ezra for a few years. He got me listening to Queens of the Stone Age, Third Eye Blind, Arctic Monkeys. Things like that."

"Are those the artists that inspired Olympus?"

Peter turns his head toward her, his forehead creased thoughtfully. "I guess so. Sort of. It was a mix of a lot of things." The corner of his mouth lifts. "But I guess I was never really able to let go of my roots. *You* probably didn't notice it, but the groovy bassline behind our song 'Galaxy' is directly inspired by the piano from 'Brandy' by Looking Glass. It's one of my dad's favorites. I think my mom got him the CD when I was like, ten, and he listened to it nonstop for a year straight."

Without thinking, she reaches out a hand to flick his nose ring. "What's that supposed to mean, *I* wouldn't have noticed?"

He laughs, the sound scraping against her like sandpaper, and holds up his hands defensively. "It wasn't an insult. Just, most non-music people don't notice the bassline in songs."

"Well, maybe I am a music person and you just didn't know it."

Peter sniffs. "Oh yeah, my bad. I'm sure. Just like I'm sure you're familiar with Looking Glass's greatest hits."

Olivia stammers trying to come up with a quick retort, then relents quietly, "I'm sure if you started singing one of their songs, I'd recognize it."

He eyes her suspiciously, "This is some ploy to get me to embarrass myself in front of you, isn't it? I knew it. I knew this was your plan all along!" He shifts under the sheets, the soft fabric sliding and then pulling taut over her body as he animatedly glances up at the ceiling, then at each wall of the room in turn. "Where are the hidden cameras?"

She can't hold back her laughter, tugging on the blankets to keep herself covered during Peter's charade. "Shut up! It's not a trick, I promise. Although, I admit, if this had still been your real childhood bedroom, I'd fully planned to snoop the first second I got. Dig up some dirt on you." She lifts one eyebrow in his direction when he finally turns back to her, his mouth askew in a crooked smile. "You never know when you might need some blackmail."

He reaches over to poke her cheek, but she dodges it and grabs his index finger in her hand instead. Somehow the single digit still seems massive in her grip.

His attention zeroes in on her grip like a laser beam, and her fingers involuntarily tighten around him. She swears she feels his pulse quicken, a tell-tale beat against the heart of her palm. Like it burned her, she hurries to drop his finger and rotates her body to lay back down in one smooth motion. She tugs the sheets up to her collarbones, leaving her hands tucked around the edge of the soft down comforter.

Peter hesitates like he wants to say something more, or like he's reluctant to go back to the way things started? Then he slowly follows suit, the mattress dipping under his weight.

A silence descends on them both and, just like she couldn't resist being the one to break it the first time, Olivia caves once again. "So..."

Peter's muscles tense like he wants to look at her, but he restrains himself. "So..." There's a soft inflection when he speaks the word, like it's a question.

"Are you going to sing it or do I need to Google it?"

He snorts and she can feel his head shake back and forth against his pillow. Like *he's* the exasperated one. She bites down on her smile and resists the sudden urge to elbow him in the ribs.

Peter waits and the room fills with a suspenseful quiet, like even the drywall is holding its breath, waiting. Right when Olivia can't take it anymore and *again* opens her mouth to fill the void, she hears Peter clear his throat.

He opens his mouth and the chorus to a song she vaguely recognizes drifts out of it.

She sucks in a sharp breath then mentally kicks herself, sure that Peter heard it. That the entire street heard it.

But she couldn't help it. His rumbling baritone is smooth. Spacious. Every note seems to climb the walls, to reflect deep hues of navy, azure, and berry blue against every blank surface in the remodeled bedroom until, somehow, it brightens the pitch darkness.

Maybe Olivia's imagining it. She knows she's imagining it.

And yet her breath hitches higher in her throat, her chest rising and falling in rapid succession, her bottom lip rolling into her mouth as she convinces herself she's never seen or felt anything more real and extraordinary in her life.

And then Peter stops. The colors and the magic stop with him, the room once again bathed in darkness. *Not once again*, she reminds herself. The same state it had been.

She doesn't realize she's been unusually quiet until he raises a fist to his mouth and coughs. She imagines the pink tint to his cheeks when he jokes, "And now you see why Ezra's the lead singer."

Her nostrils flare and she's never been so thankful for darkness before in her life. She wants to reach a hand out and smack him, hard. She wants to grab him by the shoulders and shake him. She wants to yell at him, scream at him to stop selling himself short. She wants to yell at anyone who ever doubted him before.

She does none of those things, however. She keeps the word vomit to herself, despite the heat rising in her chest, and simply says, in a barely audible whisper, "I told you I'd recognize the song."

Chapter 12

Lonely Ships Passing in the Night

G auzy slats of gold drape across Olivia's face, the color molting into an oddly beautiful shade of burnt sienna behind her closed eyelids. The warmth of it gently nudges her out of her dream state and she blinks her eyes open to find the source: the slanted blinds in the window above the bed, still partially angled open from the day before.

As her consciousness creeps back in, she realizes she's laying on her side, facing the pillow opposite hers, the spot on the mattress where...

She blinks again when she realizes it's empty. But she knows last night wasn't a dream. The sheets are still bunched up from where Peter had thrown them from his large body to slide off the other side of the bed.

Sitting halfway up, she props herself on her bent elbows to take in the otherwise empty room. She looks first at her suitcase in the cor-ner, carefully packed and zipped tightly shut. Then over to Peter's belongings, the all-black, hard shell suitcase thrown open wide, a seemingly endless supply of T-shirts and shorts spilling out of it. It's hard to tell, because that's how it's looked the entire trip thus far, but it looks freshly rifled through.

Finally, she notices the tightly shut adjacent bathroom door and the steam slowly pouring out from underneath it.

Yesterday, she'd been awake for what seemed like hours before Peter. The uncertainty of being in an unfamiliar environment coupled with her anxiety about why they were here in the first place had her up not long after the sun.

But today she woke feeling relaxed. Like she could roll back over, curl the blankets over her shoulder, and drift off into a peaceful slumber all over again. It's odd. Olivia almost never sleeps in. Yet judging by the intense sunlight pouring in from behind the blinds, it has to be well past nine.

She doesn't feel tired, either. Not the type of bone-melting exhaustion she should feel, considering she and Peter had stayed up until nearly two in the morning.

Just talking.

The conversation had quickly turned from Peter and his dad's taste in music to Olivia's. Peter had only gently ribbed her for her Taylor Swift obsession. He'd also made her promise to check out two new bands. She'd had to write their names down in her notes app so she wouldn't forget: Wallows and Dayglow.

In turn, she'd assigned him two entire Taylor Swift albums as homework.

They'd talked about their dream vacations.

For Olivia: Paris.

For Peter: Montana, of all places. Something about needing to see a real working ranch before he dies.

They talked about their favorite holidays.

Christmas for Olivia. "Obviously," she'd told him with a smirk.

Thanksgiving is Peter's favorite, although he admitted it's probably tied with Christmas in reality, but he hadn't wanted to be a copycat. "Or basic," he'd added with a smirk of his own, earning himself a jabbed index finger to the cheek.

"Why Thanksgiving?" she'd asked him after he'd finished milking a fake injury from the poke.

He leveled a stare at her like he'd never heard a question with a more obvious answer before in his life. "It's an entire holiday based around food, what's not to love?"

Olivia had laughed. A full belly laugh normally only Hannah could elicit from her.

"Big fan of turkey?" she'd asked with a cocked brow.

He had wrinkled his nose in distaste and shook his head. "Nah, turkey's way overrated. Ham is where it's at."

Her jaw had fallen open. "Who eats ham on Thanksgiving? That's a Christmas food. See? Christmas is the superior holiday. Weirdo."

They'd moved on, and Peter gently made fun of her obsession with cats when she found yet another reason to bring up the one they'd met on the pier that day.

And she not-so-gently made fun of him for never trying sushi. "You've been to Japan like, a dozen times! You need to expand your horizons," she'd yelled, and he had shushed her with a hiss, explaining he's skeeved out by the idea of raw fish.

The fuzzy memories take shape and fade one after another in Olivia's mind's eye, and by the time the montage ends she can feel a strain in her cheek muscles.

The door to the bathroom opens tentatively across the room, Peter first peeking half his head through the opening, then stepping a cautious toe out onto the hardwood. He's already fully dressed in charcoal gray shorts that hug the muscles of his thighs and a deep forest green button-up that brings out the emerald in his eyes. The sleeves are cuffed and rolled back to his elbows, the top button left undone. His black hair is damp and flecked with water droplets on the ends, making it even darker than usual.

He should wear that color more often, she muses to herself, her tongue sliding involuntarily across her bottom lip. Her breath catches on the sight of his bare forearms, the curve of a vein running through it. She feels a warm sensation at her center and tears her eyes away.

When he notices her halfway sitting up in bed, his shoulders immediately drop and he straightens to his full height to say, "You're finally up."

Her mouth pops open in mock outrage. "*Finally*? It's—" she leans back to tap a finger against her phone and read the time, then turns back to face him with a narrowed gaze. "Only nine fifteen. Since when are you an early bird?"

Peter shrugs, but the corner of his full lips inches upward as he crosses the room to deposit his makeshift pajamas on top of his suitcase, only adding to the mess. "Touché. I'm usually not," he concedes as he pulls his phone out of his back pocket to check something. "But for some reason, I slept great last night. Best I have in months, maybe longer. I feel like I could run a marathon right now." He pauses to consider it a moment, then grimaces. "Not that I ever would. That sounds terrible."

Olivia continues to watch him, blankets pulled up to her chest, as he sits down on the edge of the mattress to tap out a text. "Good thing, too," he says after a few seconds of silence. "I woke up to a bunch of texts from our manager and the guys. We got asked to do a secret show at Amity Music Hall next Friday and Ezra wants us all to do a virtual practice session today."

Then he turns to her, a stricken look on his face. "Shit, are you going to be okay on your own for a few hours? I swear I'll be done before dinner."

That's right. Tonight is the night. The entire reason for their trip to Los Angeles: dinner with Peter's entire family. Well, immediate family. His older sister and younger brother would both be arriving around five for a mini Campbell reunion.

She smiles and waves him off, assuring him she'll be just fine catching up on emails and maybe grabbing a little more intel from Madison if she can reach her.

He pauses at this, brows furrowing with what looks like worry.

"Don't worry, Mom. I promise, no more freakouts," she says, her tone playfully patronizing.

And she means it. For now, at least. In fact, she hadn't even thought about work, or the promotion, since their little trip to the observatory. Maybe sometimes he did actually know what he was doing—though she'd never tell him that.

"Maybe I'll convince your mom to show me how to make those bomb meatballs from last night. I need more of those in my life," she adds, rubbing her stomach through the comforter still covering her.

His brows unfurrow as he sniffs a laugh, and something in her stomach flips, like someone tossing a pancake in the air and just barely catching it in the frying pan when it lands.

Stupid stomach.

Then another thought crosses her mind and it's her turn to knit her brows together. "How are you planning to practice? I'm no expert, but I'm pretty sure your bass guitar isn't secretly tucked away in your suitcase."

Peter scoffs and stands up to stretch his muscled arms overhead. The movement tugs his shirt midway up his stomach, revealing the deep V of muscles that point down toward... she twists her head to look away.

"I probably shouldn't be telling you this after last night's confession slash threat, but my parents did keep all my old stuff, even if they cleared it out of *this* room. I've got like, at least three basses tucked away here, among other things." He shoots her a pointed look over a sly smile, and something about it makes Olivia's pulse stutter.

"And before you ask, no, I'm not telling you where my old yearbooks are hidden."

Chapter 13

Can't Hide That Look in Your Eyes

After a gloriously long, hot shower, Olivia dressed herself in her favorite pair of midnight blue Lululemon leggings and a matching one-shoulder cropped cami with a built-in bra—the set she had splurged on after her last Christmas bonus came through. Then, true to her word, she'd scrolled through her email inbox. She'd only been gone for two work days, but the stark, red number at the top of her mobile email app screamed sixty-five unread messages at her.

It was the weekend now, though, so the influx should slow to a crawl. This was manageable. She'd dealt with worse.

She resisted the urge to immediately respond to some and, instead, filed them away in her systematic folder system to be dealt with on Monday.

After that, she'd texted Madison for an update on the interviewing process, determined not to let it bother her no matter what the receptionist had to say. They had to interview other candidates. It was all part of the process. And if they had started with Brady, she really shouldn't be worried at all. He'd started at the firm not long after her, but typically handled half her caseload. And still struggled with it. It was probably a pity interview.

Madison ended up calling her on her walk back from her Saturday morning spin class to let Olivia know they'd completed two more interviews on Friday: a younger girl she didn't know very well who primarily worked with one of the other partners and, probably her biggest rival, Vanessa Meade, a woman on her team who had come to them six months ago from another well-known firm in Manhattan. Vanessa has less time at Kaplan, Kaplan, and Westin than Olivia does, but she has more tenure in the industry. By a hair.

"Don't sweat it," Madison had told her breezily, the sounds of the city blaring to life in the background. "I'm sure they'll pull you in as soon as you're back next week."

It was all Olivia could do to believe her.

After hanging up the phone with Madison, she was determined to hold up the promise she'd made to Peter that morning and not wallow in the worry she felt creeping in at the back of her skull. Fortunately, she'd found Peter's mom already at work in the kitchen, preparing food for the family dinner that evening.

It wasn't meatballs, but she did walk Olivia step-by-step through her recipe for slow-roasted beef tenderloin. At the start of her lesson, Becca had informed her it would take almost the entire day to cook in her space-age oven once they popped it in.

How do people have the patience to cook something that takes over three hours? She had thought to herself when her stomach was already growling at the incredible aroma spreading throughout the kitchen.

The experience overall had been strange, when she let her mind wander long enough to consider it.

Olivia adored both her parents, but her mother certainly wasn't the type to spend an entire Saturday elbow-deep in chopped vegetables or spooning marinade over a slab of beef. In her family, her dad was the chef. And even he treated his *meals du jour* as though he were on a Food Network competition: thirty minutes or less!

It was soothing, sharing a cutting board with Peter's mom. Like she had stepped through a portal into a primetime sitcom from the early 2000s.

Yes, it had been strange. And a little painful, too, when she reminded herself it wouldn't last. That it wasn't real. She didn't belong in this particular crossover episode and eventually would need to return to her regularly scheduled programming.

A glance at the clock above the sink shows her four hours have passed, leaving just over an hour until Peter's siblings arrive. Olivia carefully scrapes the shiitake mushrooms she'd just finished julienning—a fancy new technique Becca had taught her—into a waiting bowl using the backside of her knife, then steps to the sink to wash the hard-earned residue left behind on her hands.

There's a massive pile of dishes there, leftover from their effort, and she frowns at it. She really should go change and find her fake boyfriend before his brother and sister get here, but what kind of impression does it make if she leaves their mom to wash up?

As though she can read Olivia's thoughts, Becca waves her off with a matronly smile and a "Don't worry, I've got this! Please go find my son." *And make sure he's ready and down here pronto*, she doesn't have to say.

She begins the climb up the Campbells' staircase back to Peter's old room, popping into the adjoining bathroom to freshen up and then changing into the only semi-formal outfit she'd brought on the trip: a backless floral print sundress that skims to a few inches above her knees. Despite the flowing fabric that drapes over her thighs, the bodice hugs her from her chest to her waist, accentuating what curves she has sprinkled throughout her athletic frame.

She pairs it with her gently worn-in, nude wedge sandals, feeling like she may just fit into this California landscape after all. A few minutes later, she's touched up her makeup and managed to tug her hair into a messy-in-a-trendy-way bun at the top of her head with two face-framing pieces hanging in front of her ears.

After one final look in the full-length mirror, Olivia steps back into the main bedroom and frowns at the bedside clock. Half an hour until Peter's siblings arrive and her fake boyfriend is still nowhere to be found. Like fate or this incredibly beautiful house is answering her thoughts, her ears prick at the sound of a low voice filtering in through the cracked bedroom door. It's muffled, but sounds close enough.

She follows the sound through the bedroom door and down the hallway to a room she hasn't been to before on the left side of the hallway. Its door is slightly ajar, and coming from inside is the unmistakable sound of Peter's deep, rumbling chuckle, followed by the springy sound of electric guitar strings being plucked without the aid of an amplifier to bring the chords to life.

Before she can stop herself, Olivia leans against the doorframe and gingerly pushes the door open a few inches further with the back of her knuckles. She peeks her head into the space it leaves behind and sees Peter sitting on the very edge of a futon folded into the couch position, a plain black bass guitar balanced in his lap. It appears to be plugged into a laptop set on a desk a few feet across the room from him, which in turn is connected through a separate port to a pair of obnoxiously large gaming headphones tugged snugly over his head.

He's completely focused on the laptop screen and, although she can't see it from her vantage point, she can hear his bandmate and best friend Ezra Bell talking, his voice bubbling up into a laugh so loud it carries clearly through the soundproof headphones.

Her attention snags on the way Peter's fingers move gracefully up and down the frets of his bass, hugging the neck delicately with one hand while his other picks at the strings. A sensation like vertigo stirs her stomach at the sight of how gifted he is with his hands.

Olivia bites down on her bottom lip to squash the feeling and shifts her weight, accidentally knocking the door open the rest of the way. Immediately, Peter looks up from the laptop, zeroing in her face.

They don't stay there long, though.

His jaw falls slack as he looks her over, from the spunky bun on the top of her head, down to her pink painted toes, and all the way back up again to her chestnut eyes.

It doesn't escape her how long they lingered on her freshly self-tanned legs. Or the way they flickered over her cleavage before Peter could catch himself and move on, a flush rushing up his neck.

She sucks her bottom lip into her mouth and quirks a brow. He only grins back lazily, lifting and dropping a shoulder, accepting he had been caught.

They stand there, holding one another's gaze for god knows how long, until Olivia can hear more chatter buzzing from the headphones, like the angry, animated hummingbird from the *Pocohontas* movie she'd loved as a little kid.

She's pretty sure she makes out Angel's voice asking, "Why are you smiling like someone just walked in with a gigantic bowl of Cheerios?"

Peter shoots Angel a dirty look then beckons Olivia forward, yanking out the plug to his headphones with his other hand at the same time so the band's voices can flood the room. She's immediately greeted by cheers when she reaches the computer—plus one raging guitar chord from Zach—from the three members of Olympus on the screen. Heat rushes to her cheeks, and she hopes they can't tell through the video call.

She knows Ezra knows the truth about their little arrangement, but did he have the chance to fill the rest of the band in too?

Afraid of finding out, she shifts until she's out of frame. When only Peter can see her, she lifts her wrist to tap her Apple Watch face and tosses her head back toward the hallway she'd just come from in silent communication.

He nods his understanding and makes his excuses to the rest of the band before exiting the video call and powering down the laptop. He turns to her to say, "Wow, sorry. I didn't realize how long I'd been on for."

Olivia waves a hand and steps out of the way while he cleans up his equipment and returns the old bass to a stand in the far corner of the room. It's a little more than half the size of the bedroom they've been staying in, its walls painted a dark navy. Judging by the computer desk, office chair, old futon, and dozens of car posters framed on the wall, she guesses it must be Andrew's office.

When everything is back in order, Peter pauses, his hands flexing at his sides as though he's wrestling with himself about what to say next. He sucks in a sharp breath, then spits it out in a rush so the syllables all seem to mash together. "You look beautiful."

She blinks her surprise, her hands self-consciously smoothing over the ruffled fabric of her dress. She opens her mouth to say something, but instead her eyes snag on a photo atop a bookshelf just over his shoulder. She crosses the room in a near-sprint and picks it up, holding it less than a foot from her nose. Her face splits into a grin.

"Aww, come on. I knew I should've locked the door," he groans behind her.

Three siblings lined up in front of a cherry red Ford Mustang in mint condition. A girl no older than twelve with messy light brown hair towers over the two black-haired boys beside her.

Dead in the center is, unmistakably, Peter. His thousand-watt smile gives him away, despite the missing front tooth.

"You were freaking adorable!" she coos, turning to look over her shoulder and make a baby face at him.

She hadn't expected him to be standing so close to her, his broad chest no more than an inch from her back. When Peter reaches an arm across her body to point at the photo in her hands, she inhales the deep scent of cedar and rain, and her grin falters.

"God, I must've been like, eight in that photo. I'd knocked my last baby tooth out playing peewee football." He drags a finger across his face in the frame, losing himself to the memory. "That was the day Dad brought home the Mustang."

Olivia is still locked on Peter's face while he studies the picture, taking in every feature, every square inch of him. Then his gaze meet hers, the deep green in his eyes set ablaze. A forest fire that threatens at her door.

Unable to stop herself, she glances down to his full lips. He tracks the look and runs his tongue against them, making her knees shake.

He moves a fraction of an inch closer, the planes of his sculpted chest brushing her shoulder as she, in the same beat, twists her body more to the side in an attempt to face him straight on.

The sound of a door slamming open and a feminine voice booming, "Mom! Dad! I'm here!" bursts their bubble, and they both step back as though they'd been burned.

Blood rushes to her cheeks, and she's thankful for the makeup she'd just reapplied and the light coverage it offers. She dips her head to look at the carpeted floor, loosely rubbing a hand against the back of her bare neck.

Peter stiffens across from her, his eyes trained on the wall of the office, as though he can see through it to the floor below. Presumably where his sister is now hugging his parents.

Showtime, she thinks darkly, then catches the hollow look on his face when she tilts her head up. Her brows knit together and she steps up to him, lightly pressing a palm to the outside of his arm. "Hey. You ready for this?"

He sighs through his nose and forces himself to look at her. His lip twitches so minutely she almost misses it. "Do I have a choice?"

She gives his arm a squeeze and grins mischievously. "This is your party. If you want to bail and grab In-N-Out, just say the word. I'll even help make a rope out of your sheets so we can escape through the window."

He laughs, not his typical boom that fills any space no matter how cavernous. But enough for Olivia to see the ice melting.

"Thanks, Quinn," he says. He stretches out to thread his fingers through hers, then lowers their joined hands so their arms dangle loosely between their bodies. "But we came all this way. No turning back now." He narrows his gaze at her, some of the fire returning. "Are *you* ready for this?"

Olivia scoffs, waving her free hand through the air. "Wowing your parents was the hard part. This should be a cakewalk."

Peter blows a *pfft* sound through his mouth and shakes his head, a stray piece of black hair falling across his temple. "Clearly you've never met my siblings."

Chapter 14

Getting It All Wrong

Peter's hand stays tightly clasped around Olivia's as they make their way down the stairs. She's sure part of it is for show as they move to make their entrance, but based on the heat radiating from the center of his palm and the taut muscles in his fingers, she sees the truth behind the facade. He's nervous.

And if she is honest with herself, regardless of the family dynamics she still doesn't fully understand, she would be too if the tables were turned.

Faking a relationship in front of a group of colleagues, most of whom she barely knows nor cares about on a personal level, is one thing.

Lying to your family, the people who are supposed to know you better than anyone else in the world? That's something else entirely.

"Oh good, you're done up there," Peter's mom crows as the two of them materialize at the bottom of the staircase. "Your sister's just arrived."

Together they round the bottom of the stairs and head to the kitchen. Immediately, Olivia is greeted with the fragrant scent of the beef tenderloin she helped prepare earlier in the day, and her mouth waters.

A second later, she's face-to-face with a woman who looks to be in her late thirties, dressed in a pair of black high-waisted, waffle-knit trousers and a plain white blouse with a scooped neck tucked into them. It looks like something Olivia might wear to the office. In fact, she makes a mental note to scour the sale section of her favorite online clothing stores to find something similar.

"You must be the new girlfriend," the woman says, her voice low and throaty. There is a slight uptilt to one corner of her mouth as she takes in Olivia in a quick pass, her gaze pausing only a fraction of a second on the hand Peter's still grasping onto for dear life. She shifts the wineglass in her hand, the red liquid sloshing up the curved sides.

Olivia smiles, but not too brightly, and dips her head once as she shoots back, "Olivia. And you must be the sister."

There's a flicker of something like amusement mixed with approval on the woman's face—they're almost the same green as Peter's, but several shades darker—when she answers, "Jennifer." She gestures over a shoulder with her head to the kitchen island where an uncorked bottle of red sits, waiting. "Wine?"

Olivia's smile widens a hair. "Please."

When Jennifer turns around to pour a glass of whatever she'd brought along, Peter glances meaningfully between the two women, then stops on Olivia with widened eyes.

After a beat, he leans down to whisper in her ear. "I'm sensing some weird girl thing just went down that I will never comprehend."

She snickers quietly enough so no one else will notice and leans over to bump her hip against his. "It went well. That's all you need to know."

He purses his lips together like he wants to pursue it further, then eventually nods his acceptance with a small bob of his head. He turns back to his sister to watch her skillfully measure a pour into one of the Campbells' bouquet glasses, then twists his face into the picture of arrogance. "Thanks for offering, sis. I'd love a glass," he says louder than necessary.

Jennifer spins around and offers the lone wine glass to Olivia, then meets her brother's gaze with a sly smile of her own. "Hello, brother. I think you're fully capable of getting one yourself."

Olivia chokes on her wine trying to suppress a laugh, and Peter shoots her a glare. She takes another sip and pretends not to notice. She also pretends not to notice how his hand left her grip to migrate up the side of her forearm and across her waist, finally coming to rest at the small of her back.

She pretends the feel of his palm, relaxed but firm, isn't burning a hole straight through her. She pretends she doesn't like the way the weight of it feels possessive, like he has a deep-seated need to let the rest of the world know she belongs to him.

It's just an act, she reminds herself while the two siblings strike up a conversation she doesn't hear. *A very convincing act.*

Jennifer turns back to Olivia, brows lifted like she's waiting for something.

She stirs, her wine sloshing almost to the rim of the glass. She completely missed the question.

Fortunately, Peter steps in for her, "Actually, she's in your indus-try. She's a paralegal." He says it with a triumphant smile and slight cock of his head. Like it's something to be proud of. Something to brag about.

It awakens something in her she's never felt before, and she sucks down a gulp of wine to smother it.

Jennifer's eyes light, her nude-lacquered lips curving. "Really? What firm?"

Olivia waves her fingers through the air and tries to regain her composure. "Kaplan, Kaplan, and Westin," she answers, not expecting Jennifer to recognize the name.

To her surprise, Jennifer nods. "White-collar and family law, right?"

Olivia's mouth drops open for a moment but she nods. "That's right."

Jennifer smiles, satisfied with her memory. "Good firm from what I hear." She seems to notice Olivia's confusion and looks to Peter, then back to Olivia. "I take it you didn't tell her about what I do?"

Peter's cheeks flush almost imperceptibly and he nods at the floor, grumbling, "I mentioned you're an attorney... and your firm represents celebrities. But that's about it."

Jennifer chuckles under her breath and takes another sip of wine. "I'm actually a partner at a firm here in LA. We have several offices in California and Nevada, and we're in the process of opening an office in New York. Kaplan, Kaplan, and Westin came up during our market research," she explains. "Looks like we might be new competition for you," she adds with a wink, her smile turning wolfish, though for some reason it doesn't intimidate Olivia. Something about it makes her feel like she's in on the joke. "I lead the family law division and I'll be heading out there to New York to open the branch in a few months."

Before Olivia has the chance to respond, Becca cuts in from somewhere over her shoulder. "Did I just hear you say you're moving to New York?" Her voice comes out high-pitched and squeaky. Olivia can tell Becca's eyes are bulging before she turns around and steps aside to let the mother of the family join the conversation.

She tunes out the mild argument that erupts between Jennifer and her mom and instead turns to Peter.

Your sister is a partner? she tries to communicate nonverbally.

He picks up on the question and shrugs, then mouths, *I tune out when she talks about work.*

Olivia shakes her head, hoping there aren't many more surprises in store when Peter's other sibling arrives. They haven't been telling people they've been together long, but these types of details seem like something a girlfriend should know.

The hissing voices coming from Olivia's left-hand side are interrupted by the sound of the front door opening and closing again, followed by heavy footfalls approaching them from the foyer.

Time to find out just how well she can act.

"Mom, this beef tenderloin is delicious," Peter's younger brother, Eric, says around another bite of the red meat. He sits across the table and one chair over from Olivia so he's directly across from Peter.

Where Peter is extremely tall and broad, Eric is shorter and wiry. He has the same blue-black hair as his brother, but it's even longer and curlier than Peter's, and he inherited his father's brown eyes. He looks a little like Dan Humphrey in the last season of *Gossip Girl* if Olivia squints.

"I can't take all the credit," Becca chirps delightedly from one head of the table, her head bobbing. "Olivia helped me prep everything on the table. She was a big help." She beams at Olivia, her thousand-watt smile and gleaming emerald eyes identical twins to her eldest son's. The warmth and approval from that gaze warms Olivia from her head to her toes, like she's standing under one of those heated lamps the Campbells have in their guest bathroom.

It's like a bucket of ice water is thrown over her when her subconscious reminds her that her place in this family, in this home, is temporary. *Don't get used to it.*

Olivia's gaze slides to Eric as he lifts his wine glass to her in a mock toast. The way only one corner of his mouth lifts reminds her so much of Bruce it makes her jaw tick.

"You already sound too good for our dear brother," he smarms, and Olivia clenches her fist around her fork so hard the stainless steel digs into her palm. She doesn't even feel it.

She forces a smile and says through gritted teeth, "Truly, I'm the lucky one in this relationship. Peter's quite the catch. You should see the way girls fawn over him when he's on stage." She tilts her head to look sideways at Peter, hoping the fire in her eyes radiates adoration and not the anger she's trying to quelch.

Eric sniffs across the table then sips his wine to cover it. But it seems he can't keep himself from saying, "I doubt many people notice the bassist."

Peter stiffens beside her, his gaze going distant.

Olivia's jaw feathers and she takes a deep breath through her nose, trying not to react. *You're here to make Peter look good. Like he has his shit together. Leaping across the table and stabbing his brother with a fork isn't going to be a good look for either of you*, she tells herself.

Out loud she says as mildly as she can muster, "You'd be surprised. He was the only one that caught my eye." She reaches over to squeeze Peter's thigh under the table, offering her silent encouragement. When she does, she feels him flex beneath her fingers.

The lie rolls off her tongue so easily because, she slowly comes to realize, it isn't a lie at all. Olivia lets her mind drift back to that balmy summer day in Chicago, when she'd come to the city's biggest outdoor amphitheater to watch Peter's band run sound checks while her best friend Hannah worked as their social media manager.

At the time, Hannah was already head over heels for Ezra, despite her best efforts to fight it because he was her client. Which was just as well for Olivia because it ensured her best friend never noticed the way her jaw had practically unhinged at the sight of Peter on stage. How she'd been drawn to his powerful form, the way his fingers climbed the frets of his bass guitar in a way that hinted at other talents.

She remembers the first time she saw Peter smile, the force of it like a magnet, drawing her in.

A pang gnaws at her stomach then, curdling the wine she'd been sipping with dinner. The way she'd stopped texting him all those months ago, so caught up in her own shit, floods her with a feeling of grief so deep one would think she truly lost him forever.

When Olivia dares a sideways glance at Peter from the corner of her eye, she startles. He's got his bottom lip caught between his teeth and the expression he wears is darker than usual. And he's watching her. He may have been for a while.

Olivia's the first to break, turning reluctantly back to Eric. "Peter tells me you're in tech?" She phrases it like a question, figuring the easiest way to get the Campbells' youngest son off Peter's case is to get him talking about himself, even though she has absolutely no interest in what he does. Or anything about him, really.

Eric smiles like a shark and launches into what sounds like a rehearsed spiel about his company and his job. Olivia nods at the right moments and smiles politely, but she hears exactly none of it. Instead, every nerve ending in her body is trained on her hand beneath the table and the way Peter's own massive palm has lowered to cover it.

He squeezes her fingers once, and she knows what it means. *Thank you.*

The dinner conversation turns naturally to what Olivia does for a living next. Skipping over the details, she describes her firm and her role there. Without really meaning to, she mentions the promotion she's currently competing for, earning her a single lifted eyebrow from Jennifer that Olivia isn't quite sure how to read.

Eventually the conversation moves on without her, and she notices with some minor distress that Peter remains mostly quiet for the rest of the meal. She can't help but remember the words he'd whispered to her in the dark the night before, the anger that flamed to life within her along with them.

Being an only child, Olivia has never known what it feels like to compete with her own family. The whole idea seems ridiculous to her. Home should be the one place you can be unapologetically yourself, without fear of judgment.

At least, that's what her parents had always told her. Even that time they were oddly surprised she decided to pursue higher education instead of joining the Peace Corps like they both had. Like that had ever been an option for Olivia. One corner of her mouth turns down at the memory. Maybe her parents' unspoken promise had been loaded too, and the safety net she'd always thought was there to catch her actually came with a catch.

"So, the big day is coming up, isn't it?" Becca asks.

Olivia tenses, her palm starting to sweat where it still sits on Peter's thigh, tucked snugly beneath his hand. She hadn't been paying attention and has no idea what "big day" they're talking about.

One corner of Peter's mouth tugs up like he can immediately sense her stress. He speaks for the first time in at least fifteen minutes, replying, "Yep! November eighth."

Olivia's grip on his thigh loosens. Ezra and Hannah's wedding. She grins at the thought of it.

"This one's already got her dress picked out," Peter says, nudging Olivia's arm with his elbow.

Both Campbell women smile knowingly, but it's Jennifer who says, "And knowing you, I'm sure you'll be picking up your tux the day of." Something about the way she says it lets Olivia know it's a shared joke, not a dig.

Peter's huffs and nods his agreement, stuffing his last fingerling potato into his mouth.

Olivia smirks. "If Peter had it his way, he'd be up at the altar in a pair of shorts and a black V-neck."

Peter's booming laugh echoes through the cavernous dining room for the first time all meal, and a flock of birds seem to take flight all at once in Olivia's lower belly. She rotates her hand in his so her palm faces up and laces her fingers through Peter's, giving them a small squeeze.

"I do hope we'll be getting some good news from you two soon enough as well," Becca cuts in from behind the rim of her wine glass, her voice pitched so low it almost can't be heard from the far end of the table.

Almost.

"Mom!" Peter and Jennifer both cry out at the same time, shooting their mother slack-jawed glares. Olivia's spine goes stock straight in her high-backed chair, eyes round with shock.

Even Eric snorts and tosses his linen napkin over his mostly-eaten plate. "They've been dating, what? Three months? A little premature to start looking at venues."

Olivia inhales sharply and looks down at her plate. Although she doesn't disagree with him, especially given the false circumstances of her relationship with Peter, something about the way Eric says it irks her. Like he's expecting them to fail.

It makes her want to charge down the aisle, dragging a kicking and screaming Peter behind her, out of spite alone.

"Well, you know, you are almost thirty-two. I just thought maybe," Becca sputters, looking anywhere but her oldest son.

"Thirty-two is the new twenty-two," Jennifer says at the same time Peter says, "How come you never get on her case about charging down the aisle?"

Jennifer's mouth falls open at the pointed remark, her hand coming to her chest in mock horror. "Hey, I was defending you. Don't get her started on me!"

"Knowing these two, I'll be the first to get married in the family," Eric says about his siblings after swallowing the rest of his wine down in one gulp.

Peter and Jennifer both shoot him daggers. Even Olivia draws back at their expressions.

"Oh shut up, Eric! I'm the only one here with a girlfriend. I'll be the first to get married," Peter says, challenge sparking in his voice like a stone struck against flint.

Olivia turns to him with arched eyebrows at the same moment he realizes what he's said. His shoulders tense, his mouth twisting into a grimace at his mistake. He tries to backpedal, adding, "I mean—never mind, I don't know what I mean." He shakes his head and looks down at his empty plate.

A booming clap comes from the head of the table opposite Becca, and her husband speaks for the first time since they sat down. "Okay, I'd say this conversation has run its course. Honey, wasn't there a game you wanted to play after dinner?"

Becca sits up taller in her chair, her smile returning. "Oh, yes! I thought we could play Forbidden Phrases again, like the old days."

"Forbidden Phrases?" Olivia asks quietly. At the same time, all three Campbell children groan as though in physical pain.

Becca turns to her and nods. "It used to be our weekend tradition when the kids were young. It's really easy to play, you'll pick up on it quickly."

"Peter never did," Eric mumbles and Olivia's head snaps to him against her will. Luckily he seems absorbed with folding and refolding his napkin, and he doesn't notice.

"Come on, it'll be fun!" Becca coos from the head of the table, pressing her palms together in prayer hands.

Jennifer, Peter, and Eric each take turns looking at the floor, the ceiling, the table, everything in the room but their mom, while their father scowls at all three of them.

Olivia shrugs her shoulders, eager to break the icy chill spreading like a fog through the dining room. "I'm in."

"Excellent, it's settled," Becca says with a grin and stands to begin clearing the dinner dishes at a runner's pace.

·❤·❤·❤·❤·❤·

Spread out on the Campbells' coffee table are a blue and orange plastic buzzer, a tiny plastic hourglass filled with beige grains of sand, and a box loaded with playing cards.

Without trying to, the group divided itself into teams. Olivia and Peter took the seats opposite Jennifer and Eric on a matching sofa and loveseat combo. Becca and Andrew have taken the two armchairs flanking the couches.

Olivia shoots quick-moving glances between each of their faces, trying to figure out why the air in the room is suddenly thick with tension. Her family wasn't really the board game type. Documentaries about the slow extinction of the Javan Rhinos? Sure. Visits to the Philadelphia Museum of Art to see their Picasso collection? You bet. Whitewater rafting trips in the Adirondacks? Been there, done that.

A quiet Saturday evening in with nothing but healthy competition driven by a stack of flimsy cardboard with words printed on it? This is new.

Sensing Olivia's hesitation, Becca starts explaining the rules. Like all games, the primary objective is to score the most points. After a lengthy explanation Olivia barely follows, Becca concludes, "You and Peter can be a team. One of you gives the clues and the other tries to guess the word on the card."

Olivia's eyes threaten to drop back in her head. It probably isn't complex, but something about her brain seems to lose consciousness when anyone describes instructions to her verbally. Unless she has a legal pad and pen.

"Do you want one of us to go first until you get the hang of it?" Becca asks mildly. Olivia nods, grateful. Maybe this woman is a mind reader. That's twice today she's come to her rescue.

She's a visual learner.

Becca flips the hourglass on the table and kernels of sand begin to fall rapidly into its empty bottom half. She wastes no time picking up the first card in the face-down deck and launches into a barrage of random words that might lead her husband to guess what's on it.

Amazingly, he does.

By the time the last grain of sand drops, he's correctly guessed six words and skipped over only three cards.

"What did it mean when Eric hit the buzzer?" Olivia asks after they've finished.

"You can't say any of these words written on the card—" Eric points to a group of five words and phrases spelled out on the bottom half of one of the cards his parents just played. "They're considered forbidden. If you say them, you have to discard the card and start over with a new one."

Olivia nods slowly, now understanding the game's namesake.

"You ready to give it a shot?" Andrew asks Olivia, looking between her and Peter from beneath raised brows.

Olivia shrugs and smiles, then turns to her partner. "Sure. Should I be a guesser or a giver?"

"You should probably guess, otherwise you'll have no chance," Eric says under his breath with a sniff.

Peter sighs and looks down at his hands where they're folded in his lap.

Olivia's nostrils flare, but she swallows most of her anger. She turns her most saccharine smile on Peter's brother. "And why's that?" She cocks her head to one side, like a cat evaluating its prey right before it pounces.

Eric seems a little surprised by the question at first, but quickly coughs into his hand and adjusts himself on the sofa, crossing one leg over the other knee. "Nothing, just... you know. I've seen my brother play this game before."

Olivia bats her lashes at the youngest Campbell, tilting her head back the other way as though she doesn't understand at all. "And?"

Jennifer clears her throat and takes a huge sip from her wine glass, averting her gaze. Mr. and Mrs. Campbell look at one another. They can tell something's happening, though from the curious looks on their faces, they're not quite sure what.

Instead of backing off, Eric doubles down. He sits up straighter and looks right into Olivia's doe eyes when he says, "Let's just say there's a reason Peter picked the instrument with only four strings."

A sound like ice breaking booms through Olivia's head and she clenches her teeth, forcing a deep breath in and out through her nose.

Another bassist joke. So similar to the one he'd made earlier. So similar to the very thing Bruce had said to her nearly two weeks ago in his office, when he'd first found out about her relationship with Peter.

That memory, the discomfort written all over Peter's face in this moment, is the final straw. And Olivia realizes where the sound in her head came from as something again snaps inside of her chest cavity.

She turns to Peter, fire blazing in her eyes. "You guess."

Peter's brows arch high on his forehead. "You sure?"

"Positive."

Eager to break the tension, Jennifer reaches out to flip the game's hour glass and Olivia picks up the first card with a flick of her wrist.

Beach. The forbidden words are *sand, swimming, ocean, bikini,* and *water.*

She smiles without her teeth, and something in it makes each of Peter's siblings stiffen across the room.

The trick isn't trying to get around the rules, Olivia thinks. *The trick to winning is knowing your teammate.*

"Ezra's back tattoo," she says, widening her eyes meaningfully. She saw it in great detail the time she visited her best friend Hannah on tour last summer. The guy was always taking his shirt off on stage.

Peter's mouth ticks to one side. Lighthouse is his first guess, but when Olivia shakes her head he immediately snaps his fingers and guesses the right word on his second try.

She picks up another card and her smirk only grows. "My favorite animal."

Peter pulls an exaggerated face. "Easy, cat."

Olivia punches the air in front of her chest, then grabs the next card. "Hannah says you play these way too much on the tour bus."

Peter's forehead creases for a fraction of a second before understanding dawns. "Video games!"

This earns a laugh from both Campbell women. Olivia doesn't dare look away from the card in her hand, but she can feel the irritation radiating off of Eric in waves.

"Your extremely weird favorite Thanksgiving Day food," Olivia says next, wrinkling her nose.

Peter chuckles and rubs the back of his neck with his hand. "Ham is the superior option. I stand by my decision."

Olivia lets out a breathless laugh as she picks up the next card. "This was me yesterday before we got lunch."

Peter's eyes widen and he exaggerates a shiver. "Hangry."

Jennifer lets out a cackle and claps her hands together.

"The thing Hannah and Ez are doing this fall," Olivia says next.

"Wedding!" Peter shouts, his confidence building with every clue guessed correctly.

Olivia's mouth twists at the next card she picks up. This one is tough. It only came up in passing once.

She takes a risk and says, "November twenty-sixth."

Peter rolls his bottom lip into his mouth to think, the bottoms of his front teeth carving a small path along its plump edge. Then he looks straight into Olivia's eyes to say, "Birthday."

Olivia's mouth ticks up, her heart beating an uneven rhythm in her chest. Pride mixed with something else. Something she doesn't want to name.

"That's time!" Andrew Campbell shouts from across the coffee table, punching the air with his fist as he clocks the last grain of sand dropping in the plastic hourglass.

"That was incredible!" Becca cheers at the same time Jennifer says with a smile, "You beat Mom and Dad by one point. And they're the reigning champs, so that's saying something."

Peter's jaw drops open and, with the grace of a black bear, he leaps up from the couch to envelop Olivia in a bone-crushing hug. She gasps at the sudden contact, but manages to snake her arms around his shoulders and hold on. As soon as she does, Peter lifts her clean off the floor, spinning her in a tight circle that has her feet skimming the seat of the couch.

"That's the first time I've ever beaten them!" Peter crows, setting Olivia back down on solid ground. She laughs, the sound tinkling through the living room like silver bells, and adjusts the straps of her dress to prevent an impending wardrobe malfunction.

"And you wouldn't have if she hadn't been feeding you inside jokes the whole time," Eric interjects, his upper lip curling. "But I guess special circumstances require a little rule-bending."

"What is your problem?" Olivia bites out before she can think better of it. She narrows her gaze at Eric, folding her arms over her chest.

The room around her plunges into silence, but Olivia can't stop now that she's started. "You've been throwing little digs at Peter all night. What's up with that?"

Eric holds up his hands defensively, the corners of his mouth turning down. Suddenly he has nothing to say.

The silence only emboldens Olivia. Stokes the flame burning deep inside of her, the same one she felt the night before. "Yeah, Peter didn't go to college. So what?" she asks, looking slowly from Eric, to Peter's dad, then his mom and sister in turn. "He's in a multi-platinum band that sells out shows around the world. He figured out what he was good at long before most any of us do and followed that path to greatness."

She turns cold eyes on Andrew. "He didn't waste hundreds of thousands of dollars chasing a dream that wasn't his. You should be thanking him."

Olivia faces Becca next, her face softening only slightly. "He's insanely creative, making music from nothing. That takes time and dedication and true talent."

She faces Eric once again. "I'd be willing to bet that when he's on tour, he works longer hours than even you. Because he's passionate about what he does. About the people out there who love music the way he does—" Olivia looks to Peter's dad again. "The way you did, too. Did you know he incorporated bits and pieces from your favorite songs into the ones he wrote? Did you even know he named his favorite bass Sally, after the car you love so much?" She turns to Becca and adds, "After the song the two of you fell in love to."

She can feel the steam running out of her, the fire burning down to embers as the reality and the weight of what she's doing sinks in. "I just..." she sputters, her volume dropping off along with her confidence. "He deserves better. From all of you."

Taking a shaky breath, she risks a glance at Peter, but his face is impassive. Unreadable. And a pit yawns open in her stomach. *What have I done?*

The Campbells are still blinking at her in a stunned silence when she backs away slowly toward the hallway leading to the staircase. "If you'll excuse me, I need to..." She lets the words trail off and darts through the open doorway.

Chapter 15

Waiting, Pining, Anticipation

Tears prick at the back of Olivia's eyes, but they refuse to fall. Even they can't stand to share the same space as her after what she's done. Her feet wear in a path on the floor of Peter's old bedroom, where she'd retreated after her explosion.

It could have been minutes or hours since she blew up at Peter's entire family like a crazy person. Time seems to move differently once you've completely lost all sanity.

She doesn't regret what she said, not one bit. Every word she spoke was the absolute truth. But it wasn't the time, nor her place, to lay into them like that. Peter brought her here for one purpose: to make him look like he's got his shit together and get his mom off his back about finding a girlfriend for a little while.

And she had been doing so well. She could feel it. They had been impressed and charmed by her, just like she'd wanted, and in turn they'd been impressed by Peter, too.

But she simply couldn't ignore the fact that the *only* reason they seemed willing to be proud of their son, their brother, was because of someone else.

She isn't the best thing about Peter. Not even if she were his real girlfriend. Not by a long shot.

Olivia chews anxiously at a loose cuticle on her index finger, threatening to tear the skin clean off, and keeps up her incessant pacing. She can't stop. If she stops, she'll completely unravel.

She may not regret the words she'd spoken, but she still sure as hell wishes she could take it all back. Undo that moment in time. Peter's family probably hates her now. The thought alone opens up a chasm inside her chest.

More importantly, Peter probably hates you now, she thinks, and that chasm splits open completely to form a vast, endless pit.

She's facing away from the bedroom door when the sound of it clicking open pricks her ears. She sucks in a sharp inhale and stops short on her trek, spine stiffening.

Biting down so hard on her bottom lip she's surprised it doesn't draw blood, she slowly turns around, just in time to see Peter step fully into the room and close the door behind him.

Olivia takes him in from head to foot, desperate for some sign of what he might be thinking. Anything but that unreadable mask she'd last seen on him downstairs.

His eyes are trained on the floor, his hands still resting on the door handle behind him. For a moment, he doesn't look up at her. Doesn't make a move to cross the room to join her.

Her face falls and she lifts a hand to her forehead. "Peter, I am so, so sorry," she rasps, her voice like sandpaper.

His head snaps up and he makes eye contact with her for the first time. It almost looks like one corner of his mouth is curved upwards, but that doesn't make sense.

In three impossibly long strides, he crosses the room to her and grasps both of her hands in his, holding them between their bodies. "Sorry? You have nothing to be sorry for."

Olivia swallows, her forehead creasing. "Did you miss the part where I yelled at your entire family?" She can't stop the sarcasm. It's her favorite defense mechanism.

Peter laughs softly, and the sound seems to curl around her like a hug from a friend. One she didn't realize she needed so badly. "Miss it? I will be replaying that moment in my head like a movie for the rest of my life every time I need a pick-me-up."

She sniffs wetly, those tears from earlier finally deigning to drop from the corners of her eyes. "You mean you're not mad at me?"

"Mad at you?" he gasps, squeezing both of her hands. They feel so warm, covered entirely in his. The sensation is so at odds with the icy coldness she'd felt mere minutes ago. "No one has ever done something like that for me. *Ever*. It was amazing."

Olivia drags her teeth over her bottom lip then rolls it into her mouth. It doesn't hide her smile. "Okay, so you don't hate me. But what about your family?"

Peter nods and drops one of her hands to gently trail his fingertips up and down her forearm. "They were, uh... surprised at first," he begins and Olivia winces. He loops his fingers around her upper arm, his thumb tracing comforting strokes against her skin. "But after you left, we talked. Like, *really* talked. In a way we haven't in years, or possibly ever."

He holds her gaze, another silent but weighted moment passing between them. "I think we still have a ways to go, but... your little outburst actually helped." A goading grin begins to spread across his face. "That's just like you, honestly. To go totally bananas on everyone and still come out on top."

Sagging with relief, her head rolls back on her neck at the same time her eyes close. She lets out a long, slow breath. "I thought for sure that would be it. You'd send me packing."

The hand stroking Olivia's arm continues up to her shoulder, then to the side of her neck, leaving goosebumps in its wake until Peter is gently cupping her jaw. "I could never let you go," he whispers, his voice barely audible. "Even if I wanted to."

Her eyes snap open, and she tilts her face back down to meet his gaze. Twin emeralds lit by a forge stare back at her, heating her from the inside out like whiskey. She licks her lips and Peter's eyes lock onto the movement. His jaw feathers, like he's clenching his teeth. His whole body seems to go taut, holding. Waiting.

Waiting for her, she realizes.

Olivia could step back right now. Drop his hand and smother the flames growing between them with a metaphorical bucket of ice water, and that would be it. They'd go back to the way things were.

The thought of it gnaws at her chest. Sucks the air right out of her lungs. She doesn't want to walk away, to let go. Even the niggling voice in the back of her head is quiet.

She moves her free hand to the back of Peter's neck, her fingertips tangling with the loose hair at his nape. He closes his eyes at her touch, his breath exhaling in a groan as she gently strokes his scalp.

The sound makes her knees quake with want. Like she's never wanted something this badly in her entire life, and she might never feel this level of desperation ever again. She has to squeeze her thighs together to keep from dropping to the floor.

While Peter's eyes are still closed, she moves that hand to the shell of his ear, following the curved shape of it until she reaches his jaw. She follows the hard line of it to his sharp cheekbone, then moves south until her fingers reverently trace over his full lips, trying to memorize every inch of his face with her touch. Those very kissable lips. Suddenly it seems impossible that this is the first time she's touched them.

She can tell Peter is barely breathing, the puffs of air through his nose coming in erratic and uneven bursts. Like he feels it too. The undeniable thread going taut between them.

Before he can open his eyes, she jerks her fingers away and replaces them with her mouth.

At the first press of her lips, his entire body goes still. The fingers that had just been gently stroking her throat a moment ago flex, pulling away from her skin as if stunned by an electric shock.

And then he melts into her.

His full lips, slightly chapped from being out in the California sun the day before, crush against Olivia's, and she is almost certain she hears him breathe a contented sigh.

No, she feels it, that caress of air tickling her lips.

Peter slides his hand up to cup the nape of her neck as he deepens the kiss, the other sliding around her waist to push against the small of her back, bringing her impossibly closer. His movements are steady but hurried—like he's been waiting for this moment for a lifetime and doesn't intend to waste any of it.

His tongue slides out to run along her bottom lip, asking permission. A fire erupts inside of her and she willingly opens for him. He tastes like the salty air blowing in from Santa Monica pier yesterday. A little like the expensive red wine his sister brought with her, picked up last fall in Martha's Vineyard, apparently. Like the tube of minty toothpaste lying right beside hers a few feet away in the bathroom.

She can't stop herself from groaning against his lips, her fingers fisting the back of his soft, button-up shirt in an effort to stave off her desire. To retain some semblance of control.

Their kiss is fierce and messy, all clashing teeth and dancing tongues and gasps of air when they forget how to breathe. Hungry. Until Olivia can taste her cherry lip balm on his tongue.

Peter is the first to pull back, his broad and muscled chest heaving to suck down air, like he just ran a marathon with no training. He rests his forehead against Olivia's, and she can feel rather than see the upward curve of his lips.

"I've been dying to know what that felt like," he whispers, his breath tickling the tip of her nose. His eyes stay trained on her mouth, like he can't bear to make eye contact with her.

"Since when?" she asks, her voice so low and thick it's almost unrecognizable to her ears.

He hesitates a moment, then whispers, "Since the first moment I saw you."

Olivia bites the inside of her cheek, feeling a flush creep up the back of her neck. She can't resist saying, "That is such a cliche," giving his nose ring a small flick with her index finger.

Peter returns it with a nip at her bottom lip. "Only when it isn't true."

Something in the way he says it turns Olivia's core molten, makes her body vibrate. A small, inconsequential part of her brain knows she should stop this. That nothing good can come from it.

But a much larger, louder part of her brain is screaming at her to keep going. To run her fingers through his dark, wavy hair. To kiss him harder. To see what every inch of his body feels like against hers.

The louder voice wins when Olivia lifts her arms to press both of her palms to Peter's chest. Slowly, she slides them down the front of his torso, feeling every inch of carefully honed muscle hiding beneath his shirt. He lets out a gasp when her fingertips eventually reach the waistband of his shorts.

She can tell by the way the unforgiving fabric is straining that he is already at full attention beneath them.

The feel of him brushing against her fingertips sends her eyes rolling into the back of her head. Liquid heat pools between her thighs. It unlocks something deep within her, a well she'd thought had long been buried beneath the pile of mediocre dates and one-sided hookups that have wasted the last year of her life.

Peter drags his teeth across his bottom lip and looks up at her from beneath lowered lashes. His voice is like gravel when he asks, "Are you sure?"

Olivia licks her lips and nods. This time, there's no scolding voice telling her to *Stop! Think! Wait!*

The flash in his eyes is pure predator when her gaze meets his. Slowly, he slides his hand down the side of her throat and along her collarbone, carving a path toward her shoulder until his index and middle finger can slide underneath the strap of her sundress.

A shiver rakes up her spine at the brush of his cool fingers against her blazing hot skin. He carefully slides the fabric strap across her shoulder and down her arm, then repeats the action with the same painstaking slowness on the other side until her torso is stripped bare. His eyes rake over every inch of her exposed skin, the tip of his tongue sliding out to wet his lips.

She nearly withers under the weight of that stare.

Olivia has never been the shy or modest type. She isn't flashy, but she isn't a prude, either. She's never been afraid to let others see her before, but something about being laid bare in front of this man in particular makes her heart hammer an uneven rhythm in her chest, beating so loudly she's sure he must hear it in the otherwise quiet room.

It's the final line in the sand that she's about to leap over and leave behind in her rearview.

"Beautiful." The word is light and breathless when it escapes Peter's lips, and Olivia is fully prepared to make a snarky comment about men and their obsession with boobs until she notices his eyes are once again locked onto her face.

Her heart stutters to a stop, and the feeling of something breaking open in her ribcage follows.

In a rush, she throws both of her arms around the back of his neck and pulls him into her body tightly, her lips colliding with his. His firm hands cradle her bare back, her spine arching against his touch as he returns her kiss.

They part only for a moment, when Olivia tears his shirt up and over his head by its bottom seam, discarding it haphazardly on the floor behind him.

Peter's lips are back on hers in an instant, even as his firm hands are pushing down at the doubled-over waist of her dress, forcing it over her hips and down her thighs until it piles on the floor at her feet. He cups his hands around her ass and lifts her into the air with ease, settling her against his hips. She locks her legs around him for balance, gasping against his mouth when she feels his hard length press against her center.

One corner of his mouth lifts at the sound, his teeth lightly grazing her bottom lip while he walks her backward to the bed. Without breaking their kiss, he lays her across the bed she'd made earlier that morning and arches himself over her body, resting on his elbows so they are completely flush. The warmth from his body seems to call to Olivia, drawing her in. She arches her back to feel more of him, every single inch of her skin tingling where they meet.

Peter begins to plant a trail of kisses down Olivia's throat, and she tilts her head to one side, exposing more of her flushed neck to him. Everything in her feels pulled tight, like she's one of the strings on his bass guitar. Ready to hum at the smallest application of pressure.

When his lips reach the hollow just below her ear, she wriggles beneath him, trying to create her own friction.

More.

It's all she can think about. Getting closer to him. Getting more of him. To satiate a desire stronger than she's ever felt before.

Peter happily obliges, lifting a hand to her breast. Olivia groans and arches into his touch as his thumb strokes tantalizing circles over her peaked nipple. His teeth nip at the bottom of her ear lobe and she sees stars flash in her vision. She throws her arms up over her head, palms pressing into the headboard like she might float away completely without something to ground her.

Before she even senses his movement, his thumb is replaced by his mouth. He sucks hard on her nipple, nipping at it gently with his teeth and then sliding his tongue around it. The combination of pressure and pain and pleasure nearly sends her over the edge.

She reaches a hand down to run her fingers through his hair, reveling in the way his cool, wavy locks feel against her skin. God, even his hair turns her on. How is that even possible?

With her dress long since discarded on the bedroom floor, she's almost completely bare to him. Only her pesky lace underwear stand in the way.

Like he can read her mind, Peter slides his free hand down Olivia's body, leaving goosebumps in its wake, until the tips of his fingers dip beneath her waistband. The first brush of his finger against her center sends a shudder up her spine that blooms into a gasp of air released from her lips.

Goaded by the sound, Peter makes quick work of removing her thong, tossing it over his shoulder. Though it takes no more than a moment, she immediately strains at the absence of his hands on her. Her hips buck, trying to will him back faster.

He slides his hand up her bare leg, cupping over her knee, then moving up the inside of her thigh until he reaches the slip of skin where it meets her hips. Without hesitation, he presses, then circles his thumb against her center and, unable to contain the sound, Olivia groans so loudly she's sure his family must hear it all the way downstairs.

He continues to tease her with careful sweeps and circles of his thumb, her hips rolling to match him stroke for stroke.

When he dips his index finger inside of her, her heart jumps into her throat. She tilts her head back, pressing it firmly into the pillows as she moans, "Oh my god."

"You're so wet," he breathes against her throat, his hand already slick with her arousal. The low pitch of his voice is filled with adoration and lust. Like he's thrilled to be the one drawing such a reaction from her.

Every nerve ending in her body homes in on that touch. That tantalizing motion of his index finger as it moves in and out of her in a steady rhythm. The euphoric pressure of his thumb against the apex of her thighs.

Peter slides a second finger inside of her and Olivia squeezes her eyes shut so tightly she sees stars. Her mouth pops open in a gasp, like she can't suck down air fast enough. He runs his nose along the hollow beneath her ear as he pumps his fingers inside of her, then he moves to press a trail of kisses along the side of her neck to her collarbones.

She moans again, louder this time, and the sound urges him on. His hips roll forward, pressing his hard length firmly against the side of her thigh, like he just needs to feel her. More of her. All of her.

She can feel him twinge against her every time she rolls her hips to match his strokes. Each time she groans with pleasure.

"You like that?" he breathes against her skin, his lips hovering over her collarbone, tickling the sensitive skin at the top of her breasts.

"Don't stop," she begs in return, her voice a high-pitch plea she's never heard before.

He groans at the desperation in her tone and pumps his fingers in deeper, faster.

It's almost too much to bear, and Olivia can feel herself quickly approaching the edge. But she doesn't want this to end. She wants more of him. So much more.

Her eyes pop open at the same moment she grabs for the back of Peter's neck, pulling his face to hers for a passionate kiss. His fingers slip out of her as she presses one of her palms firmly against the front of his shoulder, pushing him down until he's lying completely flat on the bed.

His eyebrows arch in surprise at first until she slowly drags her fingers down his torso, following the sinewy lines of muscle in his chest and his abs until they reach the dip of his hip bones. He realizes exactly why she wanted to change positions when she begins to unbutton and unzip his charcoal shorts, sliding them and his black briefs down his powerful legs in one fell swoop.

Olivia's mouth drops open when his full length springs to life in front of her eyes. Her mouth waters at the sight and she licks her lips while Peter adjusts himself on the bed so he has one arm pillowed behind his head, angling it up just enough to see her.

His eyes are steady on her, like not even a hurricane ripping off the roof of the house right now could pull his attention away.

He groans as he watches her tongue slide across her bottom lip, noticing the aim of her hungry stare. The sound sets something loose inside her. She has to taste him. It's not that she's usually selfish in bed, but something about being here, with Peter, has her desperate to please him. It's not enough for her to feel good. She needs to bring him to his knees, to make him forget anyone else he's ever been with.

She leans her head down and runs her tongue all the way up his length, from base to tip, taking her time the whole way. Peter shudders beneath her, his eyes slamming shut as he hisses a curse under his breath.

Before he can reopen his eyes, she takes him fully into her mouth and the answering buck of his hips pushes him nearly all the way to the back of her throat. Peter fists the blankets around him tightly in his strong hands, moaning with gratification. And then one of his hands dives into Olivia's hair, holding on for dear life as she begins to work him up and down with her mouth.

"God, Olivia," he breathes. He lies back partially with heavy eyelids but keeps his chin propped against his chest to watch every dip of her head and sweep of her tongue.

She lifts her gaze to his, holding his stare, and she swears she feels his length twinge against her tongue.

"Liv, I..." he starts then stops, not sure what to say. "I need..."

She sucks the tip of him and then lifts her mouth just long enough to ask, "What do you need?"

He curses loudly again and looks her dead in the eye, his eyes darker than she's ever seen them before, and says, "I need you. *Now.*"

She can't help her smugness at the desperation and command in his voice. She's had plenty of hookups in the past, the good, the bad, and the ugly. But nothing that's made her feel this way. A relentless need to satisfy him just as much as she seeks satisfaction for herself.

It's a heady feeling.

Olivia climbs slowly up Peter's body and he props himself up partially against the headboard to meet her halfway. His arms circle around her back, his palms sliding up to grip the back of her shoulders. She lifts one leg to straddle his hips until they're both sitting flush against one another.

His jaw falls open at the first caress of her against his hard length, a loud sigh exhaling from his open mouth. He quickly tilts his head forward to capture her lips in a frenzied kiss.

She's ready for him, but she still can't resist the urge to tease him. She grinds her hips into his until the tip of his length finds home against her center. Sparks fly behind her closed eyelids, and she lets out a soft gasp, grinding her hips against him again.

"Dammit, Liv," he hisses against her lips.

Tired of waiting, he slides his hands down to grip her ass and lifts up, placing her so his tip pushes against her entrance.

The feel of him so close to where she wants him forces Olivia to stop teasing. She places each of her palms against his broad shoulders, then guides her hips until she sinks down fully on him.

Peter lets out a low curse under his breath. "You feel..." he begins to say, but she cuts him off by crushing her mouth against his. She doesn't need to hear him say it, because she can already feel it.

She cradles her arm around his neck, holding on tightly as she moves up and down in his lap, setting her pace. Peter matches her stroke for stroke, his hips rolling against hers like the waves cresting just before the shoreline.

Within minutes, the muscles in her core start to tense in anticipation. She's close again, but still not ready for it to end.

Peter moves his lips to her ear and whispers, "Not yet, Quinn," and the way he says her name is nearly enough to send her over the edge, but she digs in to find the strength to obey.

A moment later, he bucks his hips and cradles Olivia's spine with one arm to flip her over so she's lying flat on her back against the bed once more. He hooks one of her legs over his shoulder and thrusts himself even deeper inside of her, eliciting a loud gasp from between her lips.

She curses under her breath and digs her nails into his muscled back at the sudden change in sensation. His pelvic bone grinds against the sweet spot at the top of her thighs with every single stroke. If she had been seeing sparks flash behind her eyelids before, now she sees explosions. The grand finale at the fireworks show.

"Peter, I..." she tries to say, but the words are thin, barely puffs of air. And then she's tumbling completely over the edge, freefalling off the side of one of LA's cliffs and into a warm, moonlit pool the color of emeralds.

Peter joins her seconds later, and Olivia immediately chides herself for not remembering a condom when he has to spill himself across her belly.

She doesn't make the same mistake the second time they find themselves in that same position.

Or the third.

Now, the two of them lay on their backs, side-by-side under the covers and blanketed by the soothing darkness of the guest bedroom around them.

Their chests rise and fall in alternating intervals, one inhaling as the other exhales, like they share the same lungs after being bonded in such a visceral way.

Her eyelids are heavy with sated exhaustion. She cradles the down comforter to her chest, her body still fully unclothed beneath the sheets.

Companionable silence stretches between them, their heart rates slowing in tandem after that last time. And as incredible and right as it felt, Olivia knows that is *the* last time. Without her lust to cloud her judgment, she knows it has to be.

Nothing more can come from it. They are just two attractive people who hooked up one time and occasionally enjoy each other's company. No more, no less.

She bites down on her bottom lip, suddenly feeling nervous. Borderline self-conscious. It's unfamiliar territory, a sensation she's not sure what to do with.

Even if there was more to it, well, she couldn't go down that road. It wasn't worth it. With her running track record, she'd probably have him dodging her texts and running for the hills after three dates max, their tenuous friendship left rotting in the dust.

It would only complicate things. Facing him after this hookup would be hard enough.

What did you just do? she thinks to herself, her pulse quickening again.

He probably thinks you're such a—

"Hey." His voice seems loud in the heavy quiet, though she knows it's barely above a whisper.

"We uh... I mean, that was," she stammers, her head rolling back and forth against the pillow as she searches for words to head him off. Of course he wants to define the relationship. The *non*-relationship. The *can never be a* relationship.

"Incredible? I know, right?" Peter chuckles instead, and the sound softens an ache in her stomach. Maybe this won't be so bad. Maybe their friendship can recover from this.

He flips over onto his side to face Olivia in the darkness and it feels so similar to the night before, when they talked and talked for hours, that her chest grows hot, like someone struck a match right in the center of her being. "Are you hungry?"

She's so caught off guard by the casual question that she can't help but laugh.

Peter reaches out to poke a finger to her cheek, mistaking the laugh for her chastisement. "Hey, a guy my size has gotta eat. I'm gonna sneak downstairs and make a sandwich. Do you want one?"

Olivia breathes a sigh through her nose, unable to contain her relief. She *is* hungry. And a sandwich sounds damn good right now.

She'd barely picked at the incredible meal Peter's mom served earlier due in no small part to the awkwardness at dinner.

"I would love a sandwich, if you're offering to make it." She wiggles her eyebrows, although she's pretty sure he can't see her in the dim lighting.

He must though, because he sniffs a laugh and then rolls onto his other side to climb off the bed. But before he does, he stops short, like someone who just remembered they left the stove on when leaving for work. He doubles back, twisting across the bed until he's nearly pressed against Olivia, only the blankets separating them.

In that moment, she becomes dangerously aware he's still naked too.

"Forget something?" she tries to quip, but her voice seems small. Anxious.

"Actually, yeah. This." Peter closes the rest of the distance between them to press a chaste kiss to Olivia's lips.

Her eyes flutter closed, her lips easing against his like they're crafted from the same clay, molded by expert hands to fit perfectly. She breathes in his scent, cedar and rain flooding her nostrils like she stepped out of this bedroom and into an enchanted forest from one of the romantasy books she covets so much.

Peter draws back inch by inch, the tip of his nose grazing hers until their eyes meet. He's smiling, and it's small and she can barely see him in the dark, but somehow it's so completely, devastatingly handsome that her heart nearly bursts from her chest.

She watches him cross the room, admiring the barely-visible outline of his masculine form as he tugs on a clean pair of sweatpants from his suitcase. She watches him turn back to look at her from the bedroom doorway, and she swears he winks at her before walking through it.

Olivia Quinn, you are so fucked.

Chapter 16

Still Friends?

Gray light blankets the room when Olivia opens her eyes, her lashes brushing against something firm with each blink. She wrinkles her nose at the tickling sensation and it suddenly floods with the refreshing scent of a rainstorm in a thick forest.

She snaps her eyes open fully to realize the "something firm" is Peter's chiseled chest, which she'd apparently decided to use as a pillow at some point during the night. Her stomach drops and she lurches back, pulling some of the covers with her. Her chest rises and falls in heaving breaths as she stares down at the man beside her, willing her nerve-endings to stop firing in rapid succession. Her brain can't keep up.

Her heart rate eventually slows to an only just elevated thrum, eyes still caught on Peter's sleeping form. She curls her legs closer to her body, carefully inching herself toward the opposite end of the bed, the impossibly soft sheets sliding easily over her skin without disturbing the sleeping man next to her. By the time she reaches her side of the bed, she's pulled the blankets down the length of Peter's torso until they pool just above his hip bones.

He's still naked, she realizes with a shock.

God, he looks good. It should be illegal for someone to look this good.

The ends of his dark hair have curled even more overnight, loose pieces falling against his temples. His lashes are irritatingly long—a trait wasted on men—brushing the tops of his cheekbones with his eyes closed. His mouth is relaxed, jaw loose as he breathes in and out methodically through his nose. That nose.

It's a little big, some might say. Longer than average, with a tip that widens a fraction instead of coming to a tight point.

But Peter's a big guy, and it suits him. Olivia likes that nose.

Her attention next snags on his chest, rising and falling in time to his deep breaths. There's a small patch of hair in the center, dark like the rest. She remembers running her hand over it last night, and her cheeks flush.

Even laying completely flat, she can see the definition of his pecs, where they cut down to dip into the top of his six-pack. Her mouth waters a moment later when she reaches the deep V of muscle just above the sheets. She has to clench her teeth to squash down the desire that flames to life inside of her.

Thankfully, her attention is drawn elsewhere when her phone vibrates on the nightstand next to the bed. She twists over to grab it, noticing two messages from her best friend, Hannah. The first must have been what woke her.

`You finally come home to me today! Sorry, I know it's probably like 6AM there, but I couldn't wait ;)`

`Can't wait to hear all about your trip!`

Olivia groans inwardly, her paranoia growing. Does Hannah somehow know something happened last night, or is that a totally normal thing to say to someone who's been away for four days?

Ordinarily, she'd be stoked to see her best friend. But what is she supposed to tell her? She girlbossed a little too close to the sun with this whole fake relationship thing and fell right into Peter's bed?

That she might be catching feelings for her best friend's fiancé's best friend?

No, she can't be. She shakes her head, strikes down the thought.

Then a small voice rears up in her head and says, *He's your best friend, too.*

Her heart sinks inside of her chest. For the first time in her life, she's pretty sure she agrees with that stupid little voice. And that's a problem. A big, big problem.

She taps out a short, vague response to Hannah and sets her phone back down on the nightstand. The sound must be enough to wake Peter, who stirs sleepily beside her.

Sucking in a sharp breath, Olivia steels herself for an awkward morning-after conversation. She usually doesn't last this long with her hookups. More of a *sneak-out-the-front-door-before-he-wakes* kinda girl. Or, in the case of Bruce, a *stomp-haughtily-out-the-office-door-swearing-up-and-down-that-it-will-never-happen-again* kinda girl.

"Morning," Peter says, and his voice is heavy and thick, like the fresh maple syrup Olivia's dad used to buy from a sweet old lady at the farmers' market, always served warm during the rare pancake breakfasts they shared when she was growing up. Something flakes off inside of her at the sound and the memory it stirs of home, like a chunk breaking free from an iceberg and plunging into the icy sea below.

She lifts her gaze to look at him fully, and he's smiling. It's just barely an upward tilt of his lips, and his eyes are so squinted against the dim light in the room that she can barely see them, but she knows he's smiling at her. That he's happy to see her. She can feel it, and it nearly kills her.

"Morning," she says back quietly, averting her gaze. She had hoped to make a break for the shower before he'd woken up, but no such luck. She thanks herself for managing to throw on a bra and underwear set last night before she drifted off to sleep. Taking a quick look down at herself, she realizes with a start that she somehow hobbled together a matching pair.

Like he possesses a sixth sense, Peter sits up halfway and reaches out to brush his fingertips against the exposed underside of her palm. "Hey, what's up?"

"What do you mean?" she asks, and she knows her voice is too high, but she can't stop it.

He lifts those same fingertips and tucks them under her chin, forcing Olivia to look up at him. His eyes aren't squinty anymore; they're round and open and so, so green. His smile turns into a lopsided grin as he says, "You look like you just swallowed a whole tube of mustard." She vaguely remembers confessing her hatred of the condiment to him at lunch on Santa Monica pier.

She waves a hand through the air, using the motion as an excuse to pull back from his grip on her chin. "Oh, you know, just thinking about our flight and having to go back to work tomorrow." She slides to the edge of the bed opposite Peter and rises to rifle through her suitcase. "Speaking of which, I'd better shower. We have to leave for the airport in less than two hours."

After grabbing her outfit for the day—a pair of cobalt blue leggings, a matching crop tank with built-in sports bra, and a lightweight, beige off-the-shoulder crew sweater—she sprints into the attached bath, closing the door behind her with a bang louder than she intended. She leaves Peter behind on the bed with elevated eyebrows and a confused twist to his mouth.

"Oh thank god," Peter groans, drool practically dripping from the corner of his mouth as he sets his and Olivia's bags down at the bottom of the staircase with a flourish. He insisted on carrying all their belongings down himself, despite her protests to help.

"Didn't think I'd let you fly all the way back to New York without a Campbell breakfast," Peter's mom calls from the kitchen, where there are piles of pancakes, waffles, sausage links, strips of bacon, scrambled eggs, and slices of toast stacked up on what must be every plate in the house.

Olivia has been dreading this moment since the night before, despite Peter's, uh... distractions. While he is already seated at the breakfast bar that makes up one half of the Campbells' kitchen island and filling his plate with a little bit of everything in the spread, she moves into the kitchen, taking each step gingerly, like a wounded animal.

At her slow approach, Becca turns around from the kitchen sink where she'd been scrubbing out a frying pan, a wide smile lighting up her face and sending small wrinkles fanning out around her eyes. In a few strides, she steps around the island and meets Olivia on the other side, pulling her in for a tight embrace that smells like chocolate chips and waffle batter.

"Thank you," Becca whispers in her ear, quiet enough that Peter won't hear, even from just a few feet away. In a louder voice, she adds, "I'm going to miss having you around the house," then pulls back. Her hands are still braced gently against Olivia's shoulders when she looks between the woman before her and her son at the island. "*Both* of you."

Peter makes a strangled sound around a strip of bacon—yes, an entire strip of bacon—that he's shoved into his mouth.

Becca narrows her gaze at him, finally letting go of his fake girlfriend to face her son directly. "Let's try not to let another year go by again before the next visit, yes?"

After swallowing his mouthful of food, he cocks a brow at his mom and says, "If you promise to make this for breakfast every day, I'll be back again in a week."

Becca restrains a tinkling laugh and moves around the island to build a plate for Olivia as the latter takes her seat on a bar height stool next to Peter.

"Woah, save some food for the rest of us," Peter's dad jokes loudly when he enters the kitchen from behind them. He rounds the island to stand beside his wife, immediately pouring himself another cup of black coffee.

"I got my appetite from you," his son tosses back, and it's so completely normal that Olivia nearly passes out. The easy banter, the lighthearted conversation. It's so at odds with the first awkward meal they shared on Thursday not ten feet from where she sits now.

After the show she'd put on the night before, she expected heavy silences, awkward pauses. Or, more likely, nothing at all. A quick run to the waiting car, breakfast grabbed at the airport.

She tenses and remains quiet beside Peter, waiting for the other shoe to drop.

But it never does. Peter's parents never bring up her outburst from the night before. If anything, they seem more at ease than they have all weekend.

"Let me help you with the bags," Andrew says when a car pulls into the driveway after breakfast.

He and his son make light work of the suitcases while Olivia hovers next to Becca just inside the front door. She can't shake the feeling that she needs to bring up the night before. Needs to apologize, even if the Campbells seem to have no interest in hearing it.

She turns to Becca while the men's attention is diverted by depositing the luggage into the black town car's trunk. "Look, about last night," Olivia begins sheepishly, tucking a piece of hair behind her ear just to have something to do with her hands. "I was completely out of line and I'm sorry." The words come out in a rush, like barely-intelligible vomit. Which is very on the nose considering how her stomach is currently in knots. It feels like a colony of bats flapping around in there.

Becca turns to her, forehead creased in a look that is equal parts confused and concerned. "Sorry? What could you possibly have to be sorry for?" She tilts her head to one side, like she needs to survey Olivia from another angle. After a moment, Becca's expression softens.

She takes both of Olivia's hands in her own, her lips curving upward as she holds Olivia's eyes unflinchingly. Well, Becca doesn't flinch. Olivia wants to run away and hide immediately at the weight of that stare.

"I have never seen someone defend my son so vehemently. Not even me, and I've been known to throw a few punches myself." Becca chuckles under her breath and rests a hand on Olivia's shoulder, giving it a reassuring squeeze. "The things you said, they needed to be said. And every last one of us needed to hear them, myself included."

Olivia loosens a shaky breath she hadn't realized she'd been holding. "I can be a little bit of a loose cannon sometimes, when I really..." she trails off, and Becca's smile widens knowingly.

"When you love something. Or someone," Becca finishes for her in a soft voice. Olivia's heart begins to race at the accusation. Because it's simply not true. It can't be.

Oblivious to Olivia's internal argument, Becca leans in to wrap her arms around Olivia in another tight embrace—her third that morning, in fact. "I can't tell you how thrilled I am that my son has found someone like you."

Guilt and dread plummet through Olivia's gut like she swallowed a hundred-pound dumbbell. She can already feel sweat beading at the nape of her neck. Her cheeks start burning, like she has a fever, and her breath is short and hot, coming in rapid puffs through her nose.

Peter's mom pulls back to face Olivia fully one final time, right as Peter and his dad are climbing the steps to the house's front porch. "You two are perfect together."

The statement hits Olivia like a gunshot to the heart, and it takes every ounce of will she has not to let her face fall.

What have I done?

What am I still *doing?*

"Alright Mom, let the girl breathe," Peter says softly from Olivia's side when he reaches the two of them. Curiosity paints his face at the sight of them, but he doesn't ask and Olivia doesn't offer.

In an instant, Becca releases Olivia to throw her arms around her son, hugging him even tighter. Normally, Olivia would laugh at the way Peter has to stoop down nearly a foot to fold into his mother's embrace.

But she can't. She feels hollow inside, and it's taking every ounce of energy she has to stay standing.

The car ride to the airport was quiet. Tense.

The inside of Olivia's head was like a thunderstorm. Every time Peter tried to make conversation with her, she shut him down with monosyllabic answers.

Their time on the plane wasn't much better.

Peter asked her what's wrong no less than five times, and each time he did, she forced a flat smile to her lips that she knew he saw straight through and tightly assured him she's fine.

At one point, while the plane beneath them sliced easily through the air at forty-two-thousand feet, he whispered, "Are you still worried about the promotion? Because trust me, you have nothing to worry about."

Olivia blew out a slow breath. She actually felt relieved. Relieved that he had no idea what was truly on her mind. She nodded her head twice and pulled her ear buds out of her bag, then popped them into her ears to end the conversation.

She knew she was being a bitch. And she knew Peter didn't deserve it.

It'll be easier this way, she told herself while Dua Lipa crooned in her ears about a broken heart. *He deserves more than a fling that will likely end in disaster.*

He'd get over it eventually, and they could go back to being just friends. Acquaintances, really. Connected by their mutual friends and nothing more. Able to walk down the aisle, arm in arm, at Hannah and Ezra's wedding, maybe share one required dance for the photographer, then move on without guilt. Without ruining everything.

Now, Olivia slips her purse up higher on her shoulder as they trudge side by side through JFK, Peter still dutifully toting both of their wheeled suitcases behind him. The sound of them rolling along the terrazzo floor is almost soothing. A lullaby trying to pull her into a deep sleep. The five-hour flight drained her.

Or maybe that was her racing thoughts.

When they reach the sliding glass doors that lead to the rideshare pick up zone, Peter stops and Olivia draws up short beside him.

Right. She'd gotten so used to them traveling together, she hadn't considered what they'd do when they landed. His apartment is in Chelsea, hers in Brooklyn. It hardly makes sense for them to ride together, and yet...

"Do you want me to, er," Peter stammers, letting go of the handle of her suitcase to rub at the back of his neck. It's a tell, Olivia had noticed over the course of the weekend, for when he's feeling nervous. "I mean, can I..."

Another crack inside her rib cage. It takes all her strength to peer up at him. "I'm actually really tired. I imagine you must be, too. Probably the time change. No need to come all the way out to mine in evening traffic. You go ahead, I'll grab my own Uber." Another thin-lipped smile.

Peter frowns down at her and tilts his head to one side like a lost puppy. "Okay, what is going on?"

Olivia pretends she doesn't know what he's getting at, like it isn't obvious. It's easier that way.

It's not enough to dissuade him. "You've been acting weird since we left my parents' house. It's been the longest seven-and-a-half hours of my life. What's up?"

She lifts and drops one shoulder, then looks out at a point just behind Peter's head to avoid his piercing stare. "Just tired, like I said." *Liar.*

"Bullshit," Peter accuses, and his tone sends a jolt of electricity through her. Her eyes snap back to his, her mouth dropping open in mild surprise.

Peter leans in, the scent of cedar and rain filling her nostrils. "Is this about what happened last night? Because if you want to talk about it, we can—"

"No!" she shouts, far too loudly, forcing him to take a step back. "No, not at all," she says again in a softer tone. She's not ready to go there. She can't go there. In fact, she needs him to never bring it up again. To never even think about it. Ever.

And yet it's all her brain has wanted to think about all day. Each time her conscious thoughts faded out, she'd feel his phantom hands on her body, the push of his calloused thumb against her center, the weight of his six-foot-five frame on top of hers.

It weakened her defenses every time, and she couldn't afford it. Not now.

Knowing she has to give him something, she says, "I'm just... as corny as this sounds, I think I'm going to miss your parents." She wrinkles her nose as she gazes up at him, schooling her face into a picture of innocence. "I liked them more than I thought I would. Probably more than you."

Peter holds back a chuckle, some of the strained muscles in his shoulders loosening. "You say that like it's a bad thing."

Because it is, she wants to scream. Because she's going to lose them along with him when this whole charade is over, and all of it's going to hurt. Badly. Worse than the time she fell out of the tree in her backyard and broke her wrist.

Because when she isn't forcing herself to think about anything else, and her mind isn't wandering to how freaking incredible Peter felt last night, she's replaying his mom's words over and over and over and reminding herself why she needs to bail.

Peter deserves everything his mom wants for him. Someone amazing who loves him and can be a part of his family.

Not someone who can't figure her own life out. Not someone who only seems to attract trouble so she swears off dating only to end up screwing her boss. Not a mess like Olivia.

Tears are starting to prick at the back of her eyes and looks down at her feet, blinking rapidly in an attempt to push them away. "You're right, I'm being crazy. I think the jet lag has fried my brain."

When she's ninety percent sure he won't notice the sadness on her face, she forces one corner of her mouth to lift and meets his gaze with unseeing eyes. "I'll text you later?"

Peter studies her face for what feels like an eternity, like he can see her every dark thought written on it like a tattoo. He doesn't smile, but eventually he nods anyway.

She watches him walk outside and climb into a black Lincoln he must've ordered for the both of them before their plane took off.

And then she lets the tears fall.

By the time Olivia arrives back at her apartment in a little corner of Brooklyn, her eyes are dry. They feel tight, like they've been stretched too far inside their sockets. It hurts to blink, but she's happy to be rid of the tears.

God, crying in an Uber. Who am I? she had thought to herself more than once during the drive.

Her key slides into the metal lock of her front door and she pushes inward to find the apartment she shares with her best friend Hannah dark. Empty.

It's quiet. Even the door swinging out against the refurbished hardwood floors barely makes a sound. Her heart squeezes in her chest as she flicks on the light switch by the door and locks herself inside.

On one hand, relief courses through her like the blood pumping in her veins. A relief she won't have to talk about it just yet, while the wound is still fresh and springy.

On the other hand, she's not ready to be alone. And she really, really could use her best friend right now. She hadn't realized how much she'd missed Hannah.

She'd had only been gone four days, but she had been feeling adrift for far longer than that.

When Olivia rolls her suitcase farther into the apartment, her attention snags on something sitting atop the apartment's tiny, makeshift dining room table. Her lips curve as she approaches it: a bouquet of flowers with a balloon floating above it, its string tied to the clear vase.

She lifts the note and unfolds it at the perfectly straight horizontal seam.

WELCOME HOME!!!

SO SORRY I COULDN'T BE THERE WHEN YOUR FLIGHT LANDED. WEDDING PLANNING HAS CONSUMED MY LIFE. I'M BARELY HANGING ON HAHA.

I MISSED YOU SO MUCH! CAN'T WAIT TO CATCH UP. TAKEOUT AFTER WORK TOMORROW?

YOUR BEST FRIEND IN THE WHOLE WORLD,

HANNAH

Her shoulders loosen when she finishes reading it. Sure, they'd been a little caught up in their own worlds for a while now—wedding planning for Hannah; dating the wrong guys, giving up on love, sleeping with her boss then deciding to end the affair in what could be possibly the dumbest scheme in the history of schemes for Olivia.

So maybe Hannah isn't here right now. They're still best friends. Olivia still has a shoulder to lean on.

This is a good thing. It gives her a whole twenty-four hours to sort through the tangled ball of feelings knotting her chest before dissecting each and every one of them with Hannah.

Leaning down, she gently cradles the fingertips of one hand around the petals of a pale pink peony—her favorite, because of course Hannah remembered. She takes a deep inhale of the flower's sweet scent, letting it wash over her.

She swiftly rolls her suitcase into her room, leaving it upturned and open on the area rug because she's far too tired to bother unpacking now. The kind of weary-tired you feel deep in the marrow of your bones, from far more than a lack of sleep.

Olivia pops a frozen supreme pizza for one into the oven, then uncorks a bottle of Chardonnay she'd pilfered from her parents' house during her last visit (she'd also made off with a bottle of Malbec, a Riesling, and tequila that day, most of which are already long gone) to pour a heaping glass for one.

Twenty minutes later, she sits on her blue-gray suede couch with her feet propped up on the coffee table. Her personal pizza, cut carefully into quarters, rests on a plate balanced against the tops of her thighs. A Harry Potter marathon on cable bellows from the television across from her.

Her phone sits beside her on the sofa, and it's relatively quiet now. She'd texted Hannah a quick thank you and confirmed their dinner plans for tomorrow while she waited for her pizza to heat up, and Hannah had responded almost immediately with a series of emojis ranging from smiling faces to party hats to champagne bottles.

But it isn't Hannah's name she's looking for on the screen when her eyes dart to it every five seconds.

You told him you'd text him, of course he isn't going to reach out, she tells herself. *This is a good thing. What could you possibly say to him?*

Her fingers itch to grab for the phone anyway, but she resists, trying to focus her attention on the television where Harry is currently battling it out with Draco for the golden snitch.

When her phone does finally light up and that glorious *ping!* rings in her ear alerting her to a new notification, she dives for it with such ferocity her fingernails practically stab through the couch. She holds it up to her face, her heart hammering in her chest.

And then it falls.

It's not Peter. It's not even a text. It's an Instagram follow request from...

She blinks rapidly at the screen. From Jennifer Campbell, Peter's sister.

Biting down on her bottom lip, she heaves a deep sigh through her nose and stares at the tiny words on the screen.

She almost wants to laugh, like fate itself decided to swoop in and remind her why this whole thing with Peter needed to end. There were real people at stake, and they didn't deserve to be caught up in her game.

She fights the urge to open the app, where she knows exactly what awaits her on her profile. The last three photos she posted. The two smiling faces in each of them.

The first is bright. Four eyes squinting at the screen from Santa Monica, two of them hidden behind baby blue sunglasses.

The second is dark and grainy, taken outside The Pier and cropped from an article on AboutTown.

And the last one is blurry and slightly distorted by the buzzing fluorescent lights overhead, snapped in a heavily creased red vinyl booth.

Olivia's finger hovers over the screen, flexing, drawn by the temptation. Then in a flourish, she swipes her finger across the glassy surface to clear the notification entirely. *Tomorrow's problem*, she thinks.

Chapter 17

I Thought I Knew It All

Olivia had debated calling off work this morning.

She'd barely slept last night, the silence of the apartment deafening in her ears. It was a far cry from the soft sound of Peter's breaths beside her, the safety net of his rising and falling chest in her peripheral vision.

It wasn't that she missed it. She certainly didn't miss the warmth of his body next to hers, either. That would be ridiculous.

It was just different. It would take some getting used to, that's all. Her constant tossing and turning during the night had left her bleary-eyed and yawning today.

Yet here she is, rising to the tenth floor in a stainless steel-paneled elevator, on her way to Kaplan, Kaplan, and Westin. Because today is the big day. *Her* day. The day she'll finally get her interview for the senior paralegal promotion.

The invite may not be in her inbox yet, but that had always been Bruce's style. He'd ambush her halfway through the day, put her on the spot without warning. His way of keeping his team on their toes, he always quipped.

As the elevator doors part, she stifles the upward turn of her mouth at the memory of the last time he'd made that speech.

He may be an asshole, but the longer you know him, the more you come to expect it. There aren't any surprises when it comes to Bruce Westin. She knows what she's getting when she walks through that front door, and a slice of normalcy is exactly what she needs right now.

The hallway echoes with the sound of her heels hitting the tiled floor, aiming for the law firm entrance. It's already lit from within, an off-white glow filtering through the frosted glass window pane of the door, creating a skewed rectangle on the marble pattern under her feet.

"Good morning!" Madison chirps when Olivia enters, looking up from her laptop. The source of the light. Many of the other paralegals don't show up until close to 8:30 a.m., the attorneys even later.

Olivia gives the receptionist a nod, adjusting the handle of her purse to rest in the crook of her elbow.

"Any news?" Madison pries, and Olivia stifles a scoff. The girl may have been kissing her ass ever since she leaked her relationship with Peter to the press, but she's still a busybody.

"Not yet, but I'm not surprised," Olivia answers, lifting and lowering a shoulder meaningfully. Madison nods, catching her drift.

Olivia leaves her with a cool parting smile and heads down the hallway to her office at the back of the firm. She takes her time booting up her laptop, moves her mouse cursor with guided slowness toward her email app.

She's not stressed. Not worried.

She's not expecting to see a meeting invite in her inbox from Bruce.

And it's a good thing too, because she doesn't find one there in the blue-and-white digital interface. Not buried amongst the case assignments he sent while she was out of town, or the copies of discovery from opposing counsel she must review *ASAP!*

It takes her nearly the entire morning to get through it all, but honestly? It's a welcome distraction. There's a profound calm in the documentation. A sense of rhythm in the files. It calls to something deep within her, like the open road might call to a cyclist.

It's crisp and clear. Black type on white page written in a dialect she's completely fluent in by now. Formatted in a perfect pattern with no room for shades of gray.

Her phone lights up from its perch on the corner of her desk just before lunch. Or, rather, the time she'd normally take lunch: one fifteen on the nose.

She grabs for it, then reclines back in her ergonomic chair, lifting it to eye level. Her heart stumbles in her chest, like it forgot how to pump. It's Peter.

Apparently blowing him off the night before hadn't been enough to deter him. Despite what her brain wants, one corner of her mouth kicks up with pride.

She presses her lips into a thin line. That's precisely the reason she shouldn't open this message. Or respond. She's cursed when it comes to relationships, and a strained friendship with a guy she once slept with in his childhood bedroom that *wasn't* his childhood bedroom anymore would be better than nothing at all.

They just need time apart.

And yet she can't resist at least opening the message, not when she sees it's an image.

Gingerly, like the phone might explode in her palm, she presses her thumb to the little gray bubble. She has to bite back a lopsided grin.

It's a photo of a large—frankly an understatement, but Olivia is not the type to body shame—orange-and-white striped cat. Its fur is absolutely luscious, wild and thick like it should be perched amongst the branches of an oak tree deep in a forgotten wood. Its mouth is open wide in a meow she can practically hear.

There's no text, just this photo. It looks like it was taken on a sidewalk somewhere in the city.

It's probably the single best message she's ever gotten in her life, aside from maybe the time Hannah texted to say she'd just signed the lease on their shared apartment. And even then, it would be a close race.

Olivia bites down hard on her bottom lip and forces herself to close the thread without replying.

There was no interview that day.

In fact, Bruce had been absent for all nine hours Olivia spent at the office playing catch up. He wasn't in court, she knew that. She would've had to prep him if he had been. Even if that hadn't made it obvious, he'd also managed to send her follow up emails on every single case assignment he'd passed on during her brief vacation.

Asshole.

No, there had been no interview, but there also hadn't been an announcement about someone else getting the promotion. At least there was that.

At the end of the day, she had blown out a long, hard breath, pushed back from her desk to stand, and packed up her things with a small ray of hope for tomorrow budding in her chest.

"Wow, look at this spread," she says now, letting out a low whistle through her lips after the last word. She scans the marble-topped kitchen island, the centerpiece of the apartment she shares with her best friend.

Olivia had been stunned to discover it was real marble when she first toured the place a year ago. It isn't a huge island—nothing in the apartment is, by any definition—just enough to fully divide the small kitchen space from the dining-slash-living room. But even back then she had known the marble top was worth a pretty penny. It proved its worth every time it held up to her and Hannah's spilled drinks, slopped-over bowls and plates of food, and that time Olivia cut cheese for a makeshift charcuterie board directly on it because she had been too lazy to wash the cutting board that lounged in the bottom rack of the dishwasher.

It would be there through it all.

Right now though, the stone-white top, cut through with veins of gray, is completely obscured by takeout boxes. On the far left, there are four black boats stuffed with sushi of all varieties, at least three of those rolls filled to the brim with cream cheese—Olivia's favorite. Next to them are bright-white foam containers, their lids flopping to the side to reveal a feast of fried food: deep fried mini tacos piled high next to little cups of salsa and sour cream; cheesesteak stuffed eggrolls sliced in half over a bed of greens, a cup of sweet chili sauce on the side; and, of course, a mountain of beer-battered french fries to round out the retinue.

Last, but certainly not least, are two foil rounds stuffed full of Caesar salad, the dressing mixed right in, just like Olivia likes it.

"Did you rob an Uber Eats guy?" she jokes, cocking an eyebrow across the island at her best friend.

A flush creeps across Hannah's cheeks, nearly hiding the spackling of freckles that sprouted there from a month's worth of weekends spent by Ezra's rooftop pool. Olivia had been there for some of it, when she could.

When she wasn't making colossal mistakes with her boss.

"I feel like I haven't seen you in a lifetime! I got all your favorites so we can stuff our faces while you fill me in on your trip to LA with Peter," Hannah hedges, a barely-there tremble to her voice. Her hands shake almost imperceptibly as she reorganizes the plastic sushi trays for what must be the fifth time. No one but Olivia would have noticed either of Hannah's tells.

Olivia's lips draw into a thin line that she tries to turn into a smile. "It was only four days, Han. Hardly deserving of such a fine, artery-clogging meal." A bob and weave of her own.

It's not like she could truthfully tell Hannah what happened in LA. Even with a full twenty-four hours to soak it in, she still isn't ready to revisit it. To say it out loud. She'd have to dodge Hannah's questions until she has more time to process.

Hannah sniffs a laugh and pulls her fingers away from the sushi, balling them into loose fists at her sides. She glances up at the ceiling, then down at the floor, and then finally forces herself to make eye contact with Olivia.

Olivia tries to keep her face open, encouraging, but the inside of her brain feels like the lights on top of an ambulance. Bouncing, loud, bright, a warning to get out of the way. She steels herself and forces her lips to turn up higher.

Hannah lets out a soft breath, her eyes so round and so blue they look like someone punched two holes out of the petals of a cornflower and glued them to her face. "Okay, confession: I brought you here under false pretenses."

Olivia fakes a gasp, clutching a hand to her chest. "You mean you *didn't* miss me?" Despite her hammering heart, she's desperate to see her best friend relax, no matter what secret is driving her anxiety.

Hannah snorts, but her shoulders visibly loosen. "Okay, maybe false pretenses is too strong. More like, I had ulterior motives." She rests a hand against the only sliver of countertop visible beneath the sea of containers and leans her hip against it. "In addition to simply missing the hell out of you, I also need to talk to you. About something important."

"How ominous," Olivia deflects, pressing the heels of her palms against the countertop on the other side. "Should I eat first for strength or will this *something* make me throw up all this delicious food?"

Hannah scowls at her, but the chinks in her armor are widening. She's relaxing.

Too bad it feels like Olivia is absorbing all of Hannah's nerves.

"We'll eat after or I think *I* might throw up trying to get the words out," Hannah says with an unsure smile. "But let's sit down. My legs feel like Jello after running, physically running, back and forth to all these restaurants."

Hannah crosses around the island and takes the nine steps that lead into their shared living room, aiming for the sofa.

Olivia follows a few feet behind and interjects, "You mean when you jumped one of those bike delivery guys, stole all his goods, then sprinted back to the apartment," earning another laugh from Hannah, this one louder.

They sit down beside one another, their knees pointed inward so they're almost touching. Olivia clutches her hands together to hide her own fidgeting, bracing her clasped fists against the tops of her thighs. She lifts her eyebrows expectantly, rolling her lips into her mouth.

Hannah releases a breath she must've been holding on the walk over and smooths her palms against the black wide-legged jeans she's wearing. "Okay, so," she starts, then stops. Her eyes roam around the room like she's trying to remember her next line. After a pause that's just shy of awkward, she focuses back on Olivia. "With the wedding less than five months away, Ezra and I have been doing a lot of thinking. A lot of talking, I mean, about what comes after."

Olivia's mouth twitches. "Hannah, do we need to talk about the birds and the bees? Because based on what you told me last fall, I thought you two were well past that."

Hannah pulls a face, but her smile grows. "Gross, and off topic. What I mean is, we've been thinking about what it means for the two of us, after we're married. Our living arrangements," she finally clarifies, her voice trailing off at the end until it's just a whisper.

Olivia lifts her head a fraction of an inch in understanding.

Of course they'd want to live together. She had considered that back when Ezra first proposed.

She had, hadn't she?

Or had she been living in a fantasy world where Hannah continued to be her best friend and roommate, commuting into Manhattan a few nights a week to see her husband?

No, that'd be crazy. Of course Hannah would move into Ezra's place in SoHo.

Hannah sucks in another deep breath, preparing to rip off a big, fat bandage. "We decided it made the most sense to move to LA."

Olivia blinks. She blinks again. She blinks so much she's surprised her eyelashes don't all fall out from such overuse. She opens her mouth to say something, but words won't come. She couldn't have heard that right. She should just ask Hannah to repeat herself.

I'm sorry, it sounded like you just said you're moving to LA. Silly me, I must have a piece of sushi stuck in my ears.

When Olivia doesn't say anything, Hannah soldiers on. "Ezra's dad isn't doing so well, and he wants to get back there to be with him. And to help his mom, however he can. However *we* can."

Olivia's throat constricts, like someone has their hands wrapped tightly around it. She can't breathe, can't remember how to.

Her best friend is moving across the country.

"I, wow... that's... wow," Olivia stammers after a few moments of silence during which she can tell Hannah is desperate for her to say something. Anything.

"It's a lot to unpack, I know," Hannah acknowledges, nodding her head too fast, too many times. Her nerves are back, but the bandage is already off, the wound already exposed.

"I didn't mean to drop it on you right after you're back, but we just made the final decision this past weekend and I wanted you to be the first to know." Hannah pauses to pick at a cuticle on her left hand that's just starting to come loose, diverting her attention toward it.

"With the lease—our lease—expiring at the end of August, I wanted to give you as much time as possible to figure things out."

Something about that statement releases the blood flow back to Olivia's brain. "You're moving to LA in two months?!"

Hannah jerks her head up with a horrified expression. "No! No, no, it wouldn't be until after the wedding. I just didn't want to lock you, lock *us*, into another lease if this is where things are heading."

Olivia tries to nod slowly, but her head feels separate from the rest of her body.

She's losing her best friend.

Not until November.

But she's still losing her best friend.

Hannah continues, trying to offer every silver lining she possibly can to ease the tension between the two of them. "Don't worry, I already checked with the landlord and he's willing to go month-to-month after August to give us more time."

By us, she means Olivia, but that's okay. Because of course Hannah looked into it, followed all the tethers, looked into their options, crossed all the t's and dotted the i's for good measure. And despite the hurt roiling in her gut, Olivia has to appreciate that.

"Sorry, I think I'm still processing," she says quietly, her gaze distant. She's looking at the TV's black screen, but she isn't really seeing it. "You in LA, I never could've pictured it."

Hannah laughs, but it sounds strained. "I know, right? But I think I'm finally getting used to the heat and the traffic from all our visits." Hannah reaches out to tenderly grasp Olivia's hand. "You could come visit all the time, any time. And I'll be back here often, I'm sure. My mom won't let me go more than two months without seeing her."

Olivia forces a smile that even she can tell looks sad and meets Hannah's gaze. "Of course, we'll make it work. It'll take more than three thousand miles to split us up."

Her heart isn't in the words, but she says them anyway. For Hannah. For herself.

Hannah smiles weakly and there are little buds of tears pricking at the corners of her eyes. The sight of them sends a wave of deep, crushing black slamming down on Olivia's inner turmoil. It pushes down on her sadness, bowls over her fear of what will happen to their friendship, drowns the pain of loss she can't seem to escape lately, until it's all trapped in a recessed corner of her mind.

Most of all, it fills the void that's begun opening up inside her. She knows that feeling of relief, of something and someone else to focus on, is only temporary. But it's enough.

"Hey, it's going to be fine. We're going to be *fine*," Olivia says with a confidence she doesn't feel, stretching out a hand to brush a tear from Hannah's cheek. "We have five months before the move, and we'll make the most of every single second."

Hannah sniffs then nods, lifting a hand to wipe her other eye. "Right."

"Come on, let's go stuff our faces on junk food until we're ready to pass out. Then I think it's time for another *Gossip Girl* binge," Olivia says, pushing herself to her feet. It takes every ounce of will she has, but she does it. "I think we can rewatch it in full at least two more times before you move," she adds lightly, pulling Hannah to her feet by her hands.

Hannah chuckles, and the sound has a little more clarity to it this time. She allows herself to be pulled up and led to the kitchen, where the mound of food that could feed a small army is waiting.

·♥·♥·♥·♥·♥·

Later that night, Olivia blinks up at the dark ceiling above her, her neck cradled by the cool satin fabric of her favorite pillow case. She's been lying awake in bed for at least an hour now, her mind racing with thoughts she'd much rather ignore.

And she's tired. So, so tired. The kind of tired you feel in every part of your being. Not just the bones, but your hair, your skin, your fingernails, too. Like every molecule in your body screams for relief that's never coming.

Turns out, spending four and a half hours pretending your world isn't falling apart around you, that a bomb didn't just go off at the center of your universe, is exhausting.

Hannah is moving across the country.

Her best friend in the entire world is getting married in less than five months, then leaving Olivia behind in her rearview.

That isn't fair. To say it that way makes it sound cruel. It isn't. Hannah's making a life for herself, a *good* one. A life that people long for and rightfully deserve.

Everyone else, at least. She sniffs sardonically, then sighs, rolling over onto her side. She looks at her phone, sitting there flush against her nightstand. It's dark right now, though she knows the clock on its face reads just past midnight, because it's only been five minutes since she last checked it.

Does Peter know? she thinks to herself.

Had Ezra pulled him aside tonight, plied him with beers and burgers or whatever the hell guys bonded over, to break the news to him gently, too?

All she wants to do is text him. It physically pains her to resist. Her muscles ache at the restraint, the same feeling she gets squatting a personal record at the gym.

He'd texted her again, just once, after she'd ignored the tabby cat. It had been another image, this time a photo of the biggest cheeseburger she'd ever seen, piled high with all the fixings and sprawled decadently across a speckled blue plate.

Different this time though, there had been a message: "Not as good as The Sand Dune, but it'll do."

Though it had snuffed out the only ray of light she still carried within her to do it, she'd ignored that one, too.

He probably grabbed a late lunch after practicing all day for Olympus's pop-up show on Friday, Olivia had thought. She could picture him, perched on the edge of a sofa in his apartment—she'd never been to it, but in her mind it was decorated in vibrant swatches of color: a bright green couch, the color of honeydew; paintings hung from every wall so you couldn't see the off-white paint behind them anymore; a burgundy and cream tufted area rug at the heart of the living space.

He'd have Sally, his favorite red bass, cradled in his palms, running over the songs from their setlist over and over until the notes and chords came as easily to him as breathing. She'd been surprised by his work ethic back in LA. She'd thought he'd been joking when, once he found out about the surprise performance, he told her not to wait up, that he'd likely be locked in his dad's office for hours to rehearse.

She sighs at her dark phone, punches her pillow to adjust her position, and tries to brush off the fantasy curling through her head like sweet smoke. She can practically smell Peter's cologne flooding her nostrils as she rolls over for the fifteenth time in as many minutes.

"Get focused," she whispers to herself, lying flat on her back again.

She needs to get to sleep. Her interview for the promotion would likely be tomorrow; it had to be. Bruce had a partner meeting in the morning. She'd seen it on his calendar yesterday, so she knows he'll be in.

She needs to get her head back in the game.

Olivia slams her eyes shut, closing them off to memories of Peter sprawled beside her, to images of Hannah boarding a plane to leave her behind forever, and despite all the odds stacked against her, she finally sleeps.

Chapter 18

Text Message Drive-By

The sky is a strange shade of blue when Olivia emerges from the subway station to cross a packed 25th street toward her office. Still bright enough that she has to blink against it, but almost white. It's only late June, but the color of it—the way it's so thick it seems to hide the sun—reminds her of the first blows of winter.

She clutches her blazer a little tighter around her torso, hiking her work bag higher on her shoulder to sidestep a man in a three-piece shouting into his phone before he can mow her down.

When she makes it around him, she finds her gaze drifting upward once more to the puffy white clouds overhead, to where they give way to more ominous gray tufts hovering on the periphery of her vision. They seem to be slowly inching their way closer to the ground, like phantom hands reaching for her. Her stomach turns over.

Hannah had left earlier than usual this morning, rushing out the door just as Olivia exited the shower, yelling something about a meeting with a bakery before work. The apartment had felt eerily quiet the second she shut the door with a loud *bang!* followed by a muffled *Sorry!* from out in the hallway.

Olivia had spent hours and hours of time in this apartment alone before. Hell, Hannah had been on tour for six weeks straight just last summer, leaving her with the whole place to herself. And that's not even mentioning her friend's countless trips to visit Ezra on tour across the country.

Yet, today felt different.

Olivia had tried to roll it off her shoulders. She was probably just feeling a little too sentimental after the news Hannah had broken last night.

But that empty feeling follows her all the way to West 25th, the masses packed onto the New York City sidewalks only making her feel more alone.

She shakes her head—*quit being so damn melancholy, Liv*—and turns her attention to the view in front of her, just in time to round a corner to her building.

When she sits down at her desk at the back of Kaplan, Kaplan, and Westin, still nothing alluring waits in her inbox. That same drop in her stomach returns, like her body can sense something's coming and it isn't good.

You're being paranoid, Quinn. Get it together.

That's what Peter would tell her if he were here.

Olivia's mouth twists as she scans an email on her desktop screen for the fifth time with unseeing eyes.

You've got this, Quinn! Stop being so hard on yourself, he'd tell her, then light up her world with that ten-thousand-watt smile.

She breathes a sigh through her nose and refocuses on her work. Tries to, is more like it, but who's here to judge?

It takes another fifteen minutes for her to enter a groove. Another ten minutes after that for her to get caught up in the familiar pattern of reviewing pending litigation memos and declaration of asset sheets. And the pleadings—they aren't going to draft themselves, after all.

Nearly four hours pass before Bruce emerges from his meeting with the partners.

That's a record, she thinks to herself as she hears the conference room door squeak open—Madison really needs to follow up with maintenance on getting that repaired or Bruce is going to blow a gasket—followed by the muffled sound of voices entering the hallway catacorner to her office.

The last sound she picks up on is Bruce's office door slamming shut with a roar just down and across the hall. *Yikes.*

Olivia sits still and stiff-backed in her office chair for a few moments that seem to stretch into days. The only sound she can hear are the soft puffs of her exhales and the blood pumping in her ears.

Ding! The sound of a new email hitting her inbox breaks her trance, and she can't help but look at the bottom right corner of her screen to confirm it's only been about six minutes since Bruce closed himself in his office, not the three days it feels like.

Something in the back of her skull starts to pulse, slow and dull at first, but gradually growing faster until it's practically throbbing. Without looking, she knows this is it.

Of course he'd want to interview her right after a marathon partner meeting, when he'll be at his absolute worst. He probably waited until now on purpose. He'll try his hardest to trip her up, but they both know better. He can't, even at his moodiest.

She fights the urge to look smug, even though no one would be here to see it if she did, then moves her mouse cursor to pop open her email tab again.

Her eyes catch on the subject line of the new email before she can fully open it.

It's from Bruce, but it's not a meeting request like she'd thought. And yet, she wasn't totally wrong. This *is* it.

With shaking hands, she opens the email.

Subject: `Congratulations to Vanessa Meade, our new senior paralegal`

`Please join me in congratulating Vanessa on her promotion. In her new role, she will report dually to myself and Rick Kaplan, overseeing both our paralegal and legal assistant teams. An all-hands meeting with more details about the changes will be added to your calendars within the week.`

`Best,`

`Bruce Westin, Esq.`

She reads it over and over, willing the words on the screen to change with every passing line, every blink. They don't.

Vanessa got the job.

And Olivia didn't even get an interview.

Her mouth falls open, her lungs straining against the cavity of her chest to draw in air, like she's been underwater far too long and they're on the brink of collapse.

How could this be possible? Sure, Vanessa was the only other qualified candidate, if Olivia's completely honest with herself. But to not even get a chance at the job? To not get an interview after everything she's done for this firm?

Stunned is too light a word. If Hannah were here, she could flip through her extensive vocabulary like a Rolodex to find the right one.

But she'll be gone soon too, that little voice in Olivia's brain hisses. She closes her eyes. Bites down hard on the inside of her cheek.

She can feel the tears pricking at the very back of her eyes so she squeezes them shut, willing them away. She can't break down, not here. They can't know, can't see her crack.

Her phone vibrates against her desk with a new text from Madison: I'm so sorry.

Olivia's throat bobs, her bottom lip shaking with the strain of holding back the sobs that so desperately want to come.

It's not just about the job. It's *everything*.

It feels like her entire life has collapsed around her in the last three days. Three days! That's all it took for everything to implode into a million tiny pieces. Whoever or whatever is pulling on the threads of her life right now must have a sick sense of humor. Or maybe she's being punished for something she did in a past life?

Whatever the reason, they can knock it off now.

Three days. Though she's never really had to think about it before, Olivia always figured it would take more than that to break her. Unfortunately, she was wrong.

Bruce's office door remains closed for the rest of the day. She's pretty sure he doesn't even leave to use the restroom.

Hers stays closed as well, the lunch she brought long-forgotten in the communal refrigerator. She couldn't eat even if she wanted to.

The clock on her computer screen finally rolls over from 3:29 to 3:30, and her body shakes with the watery sigh she exhales. Her quitting time, technically, though she hasn't left the office before four since... ever.

Screw it, she thinks to herself as she gathers her things.

Screw him, she says to herself again as she walks silent as a cat through the office to the front door.

What little bravado she could muster fades as she trudges blindly toward the subway station, though. Those gray clouds from earlier have multiplied over the past few hours to blanket the sky. It looks like it should be seven at night, the sun no match for them any longer.

The air is thick and musty as she inhales it through her nose, and she knows what's coming just a second too late: that charcoal sky opens up on her and the rest of New York City, thick, cool droplets pelting her head, her face, and soaking her clothing.

Oh, perfect. What good is being devastated if you aren't also caught in a torrential downpour that soaks you to the bone?

She awkwardly runs the three blocks to the subway.

Drip, drip, drip. The sound is hollow in her ears as she stands with her hand braced against one of the vertical metal rails on the metro car. Water falls from the ends of her hair onto the cruddy floor beneath her feet.

Olivia can't imagine what she must look like, and honestly? She doesn't care. Mascara running down her cheeks—she hadn't had the foresight to use waterproof that morning—brown hair so damp it's nearly black where it's stuck to the sides of her face.

At least she doesn't have to hold back the tears anymore. No one could tell them apart from the rain anyhow.

The rain is still coming down, but at a slower clip, when she climbs the three flights of stairs to her apartment. It's empty, and she isn't surprised this time. Hannah won't be back for a few hours, if she'll even return tonight at all.

No, Olivia is not surprised to find it dark and empty, but she is surprised at the sharp, stabbing pain that shoots through the center of her chest when she sees it. Because it's yet another reminder of the losses she so recently suffered, those impossibly fresh wounds for which there is no bandage or tourniquet.

She drops her work bag at the closed door, takes three steps into the living room, then sinks to her knees as the tears begin anew.

Why? she asks the empty room, cradling her head in her hands. Her spine feels like it might split in two, racked so heavily by the sobs coursing through her.

I'm just as qualified as Vanessa, and I didn't even get a chance.

Is it because of Bruce? Was he in that meeting this morning blocking my chances? And why, because I slept with him and then...

Olivia lifts her head, her eyes widening in mute horror. Out loud she asks the darkness, "Is it because of Peter, because I went to LA with him? Because I got a 'boyfriend'?" Slowly, she shakes her head.

Bruce can't be jealous. It's impossible. The two of them meant absolutely nothing to one another, that had been the agreement from the start.

He's an asshole, but he wouldn't do this... would he?

That train of thought is broken by the sound of her phone buzzing in her bag behind her. She leaps for it, a piece of her unwilling to let go of hope. The hope that maybe the announcement was a mistake, or a cruel joke, or maybe they were lining up Olivia for something bigger and better so Vanessa could take that shitty senior paralegal job and shove it.

But it's none of those things, she soon realizes when she reads the incoming text. It's Peter.

`I guess my last few hints were too subtle so here's me being blunt: I want to hang out with you. Dinner at Casa Sabor tonight? I'm buying.`

Olivia swallows hard and clenches her jaw. Those malicious thoughts come coursing back like a rushing river with a broken dam.

Peter. Her fake relationship.

God, she'd been so stupid. She'd hatched this scheme to give her a chance at the promotion and it was likely the very thing that damned her.

Something ugly cracks open inside of her.

She wasn't getting Peter's hints? No, he wasn't getting *hers*.

An instant later Olivia fires back: `I think it's for the best if we cool it for a while.`

Impossibly fast, a typing bubble appears on the other end, followed by: `Cool it? What are you talking about, Quinn?`

That striking ache, the sadness like a chasm inside of her, seems to roll over all at once into something else. Something stronger. Her hands shake, this time with anger, as she writes: `This charade had to end at some point. Better we make a clean break now than draw it out.`

`I don't understand, what's wrong? This`
`doesn't sound like you. Can we please just`
`talk about this, like in person?`

He tries again when she doesn't answer: `Just come to`
`Casa Sabor tonight so we can talk. Even a`
`"charade" relationship shouldn't end over`
`text.`

Her heart thrums, and the corner of her mouth wants to lift at his attempt at humor. But that part of her is too far buried behind the hurt and the betrayal and the rage at the unfairness of it all.

Her entire life, her one fear had been ending up alone.

She'd never compromised herself, never pretended to be something she wasn't—not exactly, at least. But something deep within the well of her being had always taunted her, "You don't deserve these people. Someday they'll realize that."

So she'd become a fierce friend, the type that would drop everything and drive two hours to another state to pick you up when your heart had been broken. She'd become a dedicated employee, the kind that came in early and stayed late and took on more cases than she could possibly handle. Maybe she hadn't been the most dutiful daughter over the years, but her free spirit parents probably would've rejected that anyhow.

Olivia had a knack for figuring out what everyone else needed from her and delivering it on a silver platter.

Imagine her surprise when she'd thrown herself into every relationship with every guy that came along, only to find it was never good enough. It didn't matter, though. She ate up even the smallest crumbs of affection when they came her way, enough to sustain her for weeks, even months.

When she talked about it with Hannah, she blamed *them*. They didn't have their priorities straight, they weren't ready for commitment, they were potential sociopaths. And sure, much of that had been true. The modern dating dance is toxic at best, downright diabolical at worst.

But that little voice hissing at the back of her head had whispered something else: that she deserved what she got. Nothing at all. And soon, everyone else would abandon her too.

Well, her time is finally up.

She sends one last message, then tosses her phone across the room: `See you around, Peter.`

Peter, on the other hand, isn't content to give up. He sends probably a dozen more messages after that, most of them saying different iterations of the same thing.

At 5:22: `Olivia, come on. Just talk to me.`

At 6:03: `I'll be at Casa Sabor at seven. Please meet me.`

At 7:11: `I'll wait all night if that's what it takes.`

At 7:57: `Quinn...`

She puts her phone into focus mode at eight and crawls into bed.

Chapter 19

Is This What Broken Feels Like?

On Wednesday, Olivia takes a sick day.

It's the first one she's taken all year, so there is no polite request in her email. No ask. Just notice.

Prepare the others because I won't be there.

Then she shuts her firm-issued laptop and crawls back into bed.

Hannah would be gone all day at work, possibly the entire night as well. She hadn't come home from Ezra's the night before.

Home.

Is this still Hannah's home? Is it Olivia's?

Rolling over in bed, her cool cotton sheets slide smoothly against the bare patches of skin sticking out from her sweats. She reaches for her phone on the bedside table, then hesitates, pale pink fingertips hovering in the air, like a toddler caught sticking their hand in the cookie jar.

She knows what likely waits for her there.

She had been a coward last night. She knew that.

But she'd also been angry. *So* angry. And that had fueled her resolve, made it easier—barely, but enough—to ignore Peter's texts. Then the missed calls that followed.

That anger had burned out overnight, though, tossed aside as she stretched and strained and struggled through a fitful night's sleep.

All that remains now is the ache.

And the fear. The fear that had lingered within her for as long as she could remember.

What do I do next? Where do I go from here?

Not only had she failed, she'd failed publicly. Everyone at Kaplan, Kaplan, and Westin knew she wanted that job. Hell, they probably even knew she'd been cocky enough to think herself a shoo-in. Until very recently, she had expected it to fall right into her lap.

Could she face them again?

What choice does she have?

Today, she'll be a coward again. Just for a little bit longer, she decides, she can hide from her problems. Stay in the safety net of her little shoebox bedroom in Brooklyn for what could be one of the last times.

Olivia sighs so deeply it feels like her chest may cave in when the last puff of air leaves her lungs.

Add apartment hunting to the to-do list, she thinks to herself, and she can hear the sarcasm masking the defeat even in her own mind. Defense mechanism, works every time.

She finally gives up her resolve and reaches for her phone. She hadn't had the guts to turn it off completely the night before—what if Hannah had needed her?—but she had muted her notifications from everyone else, including Peter.

Especially Peter.

Now, she scrolls right past them without looking, though the bright red number blaring like a stop sign at the top right corner of her messages icon doesn't escape her notice.

Twenty-two.

Olivia swallows and it feels like sandpaper, but she doesn't have the energy or the will to get up and refill her water bottle. Instead, she swipes to the Spotify app and pulls up Taylor Swift's *Folklore* album, her go-to when she needs a little time to wallow in self-pity. She presses shuffle, then the replay all button, then play.

She stays there for the rest of the day. No one disturbs her.

Chapter 20

Snapped My Delusion

Olivia blinks at her haggard reflection in the wide, frameless bathroom mirror. It's dim overhead. The fluorescent bulb that normally lights this sink has been burned out for over two weeks, since well before she left for Los Angeles.

The lack of light isn't enough to hide the bags under her eyes. If anything, they look more stark in the shadows cast on her paler-than-usual skin. That California tan faded quickly.

Hiding in your bedroom for over twenty-four hours will do that to you.

She studies her mirror image a little longer and notices a messy line of white powder near her scalp—dry shampoo she hadn't fully lathered in before rushing out of the apartment that morning. It's unlike her to show up to work so unkempt, but desperate times and all that. Nothing about the past few days had been normal.

She'd been running late because she had almost called out of work again, then decided against it. If this is to be her life now, taking case assignments from freaking Vanessa Meade, then it's time to get on with the show. She can't lose the job she has, not if she wants to rent a place without roommates.

Olivia heaves a sigh, her breath fogging up the mirror, and slashes her fingers through her roots to clear up the residue gathered there. Next, she swipes her fingertip along the outer edge of her right eye, sloughing off a dark dab of mascara that had dried on her skin. Then she adjusts the place where her pale blue blouse tucks into her gray, cropped knit pants, smoothing down both articles of clothing until their wrinkles are nearly invisible.

With her teeth clenched and her jaw leveled high, she makes her way out of the ladies' room at Kaplan, Kaplan, and Westin and pads as quietly as she can down the hallway to her office. She reaches it just in time to see Bruce sneaking into his own across the hall, closing the door with a whispered *click* behind him.

Is he avoiding me? she thinks. Then adds, *Good. He should be.*

Olivia takes a seat at her desk and navigates to today's project: pulling together and redacting hundreds of pages of bank, investment, retirement, and credit card statements to send out to opposing counsel for discovery in a particularly nasty divorce. In moments, she's knee-deep in the monotony of her work, all other sights and sounds and—thank god—thoughts blocked out except for the soft coffee shop beats playing from her Spotify playlist.

Her deep focus is interrupted by an incoming call on her office line. She furrows her brows at the black box ringing at her and the unfamiliar number on its display.

It's pretty rare that she gets calls here from outside numbers unless they're transferred from the front desk first.

Curious, she reaches for it and yanks back the phone just before the last ring screams through her quiet, closed office.

"Hello?" Her voice cracks on the second syllable from lack of use.

"Finally!" a female voice cheers on the other end, something about the word dripping with sarcasm. "For a second I was starting to think this wasn't worth the hassle."

Olivia twists her mouth, her eyebrows knitting together further. The voice sounds oddly familiar, but she can't quite place it. "I'm sorry?"

The woman laughs, the sound more like a puff of air through the phone. "Right. It's Jennifer Campbell, Peter's sister."

Olivia's mouth pops open in a soundless *Oh*. Her heart rate quickens until she feels like she's running. She's almost certain if she looked in a mirror right now she'd see it pulsing in her throat. "Jennifer, I... what can I... to what do I owe the pleasure?"

Jennifer chuckles and says, "I see I've caught you off guard, which means my *wonderful* baby brother not only refused to give me your cell number, he also didn't fill you in on my master plan."

"Master plan?" Olivia hedges. Her gaze traces circles around her office, seeking out an escape plan. If only it were that simple.

"Straight to business then. I like your style," Jennifer responds, clearly mistaking Olivia's shock and confusion for frankness. "I mentioned to you over the weekend that my firm is opening up a New York office in a few months and I'd be the lucky partner transferring out there to oversee things. It's a new market for the firm and a new-ish market for me, so I'm looking for all the help I can get. I want you on as our paralegal manager."

Olivia's mouth has gone completely dry by the time Jennifer finishes. She's surprised she even heard the woman on the other end of the phone over the sound of high-pitched ringing in her ears.

Jennifer wants to hire me?

"Why?" Olivia asks out loud, then kicks herself under her desk for it.

Jennifer's smile is apparent in her voice as she says, "Well, you put Eric in his place, for starters. I've been waiting to see someone else tell him to shut up for years." Olivia winces inwardly at the memory of her outburst after the family dinner last weekend. "Peter likes you, and everyone can say what they want about him—myself included—but he's an excellent judge of character." She laughs to herself. "But most importantly, I like you. What else is there?"

Olivia bites back the smile threatening to spread across her lips, choosing to unpack the Peter comment at a later date. "My resume, for starters," she says, adopting Jennifer's tone.

Jennifer breathes a sound that's something between a laugh and a scoff. "Didn't you know? LinkedIn has all that stuff now. Everything I couldn't learn there, I got from your boss. Once I could pin down the guy, that is."

Olivia's blood runs cold. Her boss? "I'm sorry, who did you say you spoke to?"

"I didn't. But it was Bruce Westin. Hard guy to get on the phone, but he had a lot to say about you. Helped make my decision easy."

Olivia blinks at her computer screen, which has already gone to sleep from inactivity. She can just make out her distorted reflection in the black void staring back at her. "Bruce," is all she manages to say.

"Yep," Jennifer says, popping the last letter of the word between her lips. "Bit of an ass, just like his reputation claims, but he had nothing but great things to say about you. If I hadn't already been sure by my own assumptions, he really sold it for me."

Running her teeth over her bottom lip, Olivia tries to make Jennifer's words make sense. Bruce, her asshole boss who didn't even consider her for the promotion here, talked her up to another firm?

Was it some sort of power move, trying to push her out of Kaplan, Kaplan, and Westin? Dump her onto someone else's plate like used goods?

"I'm sure you're wondering about the offer itself and next steps," Jennifer cuts in, disrupting Olivia's downward spiral. "We did our research, and I trust it'll be competitive for the market. I can send it over via email as soon as we hang up. You'd need to have a video call with the other partners before we both sign, but it's mostly a formality. What's your email address?"

Olivia is only half listening, but she manages to rattle off her email so Jennifer can jot it down, the scratch of her pen against paper audible over the phone.

It doesn't add up. It feels too good to be true, like any second Jennifer's going to yell "Gotcha!" and pull the rug out from underneath her.

Par for the course, after the week she's had.

Yet less than two minutes after they hang up, an offer pings its way into her inbox, as promised. She skims only the two-word subject line: Paralegal Manager. A reminder that not only might this email contain a life-changing pay raise, it also means an expanded role with more responsibility.

That thought is what has her standing up from her desk and slowly opening the door to her office. Her steps are stiff, like a statue brought to life, as she moves into the hallway to stop just outside of Bruce's door.

It's still shut and for the umpteenth time this year, she's grateful it's solid oak and not frosted glass as she hovers there, trying to work up the courage to knock.

Bruce wouldn't even give her an interview here but recommended her to another firm?

Why? She has to know, has to understand.

She finally raps her knuckles against the heavy wood, the sound echoing in the hall around her like gunshots.

"Come in!" Bruce's voice bellows from somewhere inside.

Olivia licks her lips and swallows. She smooths the front of her blouse down and ruffles her hair a bit to add some life back into her unwashed locks. Then she reaches for the knob and turns.

Bruce is seated in his wing-backed office chair, the side of his face resting tightly in a cradle created by his thumb and first two fingers. He acknowledges her presence with only a lift of his icy blue eyes and a quirked blond brow before his attention settles back on the sheaf of papers in his right hand.

He probably thinks she doesn't notice the upward twitch at the corner of his lips just before it's gone, but she does. She ignores it as she steps into the room and silently closes the door behind her. She presses her back against the door for a moment, her hands smushed between the fabric of her blouse and the cool wood behind her, trying to figure out what to say.

One of the reasons she chose this profession is the logic to it. You get a puzzle and you solve it using the confines of case law.

Everything follows a pattern, a rhythm, one that she's grown familiar with over the years.

There's a clear cause and effect. An action and a reaction.

You get a new case, you need to meet with the attorney to discuss next steps.

Your client files for divorce, you start reviewing the assets in the marital estate.

It just makes sense. Always.

The clients don't, and the attorneys really don't, because rarely do people ever make true sense. But the job *does*.

Yet none of today's events make sense, and it's driving Olivia insane.

"Did you come in here to stand around awkwardly, or is there a more rational motivation behind this visit?" Bruce drawls without looking at her.

It snaps something to life inside her she hasn't felt in days. "If it were the former, would you kick me out?"

Bruce sniffs and finally sets down his papers, leaning back in his chair to face her fully. "I wouldn't have become a litigator if I didn't appreciate an audience." He waves his hand through the air between them: an invitation to sit.

Olivia tries to hide her amusement as she crosses the room, her heels leaving little divots in the plush carpet with each step. She takes one of the low-backed, brown leather chairs lining one side of his desk and, for the first time, meets her boss's stare. Her current boss.

Bruce sits up a little straighter, resting one of his suit-clad elbows against his desk to scratch the bottom of his chin with his index finger. It's the closest thing the man has to a twitch, a nervous tell.

Olivia's familiar with it. It gives her the courage to plow forward; he must know what this is about.

"I just got off the phone with Jennifer Campbell."

"Ah, so this is your resignation then."

Olivia stiffens, eyes widening. "No, I haven't made a decision yet." She looks toward Bruce's office window, her mouth pinching. "I haven't even read the offer letter."

Bruce chuckles and drops his hand to shake his head. She is pretty sure she catches him mouth the word *typical* under his breath. Louder, he says, "So you're here to..."

"To understand why," she finishes for him, her jaw setting on the last word.

He lifts his brows and his mouth barely seems to move when he says, "While I am a man of many talents, unfortunately mindreading is not one of them. I'm going to need you to be more specific."

Olivia can't help but roll her eyes and she knows he sees it, but she's beyond caring at this point. "Why recommend me to Jennifer? Why praise me for a role at her firm while simultaneously not considering me for a promotion here?"

A slow, close-lipped smile spreads across Bruce's lips, and somehow it makes him look more like a shark than ever. Yet his voice drips with honey as he says, "Oh, I had every intention of considering you for the senior paralegal job here. Was I going to draw it out a bit, make you sweat during the interview process? Sure. I wouldn't be me otherwise." He leans forward until his torso meets walnut, bracing each of his hands against the top of his desk. "But make no mistake Olivia, you were going to get an interview."

Something about his posture and the force of his stare set squarely on her sends a chill up her spine. She swallows deeply and reminds herself why she's here, that she should have the upper hand in this discussion. She's the one with a job offer at another firm, after all.

"So what then? What happened? Why did Vanessa Meade get the job and I get the shaft?"

A burst of laughter escapes his lips, the force of it making his shoulders shake. When he finally calms down, he swipes a finger along the corner of his eye.

It makes Olivia grind her teeth, her fist involuntarily balling in her lap. "Not sure I get the joke."

Bruce shakes his head with a sigh, though he's still smiling. Amused. "No, I suppose not, considering you barged in here before reading the offer letter or job description." He shoots her a pointed look that she's all too familiar with. It has her straightening in her chair, like a student who just got scolded by the teacher.

"To answer your question, *what happened* was a better offer came across my desk. A better offer from Jennifer. For you."

She twists her head back and forth in slow motion. His words seem to have no meaning, like he's made them up. Some secret language she was never taught.

Taking in the look of pure disbelief on her face, Bruce's face softens for what might possibly be the first time in his entire life. It's a fraction, the change subtle, but it's there.

He tries to cover it by pinching the bridge of his nose between his thumb and forefinger. "Look. I know who I am and what other people think of me. I am probably the villain in what I'm sure is an exorbitant amount of people's stories." Bruce drops his hand and heaves a sigh, then locks his gaze on Olivia's. "But I'm not the villain in your story. At least... I don't want to be."

Her mouth opens like she wants to speak, but she can't even form a coherent thought, let alone give it a voice. Her throat feels as dry as a desert, like Bruce's words sucked all the moisture out of her.

Seeing her so caught off guard must remind Bruce of who he is, because his smirk returns. He reaches a hand out to mindlessly push the papers around on his desk as he says, "When Jennifer called to ask about you and told me what she was planning, I couldn't say no. And only partly because that woman is persistent as hell." His smile widens after his last sentence, and Olivia can't help but wonder how that phone call went down. How much wine—Jennifer's—and whiskey—his—were consumed afterward.

"So you're saying I should take the job?" she whispers, unable to repress the slow spread of a smile across her lips.

Bruce snorts at that and raps his knuckles on his desk twice. "You're bright, but you're young. You have a lot to learn and even more to do. You can't do that stuck at one firm for the rest of your life. Campbell, Saxton, and Woods has offices across the country, literally. In addition to family law, they have departments dedicated to construction, estate planning, criminal litigation, just about everything under the sun." He ticks a finger off with a practiced flick for each area of specialization he names. "That means new experiences, new connections, new chances for someone willing to take them."

He cocks a brow at her, blue eyes sparkling in the light of the sun streaming through the window. "So yeah, although it pains me to say it out loud and sacrifice my own best interest, I think you should take the job."

Chapter 21

Clouded Memories and Tired Eyes

Olivia shuffles her feet over the threshold of her apartment, not quite feeling them connect with the floor. She had floated home. Not on a cloud, not on sunshine. More like one of those moving platforms at the airport. Everything around her seemed to move at a slower pace, a silent, droning rhythm replacing the normal chaos of bustling streets, angry car horns, and shouted greetings of New York.

Bruce hadn't been kidding about Jennifer's offer. Olivia's eyes had practically popped out of her skull the moment she opened it, his taunting chuckle echoing in her ears.

She wasn't quite sure how he'd known. Had Jennifer told him outright, just to shove it in his face—she could totally picture her doing that—or was it to plead her case, solicit the information she wanted from between his tight, unwilling lips?

Either way, the job pays almost twenty percent more than she currently makes, and that isn't something to bat an eye at.

She drops her work bag to the hardwood floor of her apartment with a thud and glances around. It's already well-lit, lights turned on in nearly every room, telling her Hannah beat her home for once. She rolls her lips into her mouth, studying, thinking.

The bump in pay wouldn't be enough for her to keep the two-bedroom on her own, but she could likely afford a similar studio, or possibly even a one-bedroom, in the same neighborhood.

Relief washes over her like a gentle summer rain, from the top of her head to the soles of her feet, still aching in her heels. Like maybe, just maybe, things could be okay again. It's a sensation she hasn't felt in what seems far too long.

"Hey! What are you doing, standing in the open doorway like a weirdo?" Hannah's bright voice calls from the far side of the living room where she's just appeared, jerking Olivia back to reality.

"Sorry, lost in thought," she replies gruffly, shutting the door behind her.

Hannah leans one shoulder against the doorframe separating their living room and the hallway to their bedrooms and folds her arms over her chest. Her mouth is twisted to one side, her eyes narrowed. "Something's happened." It isn't a question.

Olivia tilts her head and lets her gaze fall to the side, considering the statement. "Something" would be putting it mildly. It's almost laughable. Has it really only been one week since her life totally upended, then—by some twist of fate—started to right itself again?

She makes a quiet humming sound and looks back at her best friend, a light blinking back to life inside her. "We should probably talk."

The two of them sat on their small, blue-gray suede sofa, legs tucked beneath them criss-cross-applesauce style, for over an hour while Olivia recounted everything.

She told Hannah about her trip to LA with Peter. About the way she'd fallen in love with his parents, about their trip to the observatory sat high on a California hill overlooking the city, about her (*extremely on-brand*, chided Hannah) outburst at dinner with his family.

Olivia had cringed more than once during that part of the story.

When she got to Saturday night, her throat had all but closed up, so strong had been her desire to hide that earth-shattering night with Peter. To keep it all to herself. But she forced herself to plow through.

Hannah's mouth had gaped open so wide Olivia thought her jaw had unhinged, but she'd held her tongue, allowing her friend to continue.

Olivia told her about the next morning, the words Mrs. Campbell had whispered to her just before they'd departed. How they'd struck her like summer lightning, told her what she needed to do.

Hannah's frown deepened with every word, that tiny voice in her head urging her, *Interrupt! Shout! Wallop Olivia over the head* so loudly Olivia could almost hear it.

Still, Hannah held her tongue.

Olivia moved on, telling her about not getting the promotion at work, not even getting interviewed.

Tears pricked the backs of her eyes to say it out loud, then fell down her cheeks in slow-moving rivers, as she confided in her best friend how it had broken her further than she thought possible. To feel like everything was collapsing in a line of dominoes: first her fake breakup with Peter, then Hannah's moving announcement, then losing the promotion she had so desperately wanted.

Hannah had reached out, taking both of Olivia's hands and squeezing them firmly. Reassurance and a plea to keep going.

Finally, she told her about today. Jennifer's out-of-the-blue call, her insane offer, Bruce's sneaky way of helping her—because god forbid the guy clues her in before she has a mental breakdown.

By the end of it, the two of them were laughing through tears, Hannah's arms wrapped snugly around Olivia's shaking torso as she cooed, "I can't believe my best friend went through all that and I had no idea."

Now, Olivia makes a sound halfway between a cough and a hiccup, reaching a hand up to wipe away the tears falling down her cheeks.

Hannah pulls back until her hands grasp Olivia's shoulders and she can meet her best friend's gaze. "I'm serious! I've been a shitty friend. The worst. I should've known all of this, I should've been there!"

Olivia smiles wetly and shakes her head, reaching up to pat one of Hannah's hands with her own. "I wasn't ready to talk about it. For anyone to be there for me. I needed to do some processing on my own. It's not your fault."

"Still, I wish I hadn't added to the pile with all my talk of moving across the country."

"I wouldn't have wanted you to hide that from me, though. I needed to know, and I'm glad you told me." That is the honest truth. Putting it off would have only made things worse, for both of them. She could tell the guilt had been eating Hannah up. Guilt she shouldn't even feel, because in spite of how much Olivia would miss her, she's also happy for her too. No one should have to regret doing what's best for them.

Hannah's frown eases and although Olivia can tell her best friend is still beating herself up internally, she sees her coming around. "Are you going to take the job?"

Olivia shrugs and blows out a deep breath. Speaking of doing what's best for oneself. "I think so?" She pauses to chew on the inside of her cheek then continues, "I still need to meet with some of the other partners, but Jennifer says it's a formality. It seems like a smart move to take it. The right move."

Hannah nods emphatically. "I think you should do it. It'll open up new doors for you, let you try new things."

"You sound like Bruce."

Hannah snickers. "Hey, give the man his win." She lightly shakes her friend's shoulders, then releases them. "He did good."

Olivia laughs, the sound more air than anything, and nods. "Fine, fine. He did the right thing, *for once.*"

Hannah cocks an eyebrow, her grin going crooked. Oh no, Olivia's seen that look before. "So... that just leaves you and Peter to resolve then."

This makes Olivia freeze. When she finally speaks, her voice is hoarse. "What do you mean, *resolve*?"

Hannah kicks out one of her legs to nudge Olivia's knee with her big toe. "Come on, Liv. You gave me the barest of details and I could still tell there's something there. Possibly a really big something." She pauses, likely for dramatic effect. "You have feelings for him. Real feelings."

"So?" Olivia shoots back, sticking her chin out, a toddler fighting not to finish her broccoli.

Hannah only shakes her head. "*So*, from what little you told me, it sounds like he has feelings for you too." Olivia pops open her mouth to protest, but Hannah holds up a hand. "You should at least talk to him about it, tell him the truth."

Olivia's voice is small when she says, "He could have anyone he wants. I'm sure he'll find someone far better than me. Someone who listens to the same music, someone who likes classic cars, probably some cool chick who has tattoos and plays bass guitar."

Hannah wrinkles her nose. "You think Peter wants to date... himself?"

Olivia tries and fails to stifle a barking laugh and quips, "Peter doesn't have tattoos."

Hannah grimaces. "I'm going to pretend I don't know how you know that."

Olivia merely shrugs, looking a little pleased with herself.

Hannah furrows her brows thoughtfully. "Where is this all coming from, this... insecurity? I've seen you work a room before and turn down every eager gaze in it without a second thought." She leans over to poke Olivia's rib. "What gives?"

Wiggling away from Hannah's finger, Olivia sighs and looks down at her lap to pick at a speck of lint on her pants. "I don't know. It just seems different with Peter. Bigger. More important."

Hannah draws back, her nostrils flaring like a beagle on the scent of something. "Olivia Marie Quinn are you... do you love him?"

Olivia looses a mournful wail, flinging her arms out to her sides. Her head tilts back until she's gazing at the ceiling. "No!" She hesitates. "Maybe? Gah, I don't know! He just... he got under my skin. I can't get him out of my head. When something happens during my day, I want to tell him about it. When I see a cat in an apartment window, I want to snap a photo and send it to him. When I fall asleep at night, I want him to be there. Just... be there. For all of it." She frowns and looks back down at her lap.

Hannah gingerly reaches a hand out, resting it on Olivia's knee. "You have to tell him."

After chewing on the inside of her cheek for a long, thoughtful moment, Olivia says quietly, "What if he doesn't feel that way? Or what if he did, and then decided I wasn't worth the headache after I pushed him away? What if we try and fail and then it becomes so awkward between us that I'm never allowed around the band, meaning I never get to see you again?"

Hannah blinks slowly and cocks her head to the side. "Slow down there, Miss Doomsday. First of all, no one would ever come between the two of us. Ever." She reaches out to lift Olivia's chin gently with her thumb and index finger. "Second of all, who was it that told me not so long ago that being afraid of the future, of what might happen, wasn't a good enough excuse to stop living for it?"

Olivia groans under her breath and wrinkles her nose, remembering vividly the day she offered Hannah that advice, when their roles were reversed and it was Hannah who wasn't sure about a relationship with her then-client and now-fiancé Ezra. "Sounds like an idiot told you that."

"*No*," Hannah emphasizes, squeezing her best friend's chin before letting it go. "It was a very wise, very amazing, and very beautiful friend. And she was right. If I hadn't listened to her, I wouldn't be marrying my second-best friend in the entire world in a few short months. And now it's my turn to offer you the same sage wisdom: take the leap. You may fall, and if you do I will be right there to catch you, just like you've been there for me. But you may also fly, and that alone is worth the risk.

"Besides, I can one-hundred percent guarantee you won't fall. Or fail. Because there is no one better out there for him than you. You two have been dancing around each other since I first introduced you in Chicago last year. It's giving major meant-to-be vibes."

A few quiet moments slip by while Olivia considers it.

Hannah has a point. If her feelings truly run this deep, she owes it to herself and to Peter to tell him the truth, consequences be damned.

Maybe she should listen to what Hannah, what the universe, is telling her. Maybe that someone or something tugging on the invisible strings of her life has a plan for her after all. A small thread weaving her and Peter together when they both needed it most.

At first, as partners in crime. Co-conspirators setting up their friends last summer.

Then, a big bulging shoulder Olivia could hang on to in rough waters. And a hot-headed pretend girlfriend to stick up for Peter no matter the circumstances or cost.

Whatever it is, whoever's behind it, she can't ignore the pull any longer. It's time to follow the thread.

And even if Hannah is wrong and Peter doesn't see Olivia that way, would that really be the end of everything? Surely their friendship could recover from it... eventually.

But maybe, just maybe, she'd be right. Hannah has an uncanny way of doing that.

Finally, a calculated, mischievous smile spreads across her lips. "Okay, Miss Know-It-All. The last time he talked to me, I not only blew off his dinner plans, but also told him, in no uncertain terms,

I didn't want to talk to him. In other words, I blew it, and I haven't heard from him since. How does one come back from that?"

Hannah's blue eyes darken and her lips turn up in a smirk. "I may have an idea."

Chapter 22

Feels Like I've Stood Here Once Before

The muffled sound of guitar chords reaches Olivia's ears from behind a set of twenty-foot-high, black double doors. She strains to pick out the song title, unconsciously leaning her right ear closer to the closed ballroom.

"'Galaxy,'" Hannah breathes, her lips twitching upward. She turns her head to face Olivia and adds, "I told Ez to open with that one."

Olivia wants to make a sarcastic comment, but can't hide her smile. Her best friend is hopelessly in love, and it's clear Ezra feels the same way back. It's adorable.

A few people still linger at the wide mahogany bar just inside the entrance to Amity Music Hall, their bodies creating eerie shadows where they cut into the glow of the bar's rainbow underlighting. Olivia eyes the bar for a long moment, debating if she should stop for a pint of her own liquid courage.

Hannah reads her thoughts and tugs her best friend's arm in the opposite direction. "If you want to make an entrance, now's the time."

Olivia looks down at herself, first at her bright magenta wrap dress with its deep V neckline that hugs her in all the right places. Then at the stack of white poster boards tucked against her left side, the writing scrawled on the front of it obscured by her body. Next, she scans over to her right hand, and the inflatable—

"Come on! It's now or never," Hannah interrupts her, pressing her palm against the small of Olivia's back to force her toward the thick double doors hiding the pop-up concert going on in the next room from view.

After swallowing down the fear building inside her, Olivia nods with steel in her eyes.

A security agent dressed in all black holds open the doors for the two girls to sneak through. Instantly, the sound of screaming guitars and pulsing drum beats meets them like a cresting tsunami.

The room is bigger than Olivia had expected, with old-school vaulted ceilings at least thirty-feet high. She looks up from the back of the gathered crowd to see a small mezzanine reaching into the room's rafters. It's closed for tonight's more intimate show, seats empty and overhead lights off.

Olivia turns her attention back to the crowd, watching them sway back and forth to the music. It's a private show, super fans only, so there's only about two hundred people sharing the space when it's built to handle at least twice that. With everyone pressed toward the stage, there's still plenty of room in the back and on the sides of the ballroom, and it wouldn't take much to clear a path to the front... if one wanted it badly enough.

Did she?

The stage feels a mile away from where Olivia hovers in the shadows by the door. Her palms are starting to slicken with sweat, the oversized notecards threatening to slide from her grip, and she can't force her feet to move.

Hannah looks over at her, her rosebud lips twisting in a frown. She leans over to squeeze Olivia's shoulder and whisper-shout in her ear, "You've got this."

Olivia blinks and sucks in a deep breath, then musters all the strength she has to lift her right foot. Then her left. Over and over until she's cutting a line through the roaring crowd, shoulders and bent elbows first.

She lifts the inflatable boombox she'd bought at a party supply store on the way over to her shoulder and flips the stack of poster board over in her hands so her block-letter writing faces out. Olivia isn't sure if it's because of the oversized stuff in her hands or because they can sense the determination in her set jawline, but the crowd seems to part for her.

Hannah is a brick wall at her back as she reaches an empty space about eight feet from the stage. Caging her in, probably, so she can't make a run for it.

Olivia cranes her neck to look up at the band on stage for the first time since she arrived, and her stomach flips.

The music in her ears sounds muffled again, time slowing down around her when she finally meets two solid-cut emeralds. They home in on her like a magnet.

Suddenly, it's like she's back in Chicago last summer, a still-too-hot August breeze at her back and a nearly empty amphitheater in front of her. Instead of playing for a crowd, Olympus is running a sound check for a show later that night. Olivia can feel the humidity in the air as if the vision were real, the combination of the late-summer heat and the expansive Lake Michigan right behind the venue frizzing up her hair.

In this vision, only Olivia and Hannah are there to watch, joined by a small assortment of sound engineers too entranced with their work to notice the two women walking down the cement aisle.

Olivia's gaze locks on Peter, and suddenly his hair is three inches shorter and his skin is slightly golden and a little sunburnt in places from weeks of outdoor shows. It only makes his teeth look whiter when he smiles, so wide it pulls and strains at his cheeks. His head is tipped back in a laugh, probably from something Ezra just said.

Her heart thrums and then stills in her chest now, just like it did then. She should've known in that moment she was a goner. Should've recognized that shockwave that buzzed through her body for what it was.

In front of her, the real Peter's mouth falls open, and if Olivia knew more about music, she'd be almost certain he misses at least three notes of the song before remembering who he is and what he's supposed to be doing.

She smiles to herself, her eyes sparkling under the floating spotlights, a flush creeping up the back of her neck. Then she feels another nudge from behind and tries not to scowl.

Hiking the blow-up boombox higher on her right shoulder, she carefully balances the gigantic notecards in her left hand, holding them up in front of her torso at an angle she hopes is steep enough for Peter to see from the stage.

The weight of dozens of eyes are on her, the band in front and the crowd behind, but only one pair matters. She sees a small lift to Peter's lips and knows he's read the first notecard.

I'M SORRY.

Olivia slides it to the back of the pile and angles up the second.

YOU SAID ONE DAY I'D GET MY BIG ROMANTIC GESTURE.

She drops that one to the back and moves to the next.

BUT I MUCH PREFER GIVING THEM.

Peter's lips twitch, like he wants to laugh at the inside joke. Just like she'd hoped they would.

Her heart picks up speed until it feels like she's running at a full sprint. Her hands are shaking so badly she nearly drops the stack of poster boards, catching it at the last possible moment. She moves to the second-to-last card.

THERE'S NO ONE I'D RATHER SING TO AT KARAOKE. OR SERENADE WITH A BOOMBOX AT DAWN.

When he finishes reading this card, Peter grins and shakes his head, glancing pointedly moving to the inflatable on her shoulder and then back. She is pretty sure he's all but stopped playing his bass, but Olympus carries on around him without a word.

This is it.

It takes every ounce of will she has to pull breath into her lungs, anticipating the last card. Even from eight feet away, she can feel the tension vibrating in waves off of Peter while he waits. He skims the penultimate card in her hands once, then twice more. Waiting for what comes next. She almost can't bring herself to show him.

There's a poke to the back of her ribcage, a little push of encouragement from a friend to make the final plunge.

Just get on with it already.

Olivia has never been so scared to leap in her entire life, and that's saying something considering her parents pressed her to bungee jump with them in the Redwoods of California when she had been just fourteen.

She forces herself not to pull her gaze from Peter when she finally flips to the last card in her hands. She watches his black eyebrows shoot up high on his forehead, his mouth opening wider than she thought possible. His throat bobs.

A line of sweat drips from his forehead as he takes in the five words, all capital letters, spelled out for him and the world to see. And her breath truly does stop then, held within her lungs as she waits for a reaction, any reaction.

She only lets go of that breath when she sees the corner of his mouth turn up, followed slowly by the other one, until he's beaming down at her with Olivia's favorite toothy grin.

Heat creeps up the back of her neck and into her cheeks, blooming across her face like the sun kissing her with the first rays of true spring after a brutal winter. She looks down at her words, scrawled haphazardly in black ink on flimsy white cardstock. The most important message she's ever written, and there would be no taking it back now.

PETER CAMPBELL, I LOVE YOU.

Chapter 23

I Keep Falling Again and Again

"You're sure this is where they'll be?" Olivia paces the width of the small, bright room hidden within the bowels of the music hall. Its cheerful overhead lighting and pronounced silence mark a stark contrast to the pulsing darkness of the ballroom she'd left fifteen minutes ago.

It only adds to her nerves.

When she turns at the far side of the room and begins to stalk the fourteen steps back, Hannah grips her gently by the shoulders, stopping her in place. "I'm sure. And you've got to stop pacing or I might just lose it."

Olivia lets out a ragged sigh and rolls her head on her neck to look at her best friend. "I'm nervous."

Hannah dips her chin. "I know. And that's okay. But if you take one more step, I think you'll wear a hole in the floor large enough to swallow us both, and then instead of a romantic rendezvous with Peter, you'll have a hot date with Mercy Hospital."

Olivia sniffs a laugh and looks up at the ceiling, then down at the floor, unable to stay completely still.

The door to their left opens with a soft swoosh across the hardwood floor, four pairs of feet tentatively shuffling in behind it. At the front of the pack is—

"Ezra!" Hannah's voice matches the room around them, bright. It echoes through the silence.

Her fiancé greets her with a grin, his dark eyes sparkling like shafts of light through a glass of whiskey on the rocks. Still, Ezra and the three other members of Olympus hesitate just over the threshold. From the back of the pack, Peter towers over them all.

Hannah turns back to her friend, a comforting smile slanting her lips. She mouths the words, "You've got this," and gives her shoulders one more squeeze before crossing the room to link arms with her soon-to-be husband.

The two of them lead the band's guitarist, Zach, and their drummer, Angel, from the room in a rush of whispered conversation. When the door slides shut once more, Olivia and Peter stand opposite one another, completely alone.

"Hi," she says, her voice barely audible despite the closeness of the room.

"Hi back," he answers, mouth twitching. He slides his hands into the pockets of his jeans to keep from fidgeting.

"Hi back? I go all out with the most romantic, over-the-top gesture I can think of, and that's all I get?" she can't help but tease, her lips twitching.

"I didn't realize romantic, over-the-top gestures came with a price."

Olivia shuffles one foot forward and back against the floor, the movement making her wrap dress flutter against her thighs. "Nothing comes free, especially not with me. I thought you knew that by now."

He chuckles, the sound rumbling like a growing thunderclap in his chest, and nods his head. "Apparently I'm still figuring you out, Quinn." The words are thick with hidden meaning. A polite nudge to explain herself.

Sucking in a deep breath, she tries to prepare herself for the thing she'll never be prepared for. Not really. She takes one slow step toward him, followed by another, until she's no more than an arm's length away. Until she has to crane her neck to look at his face.

Her lip wobbles when she opens her mouth to speak. "I told you not so long ago that I'd given up on love."

Peter nods.

"I meant it. I'd written it off. I was going to live vicariously through my best friend and that would be enough." The truth comes out in a rush, a raging river no longer held back by a dam. "I'd climb the ladder at work and become the only person I ever needed."

He cocks an eyebrow, as if to ask, *And then?*

She licks her lips. "And then you came along and totally blew up my five-year plan."

He lets out a roaring laugh, the corners of his eyes wrinkling under the force of his smile. Olivia's lungs fill fully with air for what feels like the first time in days. Like her head has been underwater, deprived of oxygen for every moment she's lived without seeing him like this. Hearing that belt of laughter.

With so much care, Peter slides one hand from his pocket and reaches it out to loosely grasp one of hers. His thumb slides across her knuckles, his calluses tickling her skin. His voice croaks when he finally asks, "Do you really mean it, what you wrote on that sign?"

Her pulse quickens and she's sure he can feel it in the veins of her wrist. She thinks back to the moment she'd written them, the way her hand shook so badly she had to redo it. Twice. Not because she didn't mean them. Quite the opposite. It felt like she'd been holding them back, lying to herself for so long, that her very bones itched to share them.

She nods once, twice, then meets his gaze firmly. "I mean it."

Peter's throat bobs. He looks down at their joined hands, giving her fingers a small squeeze. "Then why'd you push me away?"

Olivia twists her mouth to one side, chewing on the inside of her cheek. Though she expected this question, it still terrifies her. "I was scared. It all happened so fast. One minute we were just friends playing house to fool a couple people into thinking we had our shit together. The next, we were..."

"In bed," he rasps, his voice like gravel kicked up under a tire.

"Something like that." She smiles, but there's something a little sad about it. "I could feel it, everything changing. And it felt *good*. But also like the most terrifying thing I'd ever felt in my entire life. That morning when we were getting ready to leave, your mom told me how thrilled she was that we'd found each other, how great I was for you, and it reminded me that none of it had been real. That we hadn't found each other, not really. That we probably only seemed so good together because it was fake.

"That I'm not good for you and I was probably standing in the way of you finding something real, something better for you, with someone else. The guilt nearly killed me, right then and there."

Peter furrows his eyebrows so closely together they nearly become one, his mouth twisting to one side.

"What's that look for?"

"I'm just trying to understand how someone so smart could be so stupid."

Olivia's mouth pops open in a gasp, and she reaches her free hand up to slap his bicep. "Well, obviously I came around eventually or I wouldn't be here. I'm not *that* stupid."

Peter runs his teeth along his bottom lip and the sight of it strikes a match against her skin. In a voice as soft as velvet, he asks, "What finally made you come around?"

Her first instinct to obscure the truth rearing its ugly head, like she did in the very beginning, with Bruce. She swallows it down this time. "Honestly? My life fell apart the moment we landed. I lost the promotion I wanted, found out my best friend is moving across the country. And through it all you were the only person I wanted to talk to." Or not talk to. To just be with.

He was the net she pictured, the one she hoped could catch her before she hit the ground. She was just too scared to admit it.

During those few days when she'd felt more alone than ever, Olivia had realized running away doesn't stop the hurt from happening. The hurts will always be there. They might be small, like when someone forgets to wish you a happy birthday. Or they might be big, like your best friend moving away.

But those hurts don't make life any less beautiful, or amazing, or worth living. If anything, they make you appreciate the joy more. The laughter. The unexpected goodness of life.

And suddenly, it all made sense. Why it had never worked before.

She'd never been willing to give all of herself away, to be truly vulnerable with a man. But Peter... he slipped behind her walls like a thief in the night. Only instead of taking a piece of her heart, he gave her some of his own. Two halves now tethered together—always tugging.

Peter sniffs a laugh. "So that's when you fell in love with me, huh?" A smirk ticks up one side of his mouth.

Olivia presses her lips into a thin line. "Here we go, tell a guy you love him one time in front of a crowd full of people and suddenly he wants to talk about it."

His teeth slide over his bottom lip as his smile grows. "I'm going to want to talk about it every day. Repeatedly. In fact, I'm gonna need to hear you say those five words out loud now, just to be sure."

She throws her head back in a deep, honking laugh.

Peter moves his other hand to her arm, sliding his slender, practiced fingers around the crook in her elbow. "I could listen to that all day."

Olivia pulls a face, tilting her head back to look at him again. "I haven't even said them yet."

"I meant your laugh," he whispers, and her breath catches in her throat, something stirring in her stomach. "The wild, honking one that means you really thought something was funny."

At that last sentence, she scowls at him, but there's no fire behind it.

Peter takes a step closer, sliding his hand up the outside of her arm, over the curve of her shoulder, until it comes to rest at the nape of her neck. His thumb sweeps around to cup her jaw, just in front of her ear. "I'm pretty sure I fell in love with you the very first day you walked into my life, at that amphitheater on the lake in Chicago."

His eyes rove over her face, as if taking her in for the first time all over again. "I'll never forget it. You had your hair piled up on top of your head, and you were wearing these ripped jean shorts that showed off your legs, a blue tank top, and a look on your face that said, 'Don't even think about it. You have no chance.'"

Olivia drops her jaw and reaches out to flick his nose ring, a move that is quickly becoming her signature, but the tears filling her eyes give her true feelings away.

Peter's chest rumbles with silent laughter, and he shifts even closer to her until both of his hands cup her face. "I knew right then I was a goner. I've just been waiting for you to come to your senses or drop your standards ever since, not really sure which."

"Just shut up and kiss me," she breathes, not waiting for him to answer her command before she loops her arms around the back of his neck and pulls him down the rest of the way.

Their mouths meet in a frenzy of crashing lips and teeth and tongues. Peter snakes a hand down her spine until he can cup a hand around her behind. He lifts her with one arm until she's pressed fully against his hard body and deepens their kiss.

She wraps her legs around his waist, anchoring herself to him as her tongue slides across his bottom lip before slipping into his mouth. Her fingers twist into the loose curls at the nape of his neck, tugging gently at the roots. He lets out a low groan, the sound sending sparks flying behind Olivia's closed eyelids.

Reluctantly, she breaks their kiss to rest her forehead against Peter's, her chest rising and falling in rapid succession. She blinks open her eyes to find twin forest pools gazing at her. Embers ignite in her heart, warming her body from the inside out.

Olivia lets loose a contented sigh and whispers, "I love you, Campbell."

She can feel Peter's smile against her lips when he returns, "I love you, too, Quinn."

Epilogue

Fizzy Bubbles in All the Right Places

One year later

Olivia squeezes Peter's hand as hard as she possibly can, until she thinks her fingers may go numb. Their arms dangle between their uneven heights as they stride east on West 26th Street, through the faded crosswalk over 8th Ave in Chelsea.

Her silk wrap dress, the same one she'd worn the night she showed up to the Olympus pop-up show last year, flutters around her knees in an early summer breeze. She'd changed into it at Peter's apartment after a Friday that flew by at Campbell, Saxton, and Woods.

Her apartment, Peter kept reminding her each time she referred to it any other way.

"Can we please stop by real quick? It's on the way."

Peter dips an eyebrow at her, completely unfazed by her death grip. For all his face lets on, she could be giving him a massage right now. "We've been there three times this week already, and it's far from *on the way*."

"It's on 30th."

One corner of his mouth turns up, a restrained smirk. He keeps his eyes forward as he says, "And we're meeting Hannah and Ezra at Harvest Table. On Madison Ave. The other direction." His black button-up strains around his broad chest at the laughter he's trying to hold back. "We're their first stop from the airport, and Hannah gets almost as bad as you when she's hangry."

She huffs forcefully enough to send the curled tendrils of hair framing her face flying. "Okay, so it's a couple blocks off-route, but we're early. We can make it."

He releases a dramatic sigh that collapses his chest. He rolls his head on his shoulders to shoot her a sidelong look. Even through his narrowed gaze, that twitch lingers at the corner of his lips.

By this time, Olivia has plastered on a smile that could rival even Peter's trademark ten-thousand-watt grin. He's resigned to blinking his eyes at his girlfriend in resignation. He never could resist her. "Fine, but we have to be quick."

She squeals her excitement and leans as high on her toes as she can go to peck Peter's cheek, then quickens her pace toward their destination. She keeps her fingers threaded loosely with his the entire way to Second Chance Rescue, their hips and legs bumping naturally every few steps. Occasionally they collapse in on one another when they need to sidestep oncoming walkers on the bustling Manhattan sidewalks.

When they arrive at the shelter, the young girl at the front desk—Ashley, one of their volunteers—instantly recognizes them. She'd been working the same shift the last time they'd popped by. Yesterday.

At first, Olivia's eyes widen at Ashley, the same expression of fear she wore the day before marring her made-up face. It's gone in another instant, when the teen looks up from her computer and smiles warmly back, dipping her head in silent answer.

He's still here.

Ashley's eyes pass to Peter's next, a small knowing glow shimmering in them. He returns it with a close-mouthed smile. As if to say, *Yep, we're back again.*

Ashley stands and moves from behind the desk to open a door behind her that leads straight into the shelter's cat room. Olivia has come to know it intimately.

Straight down the center of the room. Four cages down on the right. A tiny tabby cat the color of pumpkin purée with bright, round, green eyes that pierce your heart.

They've been visiting him almost daily for the past two weeks. Olivia had fallen in love with him the first moment she saw him, that love only growing when he'd immediately brushed his small body up against the cage door, meowing very animatedly at her to pet him.

The little guy, who the shelter has named Simba, recognizes her as soon as she enters the room. He begins to bat his left paw at the lock on his cage door, loosing a low meow that seems to say very plainly, *Let me out.*

She crosses the room in two long strides, lifting her hand to pet Simba through the gaps in the cage without a second thought. He purrs at her touch, ducking and rolling his head into the press of her fingertips.

Peter stands behind her, hands in his pockets and a small smile curving his lips.

When Olivia moves her hand to slide the little latch to the tabby's cage open, a note on the door gives her pause. Her mouth falls open in mute horror.

"No," she breathes, her heart dropping out through her stomach. *It can't be.*

In small, even print written in black marker on the back of his adoption details card is the one word she had both hoped for and dreaded: ADOPTED.

"But I thought you said," she whispers, turning her head back the way they'd come in search of Ashley. She isn't there, and there are muffled voices coming from the reception area. Another patron in need of assistance.

It could even be Simba's new mom or dad.

Disappointment tugs her lips down when she turns back to face the little orange cat. "I'm so glad you found a home. I just wish we'd had more time together," she breathes to him, and his round eyes seem to widen with understanding. *I wish it were me.*

Peter clears his throat from behind her and gently nudges Olivia from behind with his elbow, one hand still tucked into the pocket of his tailored khaki dress pants. He says to her in a barely audible voice, "Why don't you hold him one more time while we're here? We came all this way. I'm sure his new parents won't mind."

With a shaking breath, she nods. This time, there's a tremor in her hand when she reaches for the lock to Simba's cage. It slides open with a ringing *click!* that fills the room and startles a few other cats awake.

In an instant Simba is purring so loudly she wouldn't be surprised if they could hear it through the closed door to reception. Olivia's smile is smaller, much more reserved, but it's back when she slowly lifts her hands to pick Simba up and cradle him in her arms. She nuzzles his neck gently with her nose, supporting him on the backside of one forearm while she uses the other to pet him in rolling strokes down his back.

Simba ducks his head into her chest like he belongs there. The movement draws Olivia's eyes down and she notices for the first time a little red collar looped around the cat's neck.

She twists her mouth to one side, curious. That's new.

It isn't uncommon for pet parents to place collars with identification information on their animals, but it is a little unusual to do it before actually taking them home.

Her curiosity gets the better of her and she slips her fingers under the red material, very gently spinning the collar around until she can see the shiny gold tag hanging from it. Her pulse thrums in her ears. What if it's the name of the person who adopted him?

She probably shouldn't look. She'd be too tempted to Google them. Maybe stalk them on Instagram, make sure they're taking good care of her little guy.

Eventually her desire to know wins out. Carefully, like it's a bomb she's defusing, she flips the tag over with her fingertips to see a few words engraved there.

Will you marry my new daddy?

Olivia's heart leaps into her throat, the sound of blood rushing in her ears so loud she can't hear her own heavy breathing.

A proposal.

She doesn't know what to feel. On one hand, it must mean the person who adopted Simba truly is a cat lover. On the other, she feels like she's peering behind the curtain at something she has no right to see.

Unable to ride this rocky emotional rollercoaster alone, she turns behind her to Peter, the little tabby still cradled tightly in her arms. "Peter, take a look at—"

Her voice croaks, the words lodging in the back of her throat.

Because behind her, Peter is down on one knee, still comically tall even at half his height. A small, black velvet box is clutched in his impossibly large hand. When her eyes catch on it, she can see it shaking. See *him* shaking.

He takes a deep breath, then says, "Olivia Marie Quinn. I have loved you since the very first moment I saw you. That love has only grown stronger with each passing moment. Each time you've suckered me into doing something crazy. Each time you've flicked my nose ring and said something totally devastating.

"I love you more every time you play your girly pop music way too loud in our apartment, or use up all the hot water in the shower."

Olivia lets go of a wet, shaking laugh at this. It comes out somewhere between a snort and the caw a large seabird might make.

It urges Peter on, his grin widening through his nerves. "I've loved you through every silly argument, through every sly smile, through every dirty look you've given me to *hide* said sly smile.

"I've fallen more in love with you every time you've looked at me like I'm the most important person in the world; listened to me like what I have to say really matters; made me feel like someone deserving of your love, not because of what I can give you, but simply because I exist.

"I can't imagine spending even a second with anyone else, let alone the rest of my life. You are the sun I orbit around and the stars that light up even my darkest night sky. You are the reason I wake up every day, and the last thing I think about before I go to sleep. I want to spend every moment of the rest of my life showing you that you'll never walk alone again. Olivia, will you marry me?"

If it weren't for the purring kitten in her arms, Olivia would've pressed her hands to her face to cover her gaping mouth. Or used them to wipe the tears streaming down her cheeks like raging rivers.

Instead, she lunges forward, crushing her body into Peter's kneeling frame. It's all he can do to wrap his arms around her back, bracing the knee he has pinned to the floor to keep them all from toppling over like an imploding high-rise.

Simba meows in protest, frustrated at being sandwiched between the two humans. Or maybe he's just mad Olivia stopped petting him.

Her voice wobbling, she crows, "You adopted him, for me?!"

Heaving a shaking laugh, Peter rubs one of his palms in a soothing line up and down her back. "Out of everything I just said, that's the piece you hang on to," he mutters, but there's no malice in it. He adds a little louder, "In case you hadn't noticed, I'd do just about anything for you."

Olivia sniffs wetly and burrows her face into his neck. "Yes," she whispers against his skin, her teeth lightly grazing him.

Peter shivers. "Yes, you've noticed or…"

This time, she nips him on purpose, but there's a smile curving her lips when she replies, "Yes, I'll marry you. I'd marry you right here, right now in this smelly animal shelter, because I cannot wait to start the rest of my life with you. I love you Peter Andrew Campbell. Forever."

She leans back just enough to press a crushing kiss to his lips. She can taste the traces of salt on them from the tears slipping from the corners of his eyes. Peter reaches a hand around the back of her neck to swipe a thumb at them, then releases her so they can both stand.

Simba shoots Peter a haughty glare for the interruption, then nuzzles his head into the crook of Olivia's elbow, earning a laugh from both of his new parents.

She breaks her maternal hold on the kitten just long enough to allow Peter to slide the princess-cut diamond he picked out onto her left ring finger. It fits like a glove, and Olivia catches a gleam in his eye, like he already knew it would. She imagines him sneaking into her jewelry box when she's at work to find her rings and bring them to the jeweler, just to be sure.

It takes all of her willpower not to stand there and stare at the shining silver band and the diamonds glittering from its center all day.

As the two of them exit the animal shelter, Simba's adoption papers tucked under Peter's right arm, Olivia bumps her hip against his leg. They'll be back in the morning to pick the little guy up, after they've bought out the entire pet store, of course.

"I can't believe you orchestrated this whole thing without me knowing. Even pretending you didn't want to go there today." She tosses a lopsided smile up at him.

After sidestepping a pedestrian on his right, Peter beams down at her. "I believe the student has surpassed the master."

Olivia scoffs and lifts her free hand to give his bicep a squeeze, her other hand threaded loosely with his. "I wouldn't go *that* far. You still have a lot to learn from me."

He chuckles and leans down to press a chaste kiss to her temple. "Luckily for me, I've got the rest of my life to do it."

Acknowledgements

Working on this book is probably the most fun I've ever had writing (and I used to write boy band fanfiction in a spiral-bound notebook with my best friend in high school, so that's a *really* tough act to follow). Olivia is a beautiful medley of so many qualities and stories shared with me by wonderful people over the years, and as such, there are many, many people to thank for helping me write her story.

To my dearest friend Bonnie, thank you for letting me (incessantly) pick your brain about the paralegal profession. Your anecdotes about attorneys produced one of my favorite characters of all time (hello, Bruce!) and your willingness to share even the most minutiae of details about your day-to-day helped immensely. Thank you for reading my first draft and helping me keep it real.

To my other wonderful beta readers Breland and Ashley, I can't thank you enough for taking the time to provide feedback on this story. While your ideas and critical feedback were paramount to getting this right, your kind words gave me the courage to keep writing, and for that I adore you. P.S. Breland, thank you for the ham idea. I am forever in your debt.

If you're wondering how this book sounds so good: I could not have done it without my wonderful editor Alexandra. Thank you for catching all my comma splices and coming in clutch with some much-needed rephrases. If you're wondering how this book looks so good, I too am amazed by the talent of my character illustrator (Nina) and my cover designer (Layla). Thank you both for, quite literally, bringing this story to life visually.

And last, but certainly not least, huge thank you to my incredible husband Kelly. Thank you for never questioning me when I disappeared into my phone to jot down a new scene idea or when I'd randomly hide in my office for hours at a time to write. Thank you for unfailingly supporting this passion of mine and doing everything in your power to give me the resources to live it every day. I love you.

Also by Rachel Pluck

Are You In?

About the author

Rachel Pluck is the author of Are You In? and Are You Falling for It? and if it wasn't already obvious, she loves a good love story. Her entire life, she's been drawn to strong female protagonists staring down complex issues, and those are the types of stories she loves to create. In addition to being an author, Rachel is a marketing strategist living in southeastern Pennsylvania. When she's not obsessively reading, writing, or streaming old CW dramas (hello fellow TVD fans!) she can be found at home with her husband, wrangling their willful young daughter and three rescue pups.

Stay up to date with the author:
www.rachelpluckwrites.com
@rachelpluckwrites

Are You Falling for It?

An Olympus Novel

Rachel Pluck